Cross Dog Blues

Book One of
A Great Long Story to Tell

RICHARD M. BROCK

Cover Illustration by Troy Hoover 2014

www.troyhooverart.com

This is a work of fiction. Any actual persons, names, places, or events are used in a fictitious way. Some of the characters are inspired by historical figures; others are entirely products of the author's imagination. Apart from the historical characters, any resemblance between these fictional characters and actual persons, living or dead, is entirely coincidental. No portion of this book is intended to be taken as the truth.

Published by Bogie Road Publishing, Ltd.

ISBN: 0991132025
ISBN-13: 978-0-9911320-2-7

Praise for CROSS DOG BLUES

Fortean Times Magazine - "Richard M. Brock paints a gripping, funny and often harrowing picture of life in the Delta, then and now. Artfully combining fact and fiction, this is storytelling at its best, with a plot that surprises at every twist and turn."

Kirkus Reviews - "Chock-full of poignant passages and insightful dialogue about the deep, affecting power of music, the alternating narratives pass quickly right up until the end. [...] A heartening read for blues fans as well as anyone interested in the history of American music and civil rights."

★★★★★ ***5 Star Amazon Review*** - "Just an OUTSTANDINGLY GOOD READ!"

★★★★★ ***5 Star Amazon Review*** - "Perhaps the best novel written about the birth of the blues. Cannot wait for Book Two."

★★★★★ ***5 Star Amazon Review*** - "Amazing and honest."

★★★★★ ***5 Star Goodreads Review*** - "I can't even begin to tell you what an impact this book has had on me!"

★★★★★ ***5 Star Amazon Review*** - "Heavenly harmony is reached in the pages of this book."

★★★★★ ***5 Star Goodreads Review*** - "This book is so good. I can hardly wait for Book Two."

★★★★★ ***5 Star Amazon Review*** - "With a first effort this writer worked a bit of magic."

★★★★★ ***5 Star Amazon Review*** - "First book I've finished in two years. Loved the characters, especially Furry."

★★★★★ ***5 Star Amazon Review*** - "Long live Furry Jenkins!"

★★★★★ ***5 Star Amazon Review*** - "A beautifully crafted page turner that really gets under your skin."

★★★★★ ***5 Star Amazon Review*** - "I love the stories, how they intertwine. It keeps you glued to the pages. I can hardly wait for the next two books."

★★★★★ ***5 Star Amazon Review*** - "Get it now. Buy it, borrow it, steal it if you have to. A great read from beginning to end." (Note from the author: Don't steal it.)

★★★★★ ***5 Star Amazon Review*** - "This is a fine accomplishment for an author's first book."

★★★★★ ***5 Star Amazon Review*** - "Like the Blues, this book is a treasure. Compelling Story! This book is historical fiction but of the highest caliber. Once I started reading it I couldn't put it down and read it all in a day. I can't wait for books two and three. Mr. Brock is a born storyteller. His characters come to life both real and fictional. Even if you're not a fan of the Blues, you will be a fan of this book. Can't recommend it highly enough."

★★★★★ ***5 Star Amazon Review*** - "I couldn't put it down!"

★★★★★ ***5 Star Amazon Review*** - "Couldn't put it down! This was a page turner right from the get-go! I loved how the author worked in some of my heroes from the beginnings of blues music but also put a fresh spin and even took liberties with their "history." The civil rights messages in this book are very important in reference to what's going on in America today....a must read for anyone who loves the blues and/or America."

★★★★★ ***5 Star Amazon Review*** - "What an amazing story! I could not stop reading."

★★★★★ ***5 Star Amazon Review*** - "A more entertaining book I haven't read. The descriptions in the book transported me back to the train station in Tutwiler. I heard Henry Sloan singing. I can't wait for the next books. Thank you, Richard M. Brock."

SPECIAL CONTRIBUTORS TO CROSS DOG BLUES

MATT SCHOENFELDER
MICHAEL T. BROGAN

THANK YOU

I WOULD also like to thank my editor, Michael Denneny, for his great work with the story, my mother, Sheila Brock, for her support as well as her editing work, my talented friend, Troy Hoover, for his art, my Kickstarter backers for their cold, hard cash, the rest of my friends and family for being altogether top-notch and supportive, and of course, my exceptional wife, Erin, for her unwavering support, guidance, and presence. But most of all, I would like to thank *you*, reader, for taking up this old rag. Now, let's get on with it.

RMB

To Erin

"When I leave this town, I'm gonna bid you fare, farewell;
And when I return again you'll have a great long story to tell."
Robert Johnson – *From Four Till Late*

Part One

THE FIRST

Hinds County, Mississippi
1903

A TRAIN whistle called out in the distance, and the door to the shack burst open. Charlie Patton looked up with a start as his father suddenly towered over them.

Sitting on a worn chair next to Charlie in the muggy Mississippi shack was his idol, Henry Sloan. Henry was in his mid-twenties and black as night, wearing worn farm clothes and a dirty hat. Cradled in his calloused hands was his whole world: a beautifully crafted Martin guitar made from the finest Adirondack red spruce and acquired by a king-high flush in a poker game in Memphis. He, too, jumped as Bill Patton barged in.

Beside him, Charlie glared at his father, unhappy to be interrupted. He was twelve years old, and small and thin with large ears and penetrating eyes. His light-brown skin colored a melancholy face in which the sharp features of his Cherokee ancestry were becoming clearly evident. Charlie clutched the cracked and worn guitar he was playing like a lion protecting a fresh kill.

"Henry, we talked about this," Charlie's father scolded Henry Sloan, paying no attention to the cold snarl Charlie was giving him.

"I ain't but playing music, Bill," Henry defended himself. "If the boy wants to learn, what am I to do?"

Bill Patton took a breath, as if to retort, then shook his head.

"The boy's got too much free time is what it is," he said, seeming to speak to himself as much as anyone else, "and that's my fault and I aim to fix it." He straightened his back and glowered down at Charlie. "Get him learned about proper God-fearing work, instead of this damning music you got him all wild about." He shot an icy glance at Henry Sloan then fixed Charlie with a hard stare to emphasize his point. "Get up, boy," he instructed Charlie before either Charlie or Henry could speak.

Charlie began to protest.

"Mind your father, boy," Henry said.

Charlie growled, but sulked outside nonetheless. After he did, his father turned back to Henry, ice still in his eyes. He was a large man and his presence alone could put a lump of fright in the throat of any man. He opened his mouth, no doubt to begin one of his verbal lashings, but Henry cut him off before he could start.

"It ain't hurting the boy to play some music, Bill," Henry said.

"I told you, Henry," Bill Patton responded, "I don't mind him playing the Lord's gospel with the Chatmons after church, but I don't like whatever this is you're playing in here. I can't rightly say why, but it just don't sound right, Henry. These sounds you're making have been touched by demons, I can hear that straight through, clear as daylight."

"Aw, Bill."

"Don't *Aw Bill* me," Bill Patton barked and waved his finger as punctuation.

Charlie kicked the dust and stewed outside as he watched the two men argue.

"It ain't hurting him, Bill, and there ain't nothing evil about it," Henry said, his voice rising.

"I disagree," Bill stated.

Henry Sloan dropped his head and strummed his guitar. Arguing with Bill Patton was futile. Charlie knew that, and so did Henry. Henry raised his eyes one last time to Bill's and shrugged his shoulders. Bill's face made it clear that the conversation was over, and without a word he turned and left the shack, closing the door behind him.

Outside, the warm Mississippi breeze carried the familiar scent of mud off the cotton fields and the sun was still strong, though it had begun its descent into the western sky. Charlie huffed and whined but knew enough to keep up with his father as he strode by.

They walked to their place at the end of the small cluster of four sharecropper shacks on the plantation. The shack next to Henry Sloan's was occupied by the large brood of Henderson Chatmon. Charlie could see Henderson beside his shack sharpening his pick on the grinding wheel. The welted scars of a whip's burr streaked out from under his sweat-soaked undershirt. Those scars had taught Charlie a lot about the world, without a word being said. He knew Henderson was a former slave but didn't know where he had heard that. It was certainly never spoken of.

The shack beside Chatmon's was home to Joe Rawlins and his family. His wife and three kids were on their small, sagging front porch and they all stared at Charlie. It was always like this, and he had grown accustomed to it. He was different, often mistaken by outsiders for a Mexican or a full-blooded Indian. And he was outcast because of it. The people here at least knew him, but the instinct to distrust had been ingrained over hundreds of years and could be hard to shake.

Aside from his mother, from whom he had received his portion of native blood -- though it didn't show in her nearly as much as it did in Charlie -- the only person Charlie had met in his young life who truly understood him was a young gypsy girl named Abilene. Like him, she and her family were unwelcome in every level of society, and Charlie thoroughly enjoyed their company because of it. He felt comfortable there.

Abilene's mother was a fortune-teller, capable of hypnotizing people and talking to their dead ancestors. She took an immediate liking to Charlie and made him feel welcome whenever he came to call on Abilene. She said he had spirits, but she never explained exactly what she meant by that. She said she could see them in his eyes and Charlie believed her because she was full of all sorts of great wisdom. He looked forward to his conversations with her nearly as much as he looked forward to seeing Abilene herself. Their gypsy band had been around all summer, encamped outside of town and moving into Jackson during the day to make their living. And most nights Charlie would be waiting when they got back. He was impressed with how they all relied on each other and he found something grand in their perseverance, despite being shunned wherever they traveled.

The thought of Abilene made him smile as he walked along beside his father. He looked forward to seeing her later that night. He had kissed her two days before, behind her mother's tent, and she had kissed him back. And now he wanted nothing more than to kiss her again.

But that would have to wait. When he and his father reached their shack, Charlie saw four burlap bundles on the dusty porch. His father reached down and picked up two of the bundles and handed them to Charlie then picked up the other two and slung them over his shoulder. Charlie's bundles were smaller than his father's, but they were still heavy. Bill Patton offered his son no explanation and Charlie knew to just follow.

An hour later, while he and his father walked down a trail in the woods, Charlie couldn't contain his curiosity any longer. "Where we going, pa?"

Bill Patton looked down at him and smiled warmly. Charlie could see he was in a good mood, enjoying the walk through the woods. It was good to get off the plantation for a while, and the shaded breeze of the forest felt awfully nice on a hot day.

"We're bringing some crop for the church," Bill Patton explained.

Charlie looked at him, confused, "Church is way back there," he said and nodded his head back down the trail.

"Not our church, Charlie."

"The white folk's church!?" Charlie asked, exasperated. "Why the hell are we bringing crop to the white folk's church?"

"You and your blaspheming mouth!" Bill Patton reprimanded.

Charlie knew he would normally get a few licks with the belt for cussing like that, but it just slipped out, he couldn't help it. Luckily the walk through the woods must have really lifted the old man's spirits because he settled for just a stern look.

"We do this because this is what the Bible tells us to do: Treat your neighbor as yourself," his father explained.

"But they ain't our neighbors, Pa. They don't even care about us."

"Well, that ain't true, Charlie. And even if it was, it'd be all the more reason. We must pray for the wicked as sincerely as we pray for ourselves."

Charlie looked up at his father and sighed, drawing a grin from his old man. He didn't know what the hell his father was thinking sometimes.

A half-an-hour further down the trail Charlie saw a large cross in the open lawn ahead and soon the whole church came into view. It was the nicest building he had ever seen -- except maybe the plantation house. But, in reality, he hadn't seen many besides that. He had spent most of his life at the plantation and most of that time in their cluster of shacks. His recent visits to Abilene were the furthest he had ever strayed from the plantation. He'd had almost no interaction with white people, aside from the men from the plantation who would come to collect their commission. And at those times his father did all the talking while he and his mother waited inside.

Charlie Patton and his father stepped into the sun-soaked clearing. Charlie was nervous but excited. He wanted to see what the place looked like on the inside. He happily skipped across the lush green lawn toward the entrance to the beautiful house of God.

Bill Patton whistled from behind his son. "This way, boy," he said and pointed around back.

Charlie stopped and looked back at him.

"You know we can't go in there, Charlie. Let's go," Bill said and waved his son along.

As he stood on the lawn, Charlie's eyes narrowed and he grimaced, the life draining from him as he followed after his father. "I don't see why we can't use the front door if we're bringing them crop," he complained.

Bill shook his head. "Just come on," he said.

Bill and Charlie walked around the church to the back door, Charlie sulking a few feet behind his father.

Bill Patton approached the door to the back of the church as if it were on fire. He cautiously stepped forward and stood a long way from the door and leaned forward on one foot to knock faintly, as if afraid to get too close.

A moment later, Pastor Grey pulled open the back door and smiled at Bill Patton.

In front of his eyes, Charlie could see his father shrink as the pastor appeared. Just like he does on collection day, Charlie thought.

"Brought some crop for the church, Pastor Grey. Got some real good onions and peppers," Bill offered, with his eyes to the ground.

"Oh, thank you, Bill," said Pastor Grey. "That's very kind of you." Pastor Grey smiled warmly and stepped outside and guided them to a weathered table beside the back door.

But Charlie didn't go in the direction he was pointed. Instead, he dropped his bundles and ran straight past Pastor Grey and into the church.

"Charlie!" Bill Patton shouted at his son, but Charlie kept going.

Bill flashed a horrified glance at Pastor Grey and ran after his child.

When Bill rounded the corner into the nave, Charlie stood in front of the pulpit, transfixed by the intricately carved life-sized wooden crucifix behind it.

Bill Patton strode at his son, "You'll get a lickin' for this when we get home."

Charlie looked over at his father but didn't move.

When Bill reached his son he turned to Pastor Grey, who was trailing behind. "I'm sorry, Pastor Grey," he said, "the boy needs to learn a lesson, and I assure you, I will tend to that directly upon our arrival back home." He shot an icy glance at Charlie, who stared back, stone-faced.

"Oh, no no," Pastor Grey replied with a fixed smile, "he's just being as children will be, doesn't know better."

Charlie was uninterested in the two men and instead stared at the bloodied Christ behind the altar.

Pastor Grey rolled up onto the balls of his feet then back onto his heels and clasped his hands in front of his robes, "So thank you very much for the crop, Bill, we'll put it to very good use," he said with a smile.

"Of course, Pastor Grey," Bill Patton replied and bowed his head, "it's the least we could do."

Pastor Grey smiled warmly. Then he sighed and rolled on his feet again, still smiling at Bill.

"Oh---yeah, sorry," Bill said, catching the drift. He turned to wrangle Charlie. "Let's go, boy," he commanded.

Charlie suddenly snapped around to the pastor, "So we ain't allowed in here, huh? We ain't allowed to use the front door? Ain't allowed to pray in your church?" he asked directly.

Pastor Grey looked down in astonishment at the sudden, pointed questions by the young boy. Charlie didn't wait for a response; he glanced back up at the crucifix and then spun and marched toward the front door. Pastor Grey took a moment to process the intentions of the wild-eyed boy then shuffled off after him.

He caught up to Charlie halfway down the aisle and grabbed him by the arm, "What do you think you're doing, young ma--?"

Charlie turned and fixed the pastor with a glare that made the pastor shudder as the child's eyes tore into him. Pastor Grey staggered back and required a moment to regain his breath before tightening his grip on the young boy's arm and turning to Bill.

"Mister Patton, I believe you should teach your boy some manners," he commanded with a shaky voice, his right hand trembling. "Now I kindly thank you for your donation and ask you to leave, sir. Through the *back* door."

Bill Patton's eyes narrowed as he looked at the pastor clutching his son. He straightened his back and the pastor shrunk as he grew. Bill Patton reached down and took his son by the hand and pulled him from the pastor's grasp. Without another word, he marched up the aisle toward the front door. The pastor watched in astonishment as Bill Patton flung the door open and stepped out into the light.

Charlie held his father's hand and smiled. He was proud of the old man. He looked up at his father and thought him larger than life.

But his father didn't appear happy, or proud. He looked scared. When Charlie followed his stare, he saw why. Getting out of a shiny automobile -- the first Charlie had ever seen -- were three white men. They didn't look happy either. They stared at Charlie's father as they marched across the manicured lawn.

"Am I seeing what I think I'm seeing?" one of them shouted.

"I think so," the other answered, "I think I just seen them two niggers coming out of our church."

"What the hell do you think you're doing, boy," the one in the lead asked Bill Patton as they approached.

"We ain't doing nothing, suh, I'm sorry, suh," Bill Patton shrunk before the three men.

"What the fuck were you doing in there, nigger?" he demanded.

"We was just bringing some crop for the church, suh, don't want no trouble, suh."

"We don't want your nigger food," he said and spat on the ground. "And if you didn't want no trouble then why the hell are you in our church spreading your nigger filth?"

"I'm sorry, suh, won't ever do it again, suh."

The man shook his head and grinned, "I know you won't," he said, then turned to the other two men. "What do you think, boys?" he asked with chuckled. Then he glanced down at Charlie. "And what is this thing, here?" he asked his friends with a snort. "Looks like some kind of red nigger boy." All three laughed and Charlie glared back at the man standing over him.

"Fuck you," Charlie said.

All the men, including Bill Patton, jumped back.

"What did you just say to me, boy?" the white man yelled and smacked Charlie in the face, knocking him back. "You need to learn a lesson." The man was on Charlie in a flash and held him by the shirt and punched him twice in the face.

Bill Patton tried to help his son but the other two men grabbed him and held him down and made him watch while their friend pummeled the child, throwing him to the ground and kicking him over and over. Bill Patton screamed and clawed but couldn't break free.

Pastor Grey stood in the partially opened doorway, watching. Bill Patton begged him to help, to stop the men. But Pastor Grey just dropped his eyes and slunk inside, closing the front door of the church.

The man kicked Charlie in the stomach, and then again, and then kicked him in the back when he covered his stomach. And then again, and again. He kicked him once more in the front and Charlie grabbed his leg and bit down hard on his shin and the man yelped and stomped and kicked him with his other foot.

Beside Charlie, his father struggled, flailing to get loose. When one of his captors stumbled, it was enough to allow him to break free. He jumped to his feet and hurtled himself at the man beating his son. He tackled the man to the ground and punched him twice in the face before the other two got to him. They tackled him simultaneously.

On the ground behind the men, Charlie shook his head and focused his wavering vision on the three men now beating his father. The sounds of impact were sickening. Over and over. But his father was still struggling, still defending himself. Charlie realized that these men were not going to stop. This is not like the drunken fights he had seen from time to time back at the shacks, where people always broke up the fight if it was too one-sided. No one would stop this; these men were going to kill his father. He shook his head again, his brain throbbing and his vision going in and out. A loud *thud!* and Charlie heard his father scream in pain. Charlie reached into his back pocket and pulled out the collapsible knife his father had just given him on his birthday. He stood shakily to his feet and gained his balance. He unfolded the knife and looked down at his father being pummeled by kick after kick.

"Run!" Charlie's father yelled to him between blows, his eyes wide with fear.

And Charlie ran. The man who had beaten Charlie had his back to him, and Charlie ran as fast as he could and leapt onto the man's back and sunk his knife into the man's throat up to the hilt. Charlie pulled out his knife and dismounted as the man crumpled to the ground.

The sudden eruption of blood stopped everyone in their tracks, and the instant of distraction allowed Bill Patton to break free.

The two other attackers watched in horror as their friend slumped lifelessly to the ground, a geyser of blood spraying from between his fingers. Their initial horror immediately turned to rage. The one closest to Charlie lunged for him -- and missed.

Charlie darted out of the path of the man's arms and made for the forest, his father tight on his heels, the two men following but falling behind.

"We're gonna string you niggers up!" was the last thing Charlie heard as he and his father disappeared into the forest.

2

Upstate New York
2002

MY NAME is Frank, Franklyn O'Connor, which happens to be the same goddamn name as my father. But I'll get into that in a second. For now, I'll tell you about how I was sitting at a bar in the train station of my little hometown and hadn't heard the question the guy beside me had asked. I was in something of a haze right then.

"What?" I asked.

"You didn't even tell her?" the man asked again. His gray hair was mushed back and the top two buttons of his loose denim shirt hung open. He was tan, like the rough kind of tan you get from spending your life outside in the sun and inside smoky bars. We were in the bar of the train station of my hometown, like I said, and we were the only ones. We had been talking for a few minutes while he drank whiskey straight and I drank coke because the bartender didn't believe I was twenty-one. And I wasn't, for that matter. I was nineteen at the time. But, when the bartender turned around, the man beside me reached over and poured half his whiskey into my coke and nodded. Then he drank from his glass in that slow thoughtful way cool guys always drink from their whiskey glasses. And he was one hell of a cool guy.

"Thanks," I said, for the drink. And then added, "And, no, I didn't tell her."

He raised his eyebrow and sipped at his drink, not saying anything for a long moment.

"What's your name, kid?" he asked after another sip and a pause. "Mine's Tony."

"Name's Frank," I said, and shook his hand. And it is, like I said: Franklyn O'Connor. Which, like I said, is the same goddamn name as my father. My father was a bluesman -- and an asshole, and my part in this great long story to tell begins at that lonely train station as I set out to tell him as much. Seems stupid, I know, but that's what I was doing. Of course, I didn't know how I was going to find him; I hadn't seen nor heard from him since he left when I was five. But I was going to find him one way or another.

Now, before we go any further, I just want to say, don't get all '*boo hoo*' and '*poor thing*' and whatnot about all that. The guy was an asshole and I was better off growing up without him. Which will probably make you get even more misty and thinking what a strong boy and feel like I need a good saving, maybe to be touched by the Lord, or maybe I need a hug. Well, I assure you, I do not, and if all you meddling people could just mind your own damn business then the world would be a better place. You're all just as fucked up as I am anyway, so focus on that, eh?

Anyway, I had a ticket in my hand for the Mississippi Delta: the place I thought I might find that old sack of shit father of mine. And if I did find him, I didn't really know. Mainly, I just wanted to tell him he was an asshole. I'm sure there was more to it than that, but that was the gist. A man shouldn't run out on his family, regardless. Any idiot knows that. And when he does, somebody like me might just track him down and let him know he isn't worth the gum on his shoe. Or maybe just shoot him in the back. I hadn't decided on which.

At the time though, the guy I was talking to, Tony, was wondering whether I should have told my *mother* that I was about to get on a train with a one-way ticket to the Mississippi Delta. I was only nineteen, like I said, and as much as my father was an asshole who had run out on his family, my mother was an angel who had raised us in his absence. So I could see Tony's point. But I guess I just didn't want to be talked out of what I was doing. And she could do that if she wanted. She knew me well.

Well, we sat there for a while, me and Tony, and chewed the fat and waited for the train. The train wasn't on time, of course.

Outside, the sky was rimmed with the last remnants of dusk when the train finally came around the bend. Sparks spit out from under the wheels as it slowed and passed under a bridge just north of the station. I could feel the rumbling vibrations traveling through the ground as it approached, shooting like lightning from my feet to my spine to the top of my head. When the whistle screamed out across the platform my hair stood on end and an intense flutter reared up in my stomach, part euphoria and part terror.

"This is me," I said to Tony, and almost puked.

"Good luck, kid," he said with a smile. He hardly turned his head, and just looked at me out of the corner of his eye as he took a sip of his whiskey. He was a very cool guy. And I felt like the opposite of cool right then. I felt like I was going to puke.

But without a look back I ran to the train and jumped over the yellow step that was just being placed outside the door by a dapper conductor who swung down from the glimmering chrome car like a carnival director.

"All aboard," he shouted, and I was glad he said it. I didn't know they still did.

I moved down the narrow aisle, and as I did, I was Chris McCandless and Sal Paradise and Huckleberry Finn. I was rip-roaring *ready* for the road that lay ahead. Or at least I thought I was. As it turns out, I wasn't at all. But we'll get into that later.

I took a seat near the back of the third car. The train wasn't full so I had two seats to myself. I sat down and looked out the window at the white puffs of air from the train's brakes floating along the platform, engulfing the line of passengers arriving at the door behind me.

There were a few other people on the train car. I looked around and chuckled at the happenstance that would forever embed these people in my memory. They were unwittingly a part of the biggest day of my life, and I found that amusing. I can still picture the elderly lady that sat very upright a few rows in front of me. I remember wondering how long she could sit like that before becoming too tired to be proper. I like how old people are proper. People had class back then. Not like today.

Slowly, the train rolled into motion and I watched with a feeling I'll never be able to explain as the multiple tracks of the rail yard merged into one and the train passed under the bridge south of the station and out into the night.

Within a few moments, the train was rumbling through the darkness and I was excited beyond belief. The conductor walked by a few times, once checking tickets. I smiled and nodded each time he passed. Today was just a normal day for everyone else in the car. This made me laugh out loud, which drew a worried glance from the just now woken up girl sleeping across the aisle from me. *What's that strange boy giggling about?* she seemed to be thinking. *Where did he come from?*

I glanced at her and tipped an imaginary cap and giggled some more. I carried on like this for the next half-hour or so, my excitement growing the further from home the locomotive carried me.

Then the train shook and the lights dimmed slightly as the brakes were applied, the locomotive shuddering in a domino effect of shifting cars as we slowed into a brightly lit station with a long platform. The conductor was walking up the aisle, talking to people as he went.

"Transfer to Chicago, here," he said when he reached me.

I stared up at him. "What?" was the best I could come up with.

"Transfer to Chicago here," the conductor repeated with the first speckles of annoyance. "Board at Track Four on the left. The train should be here in about an hour."

"In an hour?" I parroted. I was shocked. I knew nothing of this. "I knew nothing of this."

The conductor just cocked his head and raised his eyebrows as if to say: *Read your fucking tickets, moron.*

I blinked and gathered my backpack and the bag of food I had thrown together and stepped off the train.

The lights inside the empty station were too bright and fluorescent and the walls were grimy and the tiles on the floor worn. The station was old enough to be dirty and run-down, but not old enough to have any charm or to have been built during a time when craftsmanship and artistry actually meant something.

I set my bag on one of the hard plastic seats and sat down next to it as the train I had just been on glided back out into the darkness. And then I was alone in the dreary station. The old television in the corner of the deserted, white-walled room was tuned to a news channel. I looked out the windows of the station. I was half an hour from home. *I go to the fucking movies five minutes from here,* I thought and stared down at the floor.

With each passing minute I remained in the familiarity of the life I had just left behind, the more the possibility that 'better judgment' could invade my mind and flatten my will to follow through with this hare-brained plan. I had the required gusto right then, but that momentarily explosive gusto could quickly fizzle out. I knew that all I had to do was walk to the payphone in the corner of the room and my mother or brother or sister or any of my friends would be down to pick me up in half an hour. I didn't have to go through with it. It *was* kind of stupid.

I had an hour for these kinds of bad thoughts to bombard my mind. I stared at the floor and tried to focus on the over-done voice of the news anchor coming from the old television in the corner. A town parade was lovely and had gone off without a hitch; the new mall will have its grand opening this weekend; Mayor Daniels was arrested for embezzlement. My knee was bouncing. *This is cruel,* I thought.

The metallic crash of a set of double doors opening startled me and I spun my head around to see what had caused it. It was a security guard. He walked lazily along the back of the room and out the doors on the other side, never looking up at me. I was again alone.

I got up and walked outside to the train platform where I came upon a bright yellow line with bright yellow letters instructing everyone to 'STAY BEHIND THE LINE'. I stepped over the yellow line and peered down the tracks at darkness. Nothing stirred.

The air was cold, and through the foggy windows of the train station I could see the shape of my rucksack resting inside. My bag was packed to the point of bursting. I kept myself from thinking about anything I might have forgotten. I was on my own.

Although, I thought as I scratched my chin, *I AM only half an hour from home.* I glanced at the old clock on the wall of the platform.

My breath made white puffs in the evening air as I looked at my rucksack through the fogging window, now contemplating a closer inspection to see if I'd forgotten anything. Then I shook my head and turned away from the window and surveyed the long, brick buildings across the railroad tracks. *A goddamn layover here?* These are the things I hadn't thought of. In fact, I hadn't really thought much further than buying the ticket. And that plan had gone from idea to implementation in the span of about two-tenths of a second.

I was passing the train station on my way home from work as *Cross Road Blues* by Robert Johnson played through my mother's car speakers. This was one of the few things I remembered of my father. When I was very young, he would sit me on his lap on the front porch and we would listen to old blues records for hours on end. When that song came on, at just the moment I was approaching the train station, something happened. Maybe it had been coming all along. Maybe it had been waiting out there in that cagey ol' future for the day, *the* day, and *that* song. I can't say. What I can say is that without a whole lot of thought, I pulled into the train station, stepped out, and strolled in, completely calm, as if by some light-switch the decision had been made already. Those rotten thoughts that may have previously killed my courage were quietly absent. It was just as it was, and that was that: I was at the counter buying a one-way ticket to the Mississippi Delta with half the money I had to my name; I was packing a bag and going back to the train station; and now, I was here, at another train station, half-an-hour from home.

I kicked the concrete, my breath puffing in the cold. I felt like I would never escape the blandly confining grasp of my home.

*

I woke up as the sun was rising, the train car floating fairly smoothly down the track and the orange and pink morning quietly drifting by my window. I guessed we were still a few hours outside of Chicago. Pure white puffs of smoke poured into the morning chill from the chimneys and tractors on the farms that had just begun chores for the day. I stared out the window in a comforted wonder I had never before felt. I had a plush blanket with an Amtrak logo pulled up over my shoulders and I pulled it a little tighter, drawing my knees up further. I felt like I was tucked-in watching a movie like I used to when I was home sick from school. This time, though, the movie was real and playing right outside the window of my warm train car.

The night before, I had nearly gone nuts waiting out my layover. When I finally did get on the train for Chicago I was even more excited and nervous than I had been before, I sat there looking around the car with my knee bouncing. There were more people on the Chicago train than the first train, but I still had two seats to myself. Most of the other people were sleeping at that hour of the night.

I sat there with bouncing knees for what seemed like hours, staring at the blackened window beside me, the prospect of sleep far off from adrenaline.

I visited and returned from the smoking car a few times, attempting to calm my nerves. Despite the general sleepiness of the rest of the train, the smoking car was still full with people carrying on in all manners of tobacco consumption. They talked slowly and rubbed tired eyes, but they seemed to be the only ones awake.

I love smoking rooms. They're as real as it gets, full of life. *Real* life, that is, in the sense of pain and desperation. Rarely will you find a boring soul in a smoking room. Everyone has a story, most of them tragic, but all of them interesting. And they're all bunched together into a designated area, shunned from the rest of respectable and healthy society, stuffed into a cage to ruminate and commiserate with the other outcasts as they get their fix. I like to sit in smoking rooms and wonder what the people's stories are, what their lives are like: the airline stewardess who's seen way too many hotel rooms for one life; the out of work sheetrocker, heading to the city to make a last ditch effort to keep his wife as the bills pile up; the career criminal moving on down the line. All interesting souls. For sure you don't get the guy in the khakis who's socking away a hundred fifty-seven dollars a week into the vacation fund so that for seven days in February he and the family can go to Disneyland and suck shrimp at Benihana. You don't find that guy in smoking rooms. Maybe you do. I don't know.

Back at my seat, I rummaged through my pack, taking inventory to occupy my mind. As my hand brushed across the whistle/compass/matchstick holder my sister had given me, I remembered that inside was the end of a joint I had smoked with my brother, sister and best friend in the last minutes before going to the train station. They were the only ones I had told, and I asked them not to come to the station to see me off. My brother and sister said they would break the news to my mother in a few days. Or I might call her first. But I couldn't risk her convincing me to come home. She probably wouldn't anyway. She was pretty understanding. She had been dealing with my adventurous ways for nineteen years, after all. But, you never know.

My sister was worried. My brother and best friend thought I was crazy. But I think they all understood. My brother and sister, being older, had a more vivid memory of our father, and they didn't seem to give him much thought. Maybe it was because my picture was more fuzzy, maybe the unknown piqued my curiosity. I don't know, but either way, they seemed to have moved on while I never really could. I wanted answers, I suppose.

I held the matchstick holder and contemplated for a few minutes. Then I went forward to the bathroom at the front of the car. In the tiny bathroom I took a book out of my rucksack and laid it across my lap. *Adventures of Huckleberry Finn.* I also had *On The Road, Fear and Loathing in Las Vegas*, and *Lonesome Dove.* I brought only the essentials. I pulled out my pack of Camels and emptied some of the tobacco out of the end of one of the cigarettes, replacing it with the little bit of grass from the joint. After depositing my pack back at my seat, I went forward to the smoking car, three cars in front of mine.

For the most part the train cars were dim and sleepy with a few people reading books or magazines. I reached the smoking car and could see the cloud of smoke behind the glass. As I opened the door, the murmured sound of small talk amongst strangers drifted out of the small room. I found a seat in a corner, close to the door. I didn't want to talk to anybody and made efforts to avoid eye contact with any of the fifteen or so other people in the car.

I sat down in the corner and pulled out the 'special' Camel: the one with the weed in it. The idea was that I'd suck down the weed portion in one good drag, and then I'd be on to the tobacco and could dilute the smell with that before I even blew out any of the weed. Not a bad idea, I thought. So, after a moment of appraisal, I lit the cigarette and took a long drag---and, seconds later, nearly every person in the car stopped in mid-sentence and snapped-back, gawking at me sitting there meekly with the Camel in my lips. I tried, unsuccessfully, to blend into the wallpaper.

"Who's got the good shit?" somebody in the front yelled, and everyone laughed.

"Whattaya got in there?" another guy asked me.

I just shook my head nervously and shrugged my shoulders as if I didn't know what they were talking about.

"Pass it around," the guy continued.

My heart was racing. That hadn't worked the way I planned at all. I managed a nervous smile and shrugged my shoulders again.

The guy grunted as he waved dismissively at me, going back to his conversation, as did everyone else. No one seemed to care.

After a few moments, I started to relax, looking out the window at the dark night passing by. We were in a forest somewhere. I took a drag off my cigarette -- which was now *just* a cigarette -- and blew the smoke into the window, the trees flashing by outside. I smiled because I was there.

"Hey there," said a voice, and a beautiful girl suddenly sat down next to me, her knee touching mine as she folded one leg under the other. This startled me, and I stiffened.

She was probably twenty-five and had shoulder length jet black hair. She looked me directly in the eyes when she spoke. She seemed to be a natural beauty gone dark, was the immediate impression I got. There was definitely something about her that made me believe she had the street smarts indicative of an eventful life.

"You got any more of that stuff?" she asked and nodded at the cigarette in my hand. Her voice was very natural and provocative, with a hint of an accent I couldn't quite place. She spoke gently with piercing eyes and seemed to be studying me, making me instantly uncomfortable.

"No. That was it," I responded meekly. "You want a regular cigarette instead?"

"Sure," she said and sat back. I realized I had been holding my breath and I gulped as she finally broke her stare. "I'd *luuuuv* some weed though."

The way she said *love.*

"So, what's your name and what are you doing on this train?" she asked directly as she took the cigarette.

"Uh, I'm Frank, Franklyn O'Connor," I responded feebly, "and right now I'm smoking a cigarette on this train." I nodded to the cigarette in my hand.

She crinkled her nose into a mock scowl. "Oh, so you're a smart-ass, huh?" she said and playfully punched me in the arm.

We sat talking in the murky smoking car for two more cigarettes. Mostly, she talked and I just nodded and fumbled over the few words I was able to emit. It was the way she was looking at me. She studied me up and down like she was putting together a puzzle, her mind running background tasks that were barely visible behind her eyes as she spoke and asked questions. I wasn't able to fully breathe until after she was gone.

She left in the same abrupt manner she came. In what seemed like mid-sentence she got up and gave me a quick kiss on the cheek before turning toward the door.

"Hopefully I'll see you down the road," she said, glancing back as she walked out.

"Uhh," was all I could say; she had caught me studying her nearly perfect ass when she turned around. She just grinned and danced out of the train car.

When she left, I relaxed back into the seat and pulled out another cigarette, looking out the window. I chuckled to myself, leaning back with a grin spreading across on my face. *Trailers for sale or rent, room to let…fifty cent, no phone no pool no pets, I ain't got no cigarettes…*

I tapped my knee with the two fingers that were holding my cigarette as I sang the song in my head. I thought about the girl and smiled. I didn't even get her name.

3

Hinds County, Mississippi
1903

CHARLIE PATTON slowed to a stop on the narrow trail and turned to his father. They were both bloodied and bruised. Charlie was still holding the bloody knife in his clenched fist.

Bill Patton's eyes welled as he pulled the knife from his son's grasp. Silent and shaking, he wiped away the blood with his already crimson shirt. His face was cut and scratched and starting to swell from the beating. He cleaned the blade of the knife and then collapsed it into the handle and handed it back to his son.

Charlie looked up at his father and took the knife with shaking hands and put it back into his pocket. Bill Patton stood in front of Charlie and took him by the shoulders. Off in the distance of the forest, a long train whistle keened as Bill pulled Charlie close and embraced him. He held the boy tight to his chest and cried openly, his tears streaming through the sweat and blood on his cheeks.

"You never should have done that, boy," he said in a whisper and held Charlie tight. "You never should have done that."

"I had to, Pa, I had to."

Bill Patton just shook his head and held Charlie closer and cried. He cried for the eternal soul of his young son.

After a moment Bill held the boy out in front of him and looked him in the eyes. Charlie had blood seeping out of a nasty gash over one eye. Bill pulled out his handkerchief and pressed it against the wound. "You're a good boy, Charlie, you're a good boy," he said as he pressed the cloth to his child's forehead. "You saved my life back there and I thank you for that---but you never should have done that." He looked deeply into the boys unwavering eyes then dabbed the wound a couple more times and took a deep breath and straightened up and wiped the tears from his cheeks. He smiled at his son and squeezed his shoulders.

"You got any other spots where you're bad hurt?" he asked as he inspected him from head to toe.

"No, Pa, I feel all right."

"All right, son," Bill said and smiled again, "All right." He stood up tall and took a deep breath. "Now we gotta run, boy. They'll be figuring out where we live soon enough. You all right to run?"

Charlie nodded his head, and they ran.

*

Back at their shacks, Henry Sloan was sitting on a chair on his porch, lethargically plucking his guitar strings and waving away the flies when suddenly out of the forest, Charlie and Bill came crashing into the clearing, soaked in sweat and blood.

Henry threw down his guitar and ran out to meet them. "What the hell happened, Bill?" he asked when he reached them.

"We had some trouble at the church," Bill said, "Get Henderson and Joe, we gotta talk, quick."

"At the church?" Henry asked.

"Mountain Baptist."

"What the hell were you doing at Mountain Baptist?"

"It don't matter, Henry," Bill said sharply, "we got a heap of trouble coming our way. Go get Henderson and Joe. Now!"

Henry turned and ran off to the field.

At that moment Charlie's mother came out of their shack and saw her husband and child. She ran over to Charlie. "What happened to you," she cried and clutched his face tenderly.

"It's nothing, Momma," Charlie replied and wriggled out of her grasp.

"It ain't nothing!" she cried before turning to her husband and putting her hand over his chest. "Tell me what happened, Bill?"

"Don't matter, Annie," he replied. "We gotta get packed up.

Take Charlie inside and get his cuts dressed and set up the table for all of us to have a talk. Then pack up, only what we can carry. Got it?"

Annie Patton was visibly dizzied by the sudden turbulence. She didn't know what was going on, but she followed her husband's wishes and took Charlie inside while Bill Patton stood outside his home and squeezed his head in his hands.

Three hours later, the shacks that once housed the four families stood hauntingly vacant. The moon had risen full, and on the banks of the Mississippi River, five shadowy figures moved through the dense forest.

*

Charlie stood against the railing of the tiny ferry and stared at the Mississippi River rushing below him. His small, beat-up guitar was slung across his back. He hadn't taken much else from his home, only what he could fit into the small burlap sack that lay crumpled on the bench in front of him.

Henry Sloan stepped over beside Charlie and rested his elbows on the railing and gazed out at the massive river. "You all right, kid?" he asked Charlie, not turning his head.

Charlie looked up at Henry, his idol. His father must have told him what happened. Charlie didn't respond, but instead shuffled through his burlap sack, pretending he was looking for something. He pushed around the shirt and his journal and the two books: *Up From Slavery* and the newest Billy the Kid dime novel. At the bottom of the sack was a crystal, a gift from Abilene. It was heavy and fragile, but he didn't care, it was his only reminder of her. He sighed and rolled up the top of the sack and leaned on the railing.

Truth was, Charlie didn't know how he felt. He knew he shouldn't, but he felt pride; he was glad Henry knew what he had done. He had saved his father's life, he was a warrior. But he could also still feel the warm blood on his hands despite washing them over and over.

"I'm all right," he answered.

"All right, good," Henry said stoically, "You did what you had to do."

Charlie glanced up at him and nodded.

"So the territo', huh?" Henry said and smiled, changing the

subject.

Charlie grinned; it sounded exciting.

Bill Patton had decided during the men's meeting around his kitchen table that he, Annie and Charlie would head for the Cherokee Nation in Oklahoma. Annie's Cherokee mother still lived there and he'd heard they were offering land to tribe members. Joe Rawlins had decided to take his family south to his uncle's plot in Louisiana and Henderson Chatmon had decided to take his large family north to the Will Dockery Plantation outside Ruleville, Mississippi. Henderson claimed they were offering great leases on fertile land at the expansive Dockery Farms. Without surprise, Henry Sloan had decided that he and his wife would accompany the Pattons to the Cherokee Nation. Despite the circumstances forcing them to flee from their homes and livelihood, there had been no harsh words or complaint from any of the men. This was life for a negro in the south. They were used to it, and there was nothing to do about it.

Later, as the ferry moved across the rippled, dark waters of the Mississippi, Charlie heard a steamboat whistle shriek as it fought up the currents of the great river south of them. He and Henry stood silently along the rail. Charlie looked at the reddish-brown water and thought of the story his mother told him many times throughout his childhood. About how the river runs red from the blood of the Cherokee people who perished at Mantle Rock. She said they called it the Trail of Tears: after President Andrew Jackson signed the Indian Removal Act of 1830 and thousands of Indians were forced from their lands all over the southeast and driven west to Oklahoma like cattle. She told him that they had been forced to wait for a ferry like the one he stood on now, but the ferry operators would only take the Indians over at night and once all other peoples had been served and there was nothing else to do. And even then, the rate for the Indians was ten times the regular rate. Below Mantle Rock, hundreds of Cherokee were left to die of starvation, exposure and cold-blooded murder while waiting to be allowed passage across the mighty river. A passage they never wanted in the first place. Unable to go forward and kept from going back, many died gruesome and slow deaths, at the end of which their families were not even allowed a proper burial because the same locals who murdered them could get thirty-five dollars a head from the government for burying them in a mass pit.

Ever since then, his mother said, the river has been stained red with their blood. She told him that four thousand of the fifteen thousand Cherokee who had been rounded up and herded to Oklahoma had died along the journey, that they were not allowed into towns for food or clothing or medicine, simply left to die of starvation along the road, if not killed by pistol shot.

The proprietor of the ferry they used now had charged Bill and Henry double the posted rate for their families, the *negro* rate. But they were going across nonetheless, and in a couple days they would be at their destination. Bill planned to catch a train in Crossett, Arkansas, with the last of his money, and that would take them to Muskogee, Oklahoma, near to the Nation.

Charlie's mind wandered to Abilene. There had been no time for him to say goodbye. She would be home by now, waiting for him behind her mother's tent. But he would not show. And he would never see her again.

On the opposite bank, the passengers disembarked and the ferry plunged back out into the current. Charlie stared across the river as his family began to move down the trail. He stood mesmerized by the rushing waters of the great serpent. He'd never before stepped foot on this side of the river and he didn't know when, if ever, he would see his home state again. He gazed across to the state of Mississippi and with a heavy heart he nodded a farewell as the steamboat whistled downstream.

But as he turned to follow his family down the trail, a light caught the corner of his eye from across the river. He squinted to see over the expanse. From the blackened woods on the other side, a torch moved from the shadows. The torch's faint, yellowish glow flittered against the white-hooded creature that held it from atop a horse. Behind the creature, three more torches moved into view, then two more. Behind all the burning torches were white-hooded ghosts on horseback. The eyes of the beasts were black voids. They sat unmoving atop their steeds and the flames of their torches danced off their flowing white robes. The sight of their fixed stares sent cold shivers down Charlie's spine. The rush of the river was suddenly deafening, and he choked on his breath. The black eyes of the ghosts…

Bill Patton stepped back down the trail to gather his son, who stood like a statue staring across the river. "Let's go, Charlie, we got a long walk toni--" He saw what Charlie was looking at. The sight froze him in his tracks.

Across the mighty river one of the ghost's horses stomped and shook his mane, snorting. The sound was swallowed by the roar of the torrent between them. Bill Patton reached down and grabbed his son, and they ran.

*

Charlie Patton stepped off of the train and into the sunshine of the Oklahoma day as the engineer pulled the cord beside his window and the train let off a sky-shattering shriek as the whistle plumed white clouds from its stack. The platform in Muskogee was a flurry of frenetic activity and Charlie's mother held tightly onto his hand.

The night before, they'd hidden in a dank hole in the forest while the horses of the six ghosts had moved past along the trail. Charlie could still smell the stench of death in his nostrils. Once the ghosts were long gone, Charlie and the others had risen out of their hole and crept through the dark woods adjacent to the trail for the rest of the night. They reached the train depot in Crossett, Arkansas, just as the sun was painting the eastern sky above the Mississippi river.

The train ride was like nothing Charlie had ever experienced. He fell in love the moment he saw the thunderous engine pulling into the station in Crossett. The ride took them through the forests and prairies of Arkansas and Oklahoma and Charlie's mind could not keep up with all the new sights flashing by at speeds he'd never known.

In the sunshine of the Muskogee train platform, Charlie's mother pulled him by the hand and they followed his father. The walk to the reservation was long and hot but Charlie didn't mind. He was excited, enthralled with his new scenery.

*

They received cold stares when they reached Tahlequah, the main village of the Nation. One old woman shrieked and pointed at Charlie, covering her mouth, and had to be pulled back into a building and calmed. Others cleared away before them, while armed braves were never far. The village was preparing for a large festival, and the smell of delicious food was in the air, and the sights around the village were mind-blowing.

Bill Patton talked to some of the Cherokee men and they wordlessly pointed him in the direction of Annie's mother's place.

At Charlie's grandmother's house, Bill left to go speak with the elders at the capitol building while the rest of them were treated to a feast. When Bill returned he said the elders had told him they would consider and then give an answer later that night. And that in the meantime they were welcome to enjoy the powwow for the evening.

Charlie couldn't wait. On the walk in, he had seen a mind-swelling abundance of colorful costumes, and dancing Cherokee, and drums being pounded all across the town. After dinner, with his stomach happily full, he snuck outside to explore.

Set up all over the village were the drums and dancers he had seen on the walk in. He walked from circle to circle and watched as brightly clad Cherokee men pounded massive drums in wild beats that seemed to pull the air out of his lungs and draw a vice around his spine. The sounds were like nothing he had ever heard and the dancers spun and stomped like they were fully possessed. At each drum, Charlie couldn't pull himself free until the song and dance had stopped. Then he would move to another drum. The people steered clear of him and he felt their stares but he didn't much care. The sound of the drums was consuming. He walked from drum to drum and was mesmerized at each one. He desperately wanted to know more about these drums and their rhythms.

After an hour of entrancement, Charlie sprinted back to his grandmother's house. Without a word, he burst in and grabbed his guitar and ran back out. He snuck through the woods behind the row of buildings that made up the main street of Tahlequah while the sound of a pounding drum got louder and louder as he moved. He reached a narrow alley between two of the buildings and the just-slightly muffled drum beat engulfed him. A few feet out into the forest he sat down on a log and rested his guitar on his knee. His toe tapped to the rhythm of the drum and his fingers began to move about the strings.

*

In the forest behind Charlie a shadowy figure crept through the brush. He had circled around from the south when he saw Charlie. He watched carefully. When Charlie started strumming his guitar the figure stopped and crouched. He listened to the sounds. He watched as Charlie was doing something weird with the strings of his guitar, bending them. It made a sound like: *da, da-da, da-dowww, da.* The figure squatted in the woods and moved one foot in front of the other silently, inching slowly closer. He crept to within ten feet of the boy and unsheathed his long knife. Then Charlie suddenly stopped.

The figure flattened to the ground and peered out through the brush. Up on the log Charlie yanked a knife from his back pocket and flipped it open. The figure drew his knife up in front of his bared teeth and readied to strike.

But then Charlie did something that made the figure halt. Charlie placed the back of his knife blade on the strings of his guitar and started making the weirdest sound, sliding the knife back and forth on the strings. The sound was haunting, and the figure was held transfixed for a long moment.

Then the figure suddenly leapt out of the underbrush with his knife in the air.

*

Charlie didn't have a chance to react until there was a knife inches from his eyeball.

"What are you doing?" the person yelled.

Charlie looked up into the eyes of an Indian brave not much older than himself.

"What are you doing?" the brave asked again, his knife not moving.

Charlie's eyes narrowed and he clenched his own knife in his left hand.

The Indian moved his head from one side to the other and studied Charlie from head to toe, his knife never wavering from Charlie's left eyeball. The Indian moved back to center and looked at Charlie head-on.

"They think you have spirits in you," the Indian said.

Charlie just squinted, looking for an opening to strike.

The Indian tilted his head and paused for a moment then pulled his knife back. He slid it into its sheath and squatted, pulling up a blade of grass.

Charlie let out his breath. It took a moment to relax his grip on his knife.

"Who does?" he asked finally.

"The people," the brave gestured to the village.

"Why?"

"They just do," he said, pulling the blade of grass apart and offering no further explanation. "The elders won't let you stay."

"Because they think I have spirits?"

"No," he replied. "They just won't." And again the Indian offered no further explanation.

Charlie shrugged his shoulders. "What's with the drums?" he asked.

"They are very spiritual," the brave replied and held a hand over his heart, "They open doorways to the soul."

"I like them," Charlie said.

"What is this sound you are making?"

"Nothing, just playing around."

"Why do you use the knife?"

"My friend Henry taught me to do that. He's the best guitar player in the world. We're from Mississippi."

"It sounds like there are spirits in there when you do that," he said, pointing to the guitar.

"Maybe there are," Charlie replied and grinned.

"You are a strange boy," the Indian said then stood up and walked away without a word.

*

And the brave was right, the elders didn't let them stay. When Bill was told the news later that night, he went to find Charlie.

Charlie sat with Henry behind his grandmother's house and they played their guitars. In the distance the sound of the drums could still be heard, and Bill could hear Charlie and Henry playing back and forth, one trying to mimic then outdo the other.

Henry saw Bill before Charlie did. He stopped playing his guitar and eyed Bill warily. Bill's face was contorted in a scowl as he marched toward them. Charlie turned around and his eyes went wide as Bill swung and smacked him with an open hand across his face, sending him sprawling.

"Whoa, Bill," Henry said and held up his hand.

Bill paid him no mind. He grabbed Charlie by the back of the shirt while his other hand undid his belt. He drew the long piece of leather from its loops and folded it in half. He reached his arm back and lashed his son across the back with the rawhide. "You and your Devil ways!" He lashed Charlie again, "This is all your fault!" and again, "This music you're playing has brought demons down on us all!" He reached his arm back for another strike but Henry caught it from behind, pulling him off of the boy. Bill spun and grabbed Henry by the shirt and raised his belt. He held the folded leather in the air for a long moment and looked into stolid eyes of his friend.

Bill Patton scowled and pushed Henry to the ground and stomped away, the belt still clutched in his fist.

He marched away through the dried grass beside the house, and as he did he began to weep. He held his head down and ran around the front of the building. He ran to the other side and slumped against the wall and held his head in his hands. *What half a man am I?* he asked himself. He pounded his balled fists into the top of his head. His family had nowhere to go. He could not provide. He heard the elder's denial of him over and over in his head. He saw the eyes of the klansmen on horseback. He felt his empty pockets. He wept into his calloused hands.

Annie Patton stepped around the corner and saw her husband sitting against the wall in the moonlight. Bill looked up at his wife and made no attempt to hide himself. He hung his head and his wife sat down beside him and laid her arm across his hunched shoulders tenderly.

"I am no man," Bill said, and meant every word. There was nothing more to say. He hung his head and cried.

Annie stroked her husband's neck and pulled herself close to him. On the other side of the house, Charlie and Henry had returned to their guitars. Their music drifted softly through the night to Bill and Annie. Annie held her husband close and pressed her head against his, and together they listened to the deep melancholy sounds of the moaning guitars.

4

Outside Chicago
2002

THE SOUND of the train whistle cutting through the cold morning woke me from my reverie of the black-haired girl from the night before. At this point, the train was about an hour from Chicago and the landscape was changing from farmland to suburbia.

Late in the morning, the train pulled into Union Station. Unlike the terrible wait the night before, I was excited for this layover. I was truly on the road now, and looking forward to getting off the train to walk around the big city of Chicago.

After the train was properly docked, I gathered my things and leisurely made my way onto the platform. I had a two hour layover, so there was no need to rush.

Once inside Union Station, I walked to the marble stairs and then the exit, the whole time my head on a swivel, taking in everything I gazed upon with wonder. I stepped out the front doors of Union Station and the sounds of a bustling city seamlessly replaced the sterilized music of the station. I stood in the middle of the wide sidewalk and drank in the smoggy air of Chicago like it was the finest of wines.

I had never before felt like I did at that moment. It was my first bite of this wild adventure I had laid out for myself; my first taste of being alone and free. I didn't have to discuss my actions with anyone; I didn't need approval for anything; I didn't have to *be* anywhere. Except, of course, track nine in two hours. Although, I could just get off the train there if that was what I wanted. There was no one I would have to explain it to, no one would need to approve. If I wanted to, I could, it was as simple as that. I smiled more broadly than I had ever smiled in my life.

The wind funneled through the tall office buildings of Chicago's downtown as I surveyed up and down the street, but the sun was out and it kept the air relatively warm. It all looked so amazing. There was a marvelous and magnificent world out there awaiting my arrival and I wanted to run through the streets of Chicago and talk to every person I met. I didn't know where to start.

As I stood on the street deciding which way to explore, a man in a leather jacket and sweatpants walked up to me. "You got any rolling papers?" he asked, tapping me on the shoulder, waking me up from my daydream.

"Sure," I responded after a moment to come back down to the world. I opened a pocket on the front of my rucksack and pulled out three rolling papers and handed them to the man with a smile.

The guy huddled a little closer, "You want to smoke a joint?"

I couldn't believe my luck. I was getting all the breaks. "Hell yeah," I responded. "Where should we go?"

"Follow me," said the guy in the sweatpants and leather jacket. I grabbed my pack and followed. I loved Chicago.

We crossed the busy street and passed into an alley between two large office buildings. Another busy road lay at the end of the long alley.

The guy stopped halfway down the alley and started to roll a joint. "So, where you headed on the train?" he asked pleasantly as I sat down on my rucksack.

"Heading to Clarksdale, Mississippi," I responded as I took the freshly rolled joint. "The Crossroads! At least that's where I'm starting. I'm hitting the road, man."

I could barely contain myself. I was giddy. I didn't tell him about my father, though. I didn't really want to talk about it right then, and I suppose it was none of his goddamn business anyway.

Regardless, we talked and smoked the joint and I gushed and carried on as if I were talking with a long lost friend. The guy nodded and laughed at my stories.

"You know, people gotta get out and live," I preached to the guy in the sweatpants and leather jacket. "Look at this," I gestured to us and all around us, the alley, "the world is great, man."

"You got it, brother," the guy agreed.

"People!" I said and shook my head.

"Hey, I've got some of this for sale if you want some," the guy offered during a pause, nodding to the joint.

I thought about it. The security on the train was pretty lax. I weighed the options.

"Yeah, sure, perfect," I responded after a moment, "what can I get for forty bucks?"

"I got some good shit for you," he assured me and handed me the end of the joint that had gone out. "Hold onto that too."

"Thanks, man," I replied with sincerity. I was psyched. I had about an hour before my train departed, I'd just done a J, and I would have some grass before I even got to Clarksdale.

"We just gotta go around the corner down there to get it from my man." The guy pointed toward the busy street at the end of the alley.

I nodded and got up and put my heavily overstuffed rucksack on my back. I even liked the grimy smell of the alley. I pulled my money out and had a fifty, a twenty and two single dollar bills. I had another 100 dollar bill packed into the bottom of my rucksack, and that was it, but I wouldn't be getting into the hundred for a while yet. I had enough ramen noodles and peanut butter to keep myself going for a few weeks and I didn't plan on spending a lot of money on other things, so the money should last. *And this is a good purchase,* I thought to myself.

The guy in the leather jacket and sweatpants noticed the fifty I was handing him as we walked down the alley. "Oh shit, man, I don't have change," he said with genuine concern as he took the fifty. He paused for a moment of deep thought, "Here… give me the twenty too then I can make change…" he pointed to the twenty, "yeah, then it'll be all good," he nodded his head at me.

I peeled off the twenty and started to hand it to him. When the bill was halfway between my pocket and the dude in the leather jacket and sweatpants, I paused for a second as I did the math.

Then, in a whirl, the guy grabbed the twenty and punched me directly in the left ear. He then reached back, snatched the two singles from my grasp and took off at a dead sprint down the alley with my seventy-two dollars.

It took a second for me to recover from the blow and realize what was happening. When I snapped-to, my ear was ringing and the guy was already off to a three step head-start.

"Hey!" I yelled feebly and started running after him. The rucksack was heavy and bulky while running. It bounced back and forth, throwing me off my stride. The guy was fast. *And properly equipped with the sweatpants,* I thought as I struggled behind, losing ground.

I dropped the rucksack mid-stride to try to lighten my load and ran as fast as I could, but was still losing ground to the clepto-sprinter in the leather jacket and sweatpants. The guy disappeared around the corner and I slowed a step, glancing back at the rucksack that held all my worldly possessions sitting in the middle of the alley forty yards back.

"FUUUCK!!!!" I screamed in desperation, the shout reverberating off the narrow walls of the alley, walls that felt like they were closing in on me. My ear felt hot. I lost nearly half my money before noon on my first day on the road.

I went back and picked up my rucksack in the middle of the alley and sluggishly swung it onto my back, starting slowly toward the end of the alley that the thief had fled to. I didn't know where I was going. I knew I would never see the guy again, he could be anywhere by now. And what the hell would I do anyway if I did see him? I wasn't exactly a master of martial arts.

But I also couldn't stand to go back to the train station right away, giving up. It all happened so fast! In a matter of seconds, I had completely screwed myself.

That's what you get for trusting a guy in a leather jacket and sweatpants, I scolded myself as I sulked down the street rubbing my swelling ear. I hadn't even been off the train for an hour and I'd already been robbed of much of my money and punched in the ear.

Half-an-hour later, I shambled into Union Station dejected and afraid. I was so far from home. I brooded to my track with my head down, seeing nothing but my shoes kicking forward with each step. My shoulders drooped as I moved, and the pack felt like an anvil. I cursed myself relentlessly.

At high-noon, my train pulled out of Chicago and I looked back gloomily through its window at the tall buildings that seemed so exciting and interesting from afar. It's only once you're in the bowels of the beast that you notice the grease and depravity. I knew the money was officially and unceremoniously gone, donated with angst to the Windy City from which I now fled with my tail between my legs. I'd crashed and burned in my first experience in the real world. There was no other way about it.

The train picked up speed and the landscape transitioned back to suburbia. I pressed my face against the glass and sulked. *What the fuck are you doing?* I asked myself angrily. I was depressed. I was mad. I wanted to be home. I didn't care about my stupid father. I wanted to lie down in my own bed and read a book. I didn't want to be a thousand miles from the nearest person I knew; I didn't want to be without money or a place to take refuge from whichever storms doubtlessly lay down the road. I kicked myself for the brash decisions that had led to this trip. I was just a stupid kid running headlong into a fantasy world of my own making, the real world waiting behind the illusion to punch me in the ear while wearing a leather jacket and sweatpants. What a stupid fucking clothing combination.

The train rocketed down the track and my mind raced at the same speed, searching for some way out of the situation. There was none. Now I didn't even have enough money for a return ticket home. I was rim-rocked on a speeding locomotive outside of Chicago with my destination and inevitable disconnection from safety and shelter getting closer with every bump of the wheels on the track. I couldn't even make it one day just riding a goddamn train without fucking up, what the hell would I do once I got *off* the train? I kicked the seat in front of me -- then kicked it again and again and again. I wanted to punch something. I was so frustrated and scared.

"Hey, the guy with the funny smelling cigarette," I heard from beside me and turned my head abruptly. Standing there in the aisle, and now sitting down in the seat next to me, was the beautifully dark and mysterious girl from the night before. I couldn't believe my eyes.

"It's Frank right?" she asked in her fantastically natural accent. I could smell her perfume. Those piercing eyes!

"What the hell are *you* doing here?" I asked in abrupt surprise.

"Oh, I'm sorry, am I bothering you?" she asked in mock sincerity, leaning back and crossing her arms. "I'll just head back to my seat."

"Oh, no, no, I didn't... I'm sorry," I fumbled over my words, "I didn't mean it like that, I'm sorry, I just, I was surprised---I had a rough morning."

"You did? Really?" she feigned mild concern, her arms still crossed. "What happened? Tell Blue all about it," she said.

"I was robbed of seventy-two dollars trying to buy weed in Chicago," I told her plainly, not beating around the bush.

"Seventy-two?" she asked and cocked her head.

"Yeah, seventy-two."

She jutted her chin and started to ask another question, but let it go, seeing I didn't want to talk about it.

"Well, I *luuuv* Chicago," she said. "I wish we had a longer layover there."

"I disagree," I replied.

"Ohhh, you poor boy," she said with joking dramatics, "well, we should've hung out during the layover. If only I knew you were connecting to the same train." She paused. "Then you would still have your money. And I probably could have gotten you some weed."

"Well, if you're ever back there and see a grimy dude in a leather jacket and sweatpants, ask him for my seventy-two dollars back, plus interest; and don't follow him into an alley."

She tempered a smirk and I grumbled.

"So, is that your name?" I asked, changing the subject. "Blue?"

"Kind of," she replied. "That's what I've been called my whole life: Blue Deveaux. It's because of my blue eyes," she fluttered her beautiful eyes, "or the Dylan song, depending on who you ask."

I guessed it was the eyes; they gripped me like a boa constrictor. "I love *Tangled up in Blue*," was what I said though, instead of telling her I thought her eyes were the most beautifully exotic thing I had ever seen.

"My real name is Marie, Marie Deveaux. But I prefer Blue because Marie Deveaux sounds too much like Marie Laveau."

I shook my head, not knowing who she was talking about.

"You've never heard of Marie Leveau?" she asked, surprised.

"Nope."

"You've obviously never been to New Orleans."

For the rest of the day, Blue Deveaux and I small-talked and chatted and laughed and I forgot all about the money I'd lost in Chicago.

She was a fascinating girl. She was five years older than me, at twenty-four, and had traveled the country at great length, living at times in New York and Los Angeles. She was now heading home to New Orleans to stay with a mother she hadn't seen in over two years. The accent was the remnants of a creole patois spoken in her house while she was a child in New Orleans. She loved music and poetry and sang in a band. Her band had 'a dark jazzy sound with funky undertones of lust', as she put it. It was when she talked about the band that I first saw any chink in her armor. The first she seemed exposed. But she changed the subject before I could put my finger on it.

I told her about my plans -- or lack thereof. I was heading for the Crossroads in the Mississippi Delta to find my father to tell him he's an asshole. Sounds great.

"The Crossroads, huh?"

"Yep. That's the last place I know he was."

"And what after that? What if you don't find him right away?"

I shrugged my shoulders.

"No plan after that?" she asked.

"No plan."

"What are you going to do for shelter? And food?" She asked.

"I don't know," I responded with a grin after a pause to think about it. It sounded pretty stupid when I heard myself say it. I didn't even know where Clarksdale, Mississippi was.

"I figured I would figure it out when I got there."

"You're gonna be on foot?" It was more a statement than a question; I was obviously going to be on foot.

"I figured I'd hitchhike to wherever I needed to go. And I've got at least three weeks' worth of ramen noodles and peanut butter." I patted my pack and nodded assuredly. "And---" I searched my mind for something else to mention, coming up with nothing. I shrugged my shoulders and smiled.

She raised her eyebrows in amusement. "And there's no other purpose of this adventure? Just heading halfway across the country to tell your father to fuck off -- if you can find him."

"Maybe a little of that, too," I responded. "Adventure."

She chuckled, much like most people do when one talks of such taboos as adventure. But I could see that she understood.

"I might write a book about it when I'm done," I added.

"Is that right?"

"It is."

"You're a writer?"

"Nope, I'm a dishwasher."

"A dishwasher?"

"I was," I answered. "But as of today I'm an adventurer. And maybe someday I'll be a writer."

"Well," her beautiful blue eyes narrowed in deep contemplation, "it's bold, if nothing else," she concluded. "And the world has a way of rewarding the bold. So I think you'll be fine."

Then she reached out and clutched my chin tenderly, studying both sides of my face. "But you better grow as much of a beard as you can," she said with all seriousness. "You look a little young when you're clean shaven."

"All right," I said, "I guess."

Blue Deveaux and I spent the rest of the night chatting lightly. I had a flask of Yukon Jack and we passed it back and forth, taking swigs and eating peanut butter sandwiches made with bread she lifted from the dining car after we had gone for a cigarette.

Around midnight, warmed by the whiskey, she leaned over and put her head on my shoulder and moved close to me, closing her eyes as the train coasted gently through the dark night. I pulled the Amtrak blanket over the beautiful girl on my shoulder and smiled tranquilly as I looked out the window at the blackness. I sighed and rested my cheek against her head, her fragrance soothing me as I closed my eyes to sleep with her soft black hair brushing my face.

5

Somewhere in Arkansas
1903

CHARLIE AND Henry sat on hay bales in a cattle car on the train from Muskogee. Earlier, they had been up in the Negro car, but it was packed like a tin of sardines and they had moved back into the cattle cars to play their guitars. The wheels of the train thumped a metronomic beat beneath their feet as they passed over the lengths of rails at high speed. Henry and Charlie's toes tapped to the cadence and Charlie thumped on his guitar with his thumb -- mimicking the sounds he had heard the night before at the powwow -- while his fingers still picked the strings. Henry played a long slow progression and they both hung their heads and caressed their strings and fell deeply hypnotic, playing that way for about an hour.

After that hour of playing, while taking a break, Charlie shook his head and fidgeted with his feet. His mind was running, and the more it ran the deeper the scowl became on his face.

Henry studied the young boy and raised his eyebrows. What's eating you, boy," he said. "Come with it."

Charlie snorted and tore a handful of hay from the bale and threw it at the floor. "It's just---it's just---it's just this is bullshit, Henry!" he finally spouted.

"You better mind your mouth, boy," Henry said sternly.

"But it is," Charlie said without apology.

"What is, Charlie?"

"Everything, dammit. It's all fucking bullshit!"

"Boy!" Henry scolded, but then he sighed and softened on the child. "What's eating at you?" he asked again.

"It ain't right."

"What ain't right, boy? Spit it out."

"This," he said and pointed to their surroundings. Everything. We get run off our land, chased across the country, turned away everywhere we go. We gotta cram into a Negro train car, we gotta stand in separate lines, use separate bathrooms, pray to God in separate churches."

"Bahh," Henry grunted and waved his hand, annoyed, "that's just the way it is, Charlie."

"But why though? It makes no goddamn sense!"

"Aw, don't start letting your little brain wander off into pointless figuring and such," Henry said, waving his hand. "You ain't learned enough about this world, boy. You'll see. Just play that old guitar and be happy, young Charlie. We're alive."

Charlie shook his head at Henry, but gave up and stared down at his guitar, scowling. And Henry did the only thing that made sense to either of them: he started tapping his shoe and bending his strings and played another sad refrain to the train's cadence. Charlie took his lead and pulled out his knife and slid it back and forth along the strings. He used his pinky to tap the body of his guitar in a strange, cold rhythm as his fingers plucked the melody. The guitar strings rang with a tangible gloom as the knife vibrated up and down the neck.

Charlie played with a clenched jaw and felt his anger strike out through his fingertips. And as he watched the blade pass along the strings on the neck of the guitar he pictured it plunging into the neck of the man in front of the church two days before. He closed his eyes and shook the knife and hammered the strings ferociously with his open hand and the guitar screamed out just like the man had as the knife had sunk deep into his throat. Like this Charlie pummeled and pounded and exorcised his anger until he was left breathless and sweating and his fingertips bled onto the strings.

Henry and Charlie spent most of the rest of the night in the cattle car, playing guitar. Shortly after sunrise the train slowed as it came into Tutwiler, Mississippi. Henry and Charlie moved back up into the cramped Negro car to meet up with the others. Charlie hadn't spoken to his father since the thrashing the night before, and he kept away when they finally found them in the car. But his father spotted him, and walked up to him as the train stopped.

"Give me that guitar," Bill said to his son.

Charlie looked up at him and drew the guitar in closer to his chest.

"Give it here, boy," his father commanded.

The conductor opened the doors and they exited the car onto the platform.

Bill Patton snatched the guitar from his son's hands as the train shrieked twice and released the steam from its brakes. Charlie watched his father walk straight away carrying his guitar. He was in shock as he followed his mother and Henry across the platform.

*

Out on the road, Bill Patton strode down the pavement. Eventually, he reached Tutwiler's main street and turned right and kept his hasty stride. Earlier, at the Nation, he'd traded some of their few remaining possessions with the Indians for train fare back to Mississippi. He had decided to go back to Mississippi, to the Dockery Plantation, in hopes that it was as nice as Henderson Chatmon had predicted.

He walked down the street in Tutwiler and looked down at the meager sum of cash in his hand, all that was left. He shook his head and marched along and scanned the street ahead. Then, he saw what he was looking for and crossed over. He stopped in front of the pawn shop and looked down at his son's guitar in his left hand and the small amount of cash in his right. He looked up at the pawn shop and shook his head and walked in.

*

The whistle of the approaching train rang out into the air and W.C. Handy bunched his jacket up under his head and rolled over. His hips were sore from the hard floor of the train depot platform. His train was delayed for mechanical reasons with no word of how long it would take. His band had a show tonight and he couldn't be late. He had been half-sleeping in the depot for the last two hours while he waited. He covered his ear with the sleeve of his jacket to muffle the sound of the train that had just pulled in. The whistle shrieked twice and Mr. Handy pressed the jacket harder against his ear. There wasn't even a diner he could sit in. The sign over what looked to be a delicious restaurant up the street read clearly: "Whites Only". So he rested his head on his jacket.

While he lay there trying to sleep, he thought back to the days not long before when he was teaching music for the Alabama Agriculture and Mechanical College for Negroes. Shifting onto his side, he wondered if he had made the right choice to leave the College. The pay had been decent and the life much more comfortable than where he found himself now. But he couldn't stand to teach the classical European music they had required of him. He chuckled at the thought of all the traveling he'd done since then. All the places he'd been throughout the south. He had traveled everywhere in cotton country. And along the way, he listened to the music and memorized the songs he heard and then transcribed them onto paper when he got home. He smiled as he thought of all he had seen and heard in those years. But he was also happy for the opportunity he was currently pursuing as the leader of Knights of Pythias Band. The large band settled him down some, while still allowing him to travel and play music, and he was thankful for that. Though, at present, he wasn't very happy with the travel side of things. He bunched up his jacket and sighed deeply, hoping for a few minutes of sleep.

W.C. Handy was just teetering over the edge into sleep when a sound from behind him made him come to. It was the strangest sound. Mr. Handy sat up and looked about, trying to identify what was making the sound. It seemed to be coming from outside, along the platform. He got to his feet, shook out his jacket and hung it from the crook of his arm. He turned his head to better hear the sound and followed it outside.

He stepped out onto the long platform decking. Down to his left sat a man and a boy against the wall. The man was playing guitar. But he was doing something W.C. Handy had never seen nor heard. The man had an open knife in his left hand and drew the back of the blade along the strings and made the weirdest sound. Mr. Handy stepped closer to the pair. The boy was slapping an odd beat against a worn suitcase as the man slid his knife up and down the neck of the guitar. W.C. Handy was mesmerized.

He took a few more steps and the boy began to sing in a hoarse voice, unrepresentative of his years. The guitar, the rhythm, and the voice sounded so mournful and low that it needled Mr. Handy in the ribs and welled tears into his eyes. He had heard similar sounds in the ancient African songs and field-hollers of the southern blacks throughout his travels. Inherent in all of those songs was a strange slur of the third and seventh notes, providing a powerfully mournful sound. But he had never heard it done in such a way as this man and boy in front of him.

He listened from a distance as the knife flashed back and forth and he could feel the raw pain when the boy sang:

"I'm goin' away, to a world unknown;"
"I'm goin' away, to a world unkown;"
"I'm worried now but I won't be worried long."

The man terrorized his guitar, wild sounds spitting off the strings, and the boy called out:

"I feel like choppin', chips flyin' everywhere;"
"I feel like choppin', chips flyin' everywhere;"
"I been to the Nation, oh Lord, but I couldn't stay there."

The guitarist smiled at the boy and then went into another flurry of bending intonations and the boy continued in a growl that pulled darkness over the daylight.

"Every day seems like murder here;"
"Everyday seem like murder here;"
"I'm gonna leave tomorrow, I know you don't bid my care."

And the guitar rang out!

W.C. Handy took a few steps closer, entranced by the strange sound. The boy hollered:

"I'm going where the Southern cross the Dog,"
"I'm going down, where the Southern cross the Dog;"
"I'm going down, Lord, where the Southern cross the Dog."

The boy finished with a sad drop in his voice and slapped at the suitcase as the guitarist launched into a wild, gyrating spectacle as his fingers snapped his strings and the knife vibrated along the neck, the howling resonance sending chills through the air.

Handy could hardly control himself. The sound was so penetrating. When the guitarist stopped, Handy rushed up to the duo, his breath stolen. "What was that!?" he yelped.

*

Both Charlie and Henry noticed the man simultaneously and looked up at him. He looked strange, weirdly excited.

"What?" Charlie asked, eyeing the man skeptically.

"What is that that you're playing?" the man asked again.

"Just playing some music," Charlie answered.

"But what is it? You---you slur your thirds and sevenths like the ancient melodies, yet you---you…" he trailed off, not able to explain.

Charlie eyed him, thinking the man out of his mind. "Just some Delta music, mister."

"It's so sad!" he observed.

Charlie cocked his head. "Well, I tell you, Mister, in the past two days, I lost my girl, my home, and my guitar. I ain't got no food to eat. I been beat on and chased and shunned and turned away and forced on down the line and, Mister, I tell you, I'm feeling a bit blue about it, if that's all right." He nodded his head and reached down and picked up Henry's guitar. "And, well, with this thing right here," he held up the guitar, "I can get rid of my blues."

W.C. Handy stared in wonder at the fiery boy, "Yeah, I suppose you can," he agreed and scratched his chin, "I suppose you can…" he trailed off in thought, then flashed a smile at Charlie. "So, your *blues*, huh?" He chuckled at the boy. "Hey, my name's W.C. Handy," he said and tipped his cap, "pleased to meet you. Would you play me some more of your *blues*?"

And they did. Henry played guitar and Charlie tapped the strange beats on the suitcase and sang his sad little heart out, wishing he still had his guitar. Then Henry let Charlie play the guitar and Charlie played some songs by himself for the man, still tapping the rhythms on the hollow wood of the guitar while playing the slurring melody on the strings.

After some time, Mr. Handy's train finally arrived and he begrudgingly bade the two farewell, hoping to someday meet again. Henry and Charlie waved as the train pulled out of the station and blew its whistle.

*

When the train was gone, Charlie and Henry leaned back against the wall and Henry looked down at Charlie, who was staring longingly at Henry's guitar in his hands. Henry felt terrible for the kid.

"You all right?" Henry asked. The boy had been singing something powerful and Henry could feel the pain coming off him. Losing his guitar had been the last straw. He had been able to deal with the rest of the mess they found themselves in as long as he had his guitar.

Charlie didn't answer. Henry could see that the boy still thought about what his father had said the night before. And he believed it, he believed that this had all been his fault. Henry averted his eyes as Charlie choked back tears and turned his head and looked down the track. The boy sniffled and picked a sad tune on Henry's guitar.

Henry knew there was nothing to say to the boy. He rested his head back against the brick wall of the train platform and listened to the boy's mournful melodies.

Half-an-hour later, a large locomotive rolled down the tracks and its whistle rang through the station. The painted lettering along the side read: Pea Vine. This was their train. Henry and Charlie walked over and set their things with the two women. Bill still wasn't back and nobody knew where he was. Henry worried about what might have happened to him, but he tried like hell to keep his worries hidden.

"He'll be right back, sure as day," he said to Annie.

He could see she didn't believe him.

They waited for a few more minutes and Henry's anxiety was growing. He didn't take Bill to run off on his family, but you never know. Something was definitely eating at him when he took off earlier. Anything could have happened to him. And there was no mistaking the large poster on the bulletin board beside them blatantly advertising a Klan rally in two weeks. Henry swallowed.

The conductor was calling people aboard and there was still no sign of Bill. Henry reassured Annie but she was getting frantic. He didn't know what they should do if he didn't show. Go on? Stay? Neither option was good.

Annie held Charlie's hand tight to her side as the conductor called his final 'All Aboard'.

Henry was reaching out to pull Annie to the train when suddenly Bill came into view, jogging toward them. Annie shrieked with joy and Henry let out a sigh and reached down and grabbed the suitcase and the two burlap sacks. Charlie just scowled.

When Henry looked up again though, he saw to his surprise that Bill was carrying a guitar as he ran. Henry smiled, he'd brought back Charlie's guitar.

But as Bill got closer Henry could see that it wasn't Charlie's guitar. It was polished and clean, the dark wood was smooth and the body had no cracks or holes. Henry could see the tag still attached to the neck.

Bill ran up to the group on the platform and straight to Charlie as the train began to chug. He rested on one knee and grabbed his son by the shoulders and looked him in the eye. "This mess ain't any your fault, son. I'm sorry I said it was. Please forgive your stupid old father."

Charlie didn't seem to hear a word his father said, he just stared at the new guitar in wide-eyed wonder. Bill smiled and wrapped his arms around his boy and hugged him tight, then he stood up quickly and they all ran to catch the train as it crept along the platform, the whistle screaming out through the Delta morning.

Part Two

6

Dockery Farm, Mississippi
1914

"GODDAMN W.C. Handy!" Charlie slammed the newspaper onto the table.

"What the hell are you yelling about?" his wife yelled at him.

"Was I talking to you, woman?" Charlie snapped.

"I don't see no one else around," she snapped back and gestured around her. She was a large, round woman with wild eyes. Charlie had married her one year prior and they had fought ever since. She knew he was out chasing other women till all hours of the night and she didn't have any problem telling him what she thought about it. And he didn't have any problem giving her a smack to let her know what he thought about her thoughts about it.

"Bahhh," Charlie groaned and waved her away, snatching up the newspaper. Without another word, he stood and grabbed his hat and dashed out of his shack.

*

Five minutes later, Henry Sloan sat on his porch and watched Charlie marching toward him. Charlie had grown up fast. He already had wrinkles of worry in his face despite his relative youth, at twenty-four years. He was still small and thin, and, Lord, did those ears stick out, but he had a stern and stoic quality to him, and he moved with an athletic swiftness.

"You see this goddamn W.C. Handy?" Charlie hollered from across the lawn as he stomped toward Henry's shack, waving the newspaper in his hand.

From the clothesline Henry's wife threw up her hands. "Don't you come round here with that kind-a mouth, boy," she scolded.

"Sorry, ma'am," Charlie offered, but he didn't slow as he approached Henry.

Henry shook his head and waved Charlie in. "I thought you were supposed to be working the field with your father today."

"Bullshit."

"Charlie PATTON!" Mrs. Sloan yelled.

"Sorry, ma'am," Charlie replied as he darted inside. He gave Henry a look to say just how he felt about his nagging wife.

"So what's the tragedy now?" Henry asked as he followed Charlie into the shack.

"Do you see this sonofabitch?" He held up the newspaper to the full page ad for W.C. Handy's band playing at the Ballroom in Ruleville, Mississippi. The headline read: 'Come see the Father of the Blues'.

"This sonofabitch is getting rich using the name *and* the music we gave him. And he don't even play it right. He's just playing bullshit and calling it the blues. Like he fucking knows."

"My Lord, with the cussin', Charlie."

"Baaah."

"What's the big deal?"

"What's the big deal?" Charlie parroted, shocked. "The sonofabitch is a thief!"

Henry shook his head at the stubborn young man. "You get your head into them goddamn books then start thinking you know something." Henry fixed Charlie with a good, stern eyeball. The kid was too smart for his own good in Henry's opinion. He'd become a natural whiz on the guitar and could stir a morgue up to dancing with his wild performances. But he just couldn't stop there. Couldn't be happy. He kept his nose in those books about all number of questionable subjects and didn't hesitate to go spouting his mouth off about them.

"We're going down to this place and we're gonna have a talk with this sonofabitch."

"No we ain't, Charlie."

"Yes we is, Henry."

"No, we definitely ain't. That's it," Henry said forcefully and planted his palm down onto his kitchen table.

*

Two hours later they stood on the street across from the Ballroom in Ruleville, Mississippi.

"What now, Your Excellency?" Henry said to Charlie, who studied the building on the other side of the street.

Charlie grunted. "Come on." He waved Henry to follow him and moved down the street.

Twenty minutes later, Charlie crawled through the rafters above the Ballroom in front of Henry.

"This is a bad idea, Charlie," Henry whispered sternly.

"Shhh," Charlie replied and crawled forward until he reached the open front. They were directly over the room packed with white folks in evening dress. The ballroom was nice. It was large with white pillars along the walls and long, heavy drapes over the windows.

Soon the din rose and the lights dimmed and W.C. Handy and his orchestra came out onto the stage. Aside from Charlie and Henry, the only other black people in the place were the members of the orchestra. The band started with a few arrangements and the white folks swayed gently and Charlie looked at Henry with a scowl. "This is garbage."

Henry shook his head at Charlie, but didn't much disagree.

After the third song, a patron yelled, "Play some of your native music!"

Charlie turned to Henry to be sure he'd heard the same thing. And he had. W.C. Handy also seemed to pause in surprise for a moment, but quickly continued with his performance.

After the fourth song, W.C. Handy stood at center stage and called out to the crowd, "I now present a new arrangement for the very first time. I call this: *St. Louis Blues.*"

Charlie turned and growled at Henry. "Sonofabitch." The band started with a tango and Charlie spit into the dust of the rafters. But then suddenly the music changed.

Later in life, W.C. Handy himself would describe that moment when he debuted St. Louis Blues by saying: *"When St. Louis Blues was written the tango was in vogue. I tricked the dancers by arranging a tango introduction breaking abruptly into a low-down blues. My eyes swept the floor anxiously, then suddenly I saw lightning strike. The dancers seemed electrified. Something within them came suddenly to life. An instinct that wanted so much to live, to fling its arms to spread joy, took them by the heels."*

And Charlie saw the same thing. Suddenly the twelve pieces of the orchestra came together to create a sound familiar to him, a sound he'd been playing on his single guitar for years now: The blues. The *real* blues. The orchestra needed a little practice with it, but they were close. And Charlie looked out at the crowd and could see they were going wild. Stiff, white people flailing madly, possessed. He'd made black folks do the same with his guitar, and it always fascinated him, but he'd never seen the music laid on white people.

The song ended and Charlie stared down at the mass of people below him for a moment longer, just to make sure it was real, then he turned around and crawled quickly back out of the rafters without a word.

"Hey," Henry called in a whisper, "where are you go--" Charlie was scrambling away and paying no attention. Henry grunted in frustration and followed his young friend.

Henry caught up to Charlie out on the street. He had to run to catch him. "Well, that was a waste of time."

"We gotta get home," Charlie stated as he marched along. "Did you see that?" He turned to Henry with a strangely maniacal fire in his eye that made Henry very uneasy.

"Yeah, I saw it, they loved it."

"They didn't just love it, they were *possessed* by it." He looked to the ground in front of him and muttered to himself and the wheels were turning in his brain. He walked the rest of the way home like this, head down, fast stride, unconsciously rubbing his thumb and fingertips together. He didn't even say goodnight to Henry when they reached Henry's place, he just kept walking in a bee-line to his shack, his body moving on instinct as his mind remained otherwise occupied.

7

Clarksdale, Mississippi
2002

THE ENGINE roared and the wheels screeched and the train created quite a racket as the last of the blue and silver train cars passed me standing on the depot platform in Clarksdale, Mississippi.

A few minutes earlier, before departing the train, I'd bade farewell to Blue Deveaux and taken down the address and phone number of where she thought she would be in New Orleans, in case I ever made it down that way in search of my old man, or otherwise. It was high noon as the last car passed and my head was a mashed-up omelet of fear, excitement, worry, wonder and panic. Being on the road was easy when the world was but a living picture viewed from the relative safety, warmth and comfort of a train car. But now, as I watched the last car disappear down the track, I felt the true disconnect from my home and comfort zone for the first time. Home was a world away and I was entirely alone. I stood there on the platform until the train was completely out of sight in the Delta forest.

I loitered at the Clarksdale Train Depot for quite a while. I didn't know what I should do. I really had no idea where my father was or what I would actually say to him if I found him. Until then it was all in theory, and I had been putting off thinking about the moments to come for a long time, but now I was there and had to face it.

I put it off for about twenty minutes longer, just sitting on my pack on the platform, gazing up and down the track.

This was the first time in my life that I wasn't supposed to be anywhere. I had only ever been either coming or going from home, like there was a rubber band attached to my back. Its force, in the form of schedules and responsibilities, inevitably pulled me home no matter where I tried to roam. As long as I was anchored to home, all of my ventures were round trip, diminishing the outward journey and making the return a bore.

Over the past forty-eight hours I had finally snapped the rubber band I had been tethered to for my whole life and the severance rocketed me outward with a starburst of kinetic energy. But now, as I sat alone -- totally alone -- in the Clarksdale Train Depot, I wondered if the home that I had been tethered to in frustration was really that bad. Now my life was turned completely on its head. By my own doing, of course. And while it was certainly emboldening and freeing knowing that I didn't *have* to go anywhere, I also didn't *have* anywhere to go.

So I sat at the train depot in Clarksdale, Mississippi and ate some peanut butter with a spoon.

*

After some time for my anxiety to relax, I took stock of the situation. I had one hundred dollars; I had the contents of my backpack; I had a sleeping bag. And my father was out there somewhere. Besides that---well, there was nothing besides that. I didn't know anyone and I knew nothing of Clarksdale, Mississippi, except for one little fact: here lie The Crossroads.

I sat back and smiled and started to whistle as I looked up and down the railroad track. I whistled the tune of *Cross Road Blues* and my smile grew and grew. With a final glance up the curving line of the steel rails that had carried me there, I stood up abruptly and slung my rucksack over my shoulder. *What the hell are you doing?* I asked myself. I hadn't come here to wallow in self-pity over something that was entirely my own choice. I hadn't come here to sink into stagnation while telling myself all the reasons I was going to fail. I certainly hadn't come here to let fear win before the battle had even begun. Goddammit, I came to this Delta crossroads to find that sonofabitch father of mine, if nothing else, and that was what I was going to do.

I tramped out of the train station and hopped down the steps two at a time. The world had a different, brighter hue to it than it did just ten minutes ago. I still didn't know what the hell I would do, but my world settled into a proper perspective. The demons jumping out of the shadows were gone. I needed nothing more than a place to roll out my sleeping bag and a new jar of peanut butter in a week or so.

My grin was that of a bandit as I marched down the road.

8

Dockery Farms, Mississippi
1914

"HENRY, HENRY, you gotta come help," Charlie's wife yelled as she ran up the path to Henry Sloan's house, "it's Charlie, it's Charlie."

A few minutes later, Henry and Charlie's wife approached Charlie's shack. Henry saw a group of about fifteen people standing in front of it. At the head of the group, three Voodoo priestesses flailed about, talking in wild tongues with their eyes rolled back into their heads. They clutched gruesome strings of idols and various objects, and they shook their hands above their heads as they chanted to the heavens.

"What the hell is going on?" Henry asked Charlie's wife as they approached.

"He ain't been out in three days," she cried, "Oh, what did you do to him?"

"What did *I* do?" he asked, surprised.

"He ain't been out of his room since he got back from that W.C. Handy thing with you. Oh, what *happened* to him? I thought he was just sleeping the first day, but then he never came out. I can hear his guitar at times but he won't answer when I call. He's making awful sounds in there, Henry. The Voodoo priestesses think he's been possessed by demons."

"Oh, doll," Henry dismissed the girl's wild imagination. But there *were* a lot of people around as they stepped in the front door of Charlie's shack. Henry walked up to the bedroom door and banged on it.

"Charlie, it's Henry, come on outta there."

No response.

"Charlie." He knocked again.

He heard rustling inside and footsteps to the door.

Charlie flung the door open and stepped out, right into Henry's face. His hair was wild in all directions and the whites of his eyes were the blood-red color of a cardinal. His face was rough with stubble and he had a wild grin spread from ear to ear. He pulled Henry inches from his nose, "You gotta see this!" he demanded with rank whiskey breath as he yanked Henry into the room and slammed the door.

The room brought to Henry's mind the aftermath of the Mississippi flood of 1897. The room looked like it had been picked up, turned over, and dropped. There was mess everywhere. The floor was littered with dozens of books and empty whiskey and beer bottles.

"Jesus Charlie." Henry stood in the doorway, frozen.

Charlie grunted and waved him in. He reached behind Henry and pushed six beer bottles onto the floor to clear the chair for Henry to sit down.

Henry watched him scurry about, dumbfounded. "You know you got three Voodoo priestesses out there thinking you been possessed by demons?"

"Don't matter. Sit down," Charlie said and pushed him into the seat. He hopped over to the small table by his bed and grabbed a blue notebook.

He hadn't shaved and his undershirt was stained and dirty. The room stunk to high heaven. He turned to Henry with a wide grin, holding the blue notebook in both hands.

"What's that?" Henry asked obligatorily, but more concerned with not touching any of the filth around him.

"This," Charlie said with a grin, "this is a blueprint." He handed the notebook to Henry.

"A blueprint?"

"That's right," Charlie said and nodded his head. "A back door in. Read it."

"Read it?"

"Yeah, read it."

"All right, I'll take it home and read it tonight," he said and eyed Charlie with worry. "I tell you, boy, you look like shit. You should get you a bath and some sleep."

Charlie didn't listen to a word. "No. Read it now."

"Read it now?"

"Yeah, read it now." He was stone serious.

"Good Lord, Charlie, have you gone out of your head?"

"No. Read it." He offered no further discussion.

"I ain't gonna read the damn thing right now, Charlie," Henry said defiantly.

*

Two hours later, Henry approached the end of the notebook and Charlie remained seated in nearly the same position. A train whistle called in the distance as it approached the Dockery Plantation and Henry closed the final page and stared down at the blue notebook.

"This is dangerous," was all he said, worry written across his face.

9

Clarksdale, Mississippi
2002

THE FIRST thing I saw after stepping out of the train station in Clarksdale was the Ground Zero Blues Club. The building was old and worn, with grey paint peeling off the dull red brick walls. It stood alone by the railroad tracks, its dust-covered, cracked macadam parking lot being slowly devoured by the weeds in the vacant lot next to it. The place looked right enough to me. I was in search of a bluesman, after all; and a place called the Ground Zero Blues Club seemed like a good place to start.

I opened the door to the old building slowly, not sure if the club was open at this time in the afternoon. As my eyes adjusted to the dimly lit bar-room I saw a heavyset huckleberry in denim bib-overalls standing in the middle of a small, cluttered stage in the back of the club. He had one arm raised high toward the ceiling and the other holding a microphone and harmonica to his lips. All around, the scribbled ink of thousands of signatures covered the interior walls of the club, with old guitars and horns decorated over them.

With a quickness unexpected of such a large man, the huckleberry leaped and stomped his foot and dropped his arm to the floor in a flash. This queued the drummer, who had been sitting in darkness, and he flung into motion, pounding the bass drum and the high-hat at same time with only his hands and drumsticks visible outside the shadows. The nimble huckleberry crouched as his hand slapped the floor and he blew harp into his other hand with such ferocity that the world shook to the deepest depths of subconscious. He violated his harp in such a violent manner as to invoke thunderbolts from the heavens, his face turning a ghastly shade of blue and his eyes popping from his skull.

The bass and rhythm guitar entered on the second bar and the lead guitar tore through the amps, entering with a blur of clean electricity as the huckleberry spit fury back and forth through his harmonica.

I stood in the doorway with my jaw and my rucksack on the ground. There were only five or six other people in the place besides the band. A bartender was signaling a bar-back which bottles of liquor needed to be restocked for the night, a weathered soundman in a faded fedora stood behind the dials and switches of the soundboard with a half-smoked cigarette hanging from his mouth, tinkering with the levels, and there were two guys wrapping and unwrapping cords for the instruments and setting out guitars.

Then, in the same abrupt manner in which it erupted, the sound stopped in a *whoosh* and silence held for one beat before an old bluesman in a wrinkled three-piece suit stepped out from the shadows and cleared his throat in a rumble that summed up every ounce of moanin' blues in this wicked world. He kept his eyes to the floor of the stage and held the microphone under a tall, white Stetson as he groaned an homage to a long lost love. His words, so true as to clutch at my very spine, were accented by bursts of dueling guitar and harmonica.

And there was me, enthralled. The music was so guttural I felt I would burst, so moved by thirty seconds of song.

Then, violently, in the middle of a verse, someone yelled "*Stop!*" and the music fell apart into squeaks and thumps as the players halted.

When the music clunked to a halt I felt as if someone had walked up and smashed the world in front of me with a sledge hammer, shattering it into a million shards that all crashed to the floor.

"A little higher on this monitor," the rhythm guitar instructed the soundman in the fedora.

I felt abused, as if a goddess of the flesh had lured me to bed only to slip out the window before the deed was done. *Goddammit, how could they do that to me?*

"How's it sound back there?" the rotund huckleberry pointed to me, standing like a statue at the back of the bar, directly in front of the door, my rucksack at my feet.

I snapped out of my delirium.

"Uhhh---good---I mean, fucking awesome, man," I said, still recovering from having my world shattered.

"Right on," the huckleberry responded and returned to his discussion with the bassist.

I walked slowly up to the bar, feeling like an intruder, but drawn in by the blues. I still wasn't sure if they were open, but no one was telling me to leave. I took a seat at the bar and ordered a Jack on the rocks. Might as well give it a try, I thought. Without a question, the bartender handed me a tumbler filled with the golden whiskey and ice cubes. Hot dog! I dug into my pack for the hundred that I hadn't planned on accessing for at least a couple weeks, and handed it to the bartender as the band took up another tune.

The second song was just as penetrating as the first, and I sat in a trance on my bar stool. The band started and stopped a number of songs for the next half hour or so and I just sat quietly on my stool, taking everything in with a smile on my face. I avoided moving so as to not draw attention to myself, still worried that someone might ask me to leave.

The band wrapped up the first sound-check a little while later and milled about, tweaking instruments and joking with one another. The old bluesman in the Stetson seemed to be doing most of the joking, and the heavyset huckleberry in the overalls -- who, I could now see, was missing a couple of teeth -- was generally the very accommodating heel of the joke. The band made their way over to the bar in a pack. They ordered their drinks and all seemed to notice me sitting at the end of the bar at the same time.

The huckleberry leaned back and looked at my rucksack on the floor. "What's your story, kid?" he asked in a friendly tone.

"I'm Frank, I just got to town," I replied, then smiled, liking the sound of what I just said.

The old bluesman in the Stetson took some interest. "You on the road?" His eyes were slightly yellow with hard age and his skin was dark brown and leathered.

"Sure am," I replied with pride.

"Where you rolling out the bag?" he nodded at the sleeping bag tethered to my rucksack.

"Not sure yet. You know of a good place?"

This drew a raspy laugh from the old bluesman. "You hear this kid?" he jabbed the huckleberry in the ribs with his elbow, "a regular Tom Sawyer." He turned back to me with a smile on his face. "What's got you out on the road, boy?" he asked.

"I'm looking for my father," I replied. "He's an asshole. His name's Franklyn O'Connor, same as me."

The old man chuckled at my description of my father. "And he's here in Clarksdale?" he asked.

"I don't know," I said. "Might be. I have no idea. He's a blues guitarist apparently. Last I heard he was around here. It's a long story."

"I bet it is," the old man said and patted my shoulder. He turned to the huckleberry and asked, "You know a Franklyn O'Connor blues guitarist?"

"Afraid I don't," he replied after some thought.

The old man turned back to me. "Sorry, kid," he said. "I hope you find him."

"Well, he's a sonofabitch anyway, as I said."

The old man smiled at me and placed a hand on my shoulder. "Well, in the meantime, whatcha doing for scratch?" he asked.

"Nothing right now," I replied. "I just got off the train about an hour ago."

The old man thought for a second, sipping his drink. "Well, can you lift a crate?"

The question surprised me. "Yeah."

The old bluesman pulled a twenty out of his pocket and handed it to me. "When you finish your drink go help those morons get things set up," he nodded toward the two stage-hands moving things around. He then turned back to the bartender.

"The kid's with us, give him whatever he wants."

The bartender rolled his eyes, but nodded his head in acceptance of the order.

I was floored. "Thanks, mister," I said as the old man slapped my back.

"Don't mention it, kid," he said with a smile. "The road ain't an easy place to make your comforts."

"Well, I appreciate it."

The old man nodded and sighed, turning his gaze to the racks behind the bar as he sipped from his whiskey. He grew quiet and seemed to look straight through the racks and bottles to something miles away. "Yeah, I been doing what you're doing for some time now," he said. "The road ain't easy but the living sure can be its own reward."

The huckleberry leaned over. "Hell yeah, he's been at it a long time," he said, laughing. "Lewis and Clark dropped him off an hour outta port on their way up the Mizz-ooo." He laughed in a booming hillbilly roar. "Couldn't stand his croaking on the boat," he pounded his knee, doubled over. "The Injuns called him Ol' Froggy Throat and Sacagawea cussed him out for sticking his hand up her skirt." He was nearly rolling on the ground.

The old man laughed along with him. "You got that one right, at least," he chuckled. "I'd-a given her the looooong trombone."

*

The bar began filling up around seven and by ten o'clock, when the band started, it was packed wall to wall with dancing patrons.

As the band took up instruments, I pulled up a stool to take in the show. With a mellowing Jack Daniels in my right hand and a cigarette in my left, I looked around, instantly and electrically dumbfounded at the shear insanity of finding myself *here*. The magnitude of my still freefalling swan dive into another life and another world came alive in front of me in the form of a dark room with a small stage and the plasmatic sound waves of pure, moanin', Delta blues.

I couldn't believe it. I sat at a blues club a quarter of a mile from the Crossroads. The goddamn *Crossroads*! Where, on a moonless night in nineteen-thirty, Robert Johnson walked to the intersection of Mississippi highways sixty-one and forty-nine and proffered a devilish deal for his immortal soul. And where Lucifer grinned through the midnight mist and took Robert Johnson's guitar and tuned it, giving it back to him accompanied by an unworldly ability to play the blues. I sat with my goddamn drink in the center of blues history! One street down from John Lee Hooker Lane and nuzzled up to the arterial railroad tracks that once carried rambling bluesmen up and down the Mississippi

Delta. Hallowed ground of Muddy and House, of B.B., Pinetop and Howlin' Wolf. I was nestled in the maternal bosom of American music, and its rhythmic heart was still pounding wildly. The lights swirled as I tried to take it in, to know that it was real. Forget about my father, what I really wanted was to find the living blues on a Saturday night in the Mississippi Delta, and tonight, at the Ground Zero Blues Club in Clarksdale, Mississippi, the blues were on full display.

10

Texas
1915

ON A sweltering night in a small juke joint in Texas, Charlie Patton sat at the bar and sipped his whiskey. He looked at himself in the murky mirror behind the bar and saw a tired man. In the nearly ten months since he had left Dockery that night after Henry read his Blueprint, he had traveled all around Mississippi, Louisiana, and Texas, meeting and playing guitar with as many musicians as he could find. He listened to the differing styles and taught them his own and moved along, not yet finding what he was looking for. Now, sitting at the bar, he patted the inside pocket of his jacket for the hundredth time that day, and felt the folded mass of the blue notebook still in its place. He had yet to reveal its contents to anyone other than Henry.

The joint began to buzz in anticipation and filled up fast, the already sweat-covered patrons squeezing through the doors in joyous celebration. Charlie smiled at the scene; it looked to be a good one. He noticed a slender, milky fawn at the end of the bar and combed back his shock of wild hair, grinning at this newly revealed quarry.

From the front of the juke joint, whistles and shouts moved in a wave starting at the door, eventually engulfing the whole crowd as two men with guitars made their way in and to the corner that acted as the stage. The first songster came into view and Charlie could see the contradictory features of a young, lively face and head of nearly white hair. He was a big ol' buck, lean and long with bear sized hands; and, despite his white hair, Charlie figured he couldn't be much older than himself, late-twenties maybe. With his left bear paw, the prematurely white-haired songster led the other musician to the stage area. When the second man came into view it became obvious that he was blind. He was a few years younger than the first and had an elated, nearly childish smile on his face as his ears took in the sounds of the hooting and hollering around him. He was as tall as the first songster and even more massive, resembling a giant boy. And he loved the crowd, smiling happily as he sat down and rested his guitar on his knee.

As the guitarists tuned-up, Charlie could see that the white-haired musician carried a twelve-string guitar. A twelve-string was a rare sight, and Charlie looked forward to discovering what this man could do with it.

The two musicians finished tuning and the patrons readied for the show. The white-haired songster strummed his guitar one final time to make sure it was in tune, then hollered out: "Hello, folks!" in a thick Louisiana accent. "Y'all know this man," he pointed to his partner, "Blind Lemon Jefferson!"

The crowd clapped and shouted and Blind Lemon swayed in his seat and smiled out at the crowd with his eyes shut tight and his fingers plucking at his guitar stings in anticipatory delight.

"And I'm Huddie Ledbetter." He pronounced it: *Hugh-dee Ledbehh* in his Cajun tongue and Charlie could see straight away that this one had wild inside him. His eyes were light brown and wide and appeared almost possessed. His grin was that of a witch jester with a front tooth missing.

Without further announcement, the duo launched into song, their two pairs of hands moving deftly over their strings as Huddie Ledbetter sang with a moaning, emotive tenor that filled the juke joint to the rafters:

"My girl, my girl,"
"Don't you lie to me,"
"Tell me where did you sleep last night?"

He groaned and plucked a doleful, marching rhythm on his twelve-string as Blind Lemon's finger-tips danced about the neck of his guitar.

"In the pines, in the pines,"
"Where the sun don't ever shine,"
"I will shiver the whole night through."

By the end of the first song Charlie was hooked, and by the middle of the second -- a tauntingly defiant melody about the black boxer, Jack Johnson, being denied passage on the doomed Titanic -- he knew what he had to do next.

Huddie Ledbetter sang out as he hammered his strings with an open hand.

"Jack Johnson tried to get on board,"
"And the Captain, he says, 'I ain't haulin' no coal!'"
"Fare thee, Titanic, fare the well!"

Charlie loved it, and the crowd agreed and stomped to make the earth quake. Charlie forgot about the milky fawn and was consumed with the two songsters. The tandem played late into the night, and the crowd danced, and the whiskey flowed, and the temperature rose, and sweat dripped down from the roof above the extravaganza.

Well into the hours in which the Devil makes his home, Huddie Ledbetter and Blind Lemon Jefferson electrified the unwaning crowd. And then, perhaps, a little too much.

Charlie watched as a voluptuous lady in a sweat-soaked, short dress that hung off her shoulder danced provocatively in front of Huddie Ledbetter. She slithered her curves this way and that and ran her hands from her knees to her navel to the top of her head as she moaned in ecstasy. She writhed and melted and moved closer and closer to the white-haired musician, and he watched with licking chops as she danced with her hips inches from his face. With his left hand, he hammered the strings on the neck of his twelve-string guitar to keep up the melody as his right hand deftly moved from the strings and up the inner thigh of the provocateur.

"Eeee, the jelly roll," Charlie muttered to himself and knew what would come next. He knew from his own experience that the field hands didn't take kindly to the roving musicians messing around with their women. And sure enough, no sooner did

Huddie Ledbetter's hand find the smooth skin of the girl's inner thigh than a commotion erupted and the music crashed to a halt. Four large field hands were suddenly standing in the face of Huddie Ledbetter, the front man apparently the one who spoke for the young filly. They were not happy. Shouting erupted in the packed powder keg of the juke joint and Blind Lemon quickly stepped between the shouting voices of the mob and his partner.

"Now, now," Blind Lemon said and put his hand on the shoulder of the man he could hear shouting to his left.

Charlie was relieved the blind man stood in the middle. Perhaps a melee could be averted.

No sooner did that thought cross his mind than Blind Lemon Jefferson suddenly administered a gruesome head-butt onto the bridge of the jealous man's nose. The place exploded into a frenzy and fists flew and bodies sprawled and the two musicians fought for their lives in the corner of the juke joint.

Charlie snapped into motion and ran and jumped and brought down his nearly empty whiskey bottle onto the head of the field hand that was now on top of Blind Lemon. The bottle shattered and the field hand slumped to the floor and Charlie spun to face the remaining mob. He punched another patron in the jaw and helped Blind Lemon to his feet. Blind Lemon was up in a flash and immediately firing out punches in any direction he sensed danger. The blind man knocked two men clean out with a series of surprisingly well placed fists, using his left hand as a guide for his right. Huddie Ledbetter, to Charlie and Blind Lemon's right, drove a man's face into the cast-iron radiator beside him then picked up his guitar and swung it like an axe down onto the crown of another attacker. Blind Lemon also found his guitar on the chair and used the bottom to rupture the face of an approaching voice.

Women screeched and men yelled and Charlie snatched up the bottle from which Blind Lemon had been drinking and threw it at the heads of the men standing between them and the door. He grabbed Blind Lemon by the arm and pulled him toward the door, and Blind Lemon and Huddie Ledbetter swung their guitars at the advancing mob. With one final reverberant '*thwack*', Huddie's heavy, twelve-string guitar found a target and the three men made it clear of the door and took off running, the shouting mob pouring out of the juke joint as they disappeared into the night.

They ran and ran, until well away, and then stopped to catch their breath. While they rested, Blind Lemon used his hands to inspect Charlie as Huddie Ledbetter gulped for wind and turned to view the new man.

"Who we got here, Huddie?" Blind Lemon asked his partner.

Huddie studied Charlie and squinted his eyes, wary of their sudden ally. "Not sure."

"Name's Charlie Patton," Charlie said and held out his hand to Huddie Ledbetter.

"Huddie Ledbetter," Huddie replied but didn't shake his hand, still wary.

Blind Lemon was decidedly friendlier. "Mighty nice to make your acquaintance, Charlie Patton." He thrust out his hand. "Name's Lemon, Lemon Jefferson, my friends call me Blind Lemon, on account of my being blind and all." He smiled warmly as they shook hands. "I suppose we owe you a big one for helping us out in there."

"No, I wouldn't say that," Charlie said. "But I would appreciate you letting me bend your ear for a few."

"I knew he wanted something," Huddie scoffed at Charlie. But his demeanor suddenly changed as Charlie's burning eyes flashed toward him.

Huddie was taken aback but quickly regained himself and leaned in toward Charlie. "You got some kind of problem, boy?" he asked and bared his teeth. He stood a full eight inches taller than Charlie and had a crazy, devilish eye.

But Charlie glared back, unflinching, and Blind Lemon had to jump between the two, grinning as he placed a hand on each of their chests and pushed them apart.

"Forgive my apish friend," he said to Charlie, still grinning. "He's just protective."

Charlie didn't respond but kept his eyes locked on Huddie Ledbetter.

"Well, ask the fucking guy what he wants," Huddie said finally, breaking eye contact to turn and step over to his guitar. He picked it up and sat down on the ground with his back to the two other men and started strumming a tune.

Blind Lemon patted Charlie on the back and wrapped his large arm around his shoulders and engulfed the little man. "So, to what do we owe the pleasure of your help back there?" he asked as his smiling face swayed back and forth, tilted up like he was looking happily at the stars.

"Well," Charlie said, "You've heard of blues music, right?"

Blind Lemon thought for a second. "You mean the stuff Ma Rainey and W.C. Handy been putting out?"

Charlie growled to himself. "No, not exactly. But yeah. They call that shit blues, but they got it all wrong."

"All right," Blind Lemon allowed without argument.

Charlie pulled out his blue notebook from his inside jacket pocket and held it for Blind Lemon to see -- before realizing Blind Lemon, of course, couldn't see. "You see," he explained, "I've studied a great deal about music and the human mind."

"Oh yeah?" Blind Lemon asked, still smiling happily. "You an educated fella, are ya?"

"Nah, I ain't saying that." He paused and studied the two men. "What do you guys think about the state of things for us colored folk?"

"Ohh, so you're a colored fella?" Blind Lemon asked.

The question caught Charlie off guard, but then he realized Blind Lemon couldn't see his skin color. "Yeah, I'm a colored fella," he said and left it at that.

"Colored some kind of red," Huddie chimed in.

Blind Lemon didn't ask what the comment was about but instead asked Charlie, "Whachya mean about the state of things?"

"You see, I got an idea." He held up the blue notebook. "And I think you two could be just what I've been looking for."

"I knew it," Huddie spouted. "He wants something."

*

Charlie Patton, Blind Lemon Jefferson, and Huddie Ledbetter sat on the two small beds of Charlie's room at the boarding house.

"Yeah, it ain't right, but there ain't nothing we can do," Huddie replied to an inquiry from Charlie. "You think white folks are just suddenly gonna start giving a damn about us?"

"No," Charlie said bluntly. "And that's my point. They're never gonna come around to treating us right on their own."

"Exactly!" Huddie said. He was holding a revolver he had taken out of his waist band earlier and he pointed it at the wall and mimed shooting.

"But that's exactly my point," Charlie said, pointing to the gun.

"We can't fight this shit head on. We're outnumbered and the tables are stacked against us on every level."

Charlie stood up and held his hands out in front of him as he continued. "Who the hell does a black man go to?" he asked. "He wants things to change he has to talk to a white politician, elected by white men. He's got a complaint he's got to talk to a white sheriff, elected by white men. If he gets arrested by that sheriff, he goes in front of a white judge, where he pleads to a white jury and is prosecuted and defended by white lawyers, and then hanged by a white executioner."

"That about sums it up," Huddie said.

"Goddamn right," Charlie said.

"So let's kill 'em all," Huddie shouted with a crazy smile, egging Charlie on.

Blind Lemon grunted and waved at his drunken friend, "They ain't all bad," he said to both of them. "One of the best men I know is a white man, name of John Lomax, a music collector here in Texas."

"Well, that's one," Huddie said and held up one finger.

"Nah, there's more. I've known quite a few."

"Well, I tend to agree with Huddie on this," Charlie stepped forward, "but I hope you're right, because just by the numbers, we can't out-fight them and we certainly can't out-vote them. So the only option is to convert them, to make them join us, fight with us." Charlie paused and tapped his head with his fingertip and a flash of wildness came across his eyes. "And I got a plan to do just that."

"Must be one hell of a plan if you think it's gonna do *that*," Huddie said.

"It is."

"Must be some kinda magic plan," Huddie added with a sneer.

"It is -- kinda."

"Ah, hell," Huddie said and waved his hand, turning to Lemon. "This guy's a lunatic."

Blind Lemon held up a hand to Huddie before raising his eyes to Charlie. "Does sound a might far-fetched, Mr. Patton," he said.

"It ain't," Charlie stated, undeterred. "I know how. I've got a blueprint. I've got *the* Blueprint."

"The Blueprint?"

"I happen to know there are ways to all but hypnotize people with certain intonations and rhythms. I've studied this side of music for years. Used right, these techniques have powers over people, strong powers, over *any* people. And I believe they can be used to plant the seeds of a revolution -- right through the back door," he said, and tapped his head with his fingertip.

"A revolution?" Blind Lemon asked and raised his eyebrows.

"That's right, we plant the seeds of ideas and the trees will grow. This, boys," he held up his guitar, "this is a lock-pick to the back door of anybody's home and soul. And the bastards won't even know we're there."

"That shit sounds weird," Huddie said.

"It ain't, and you'll see. I know how to do it." He reached into his pocket and pulled out the blue notebook. "I can make a person feel just about anything I want, practically control them like a puppet." He moved his fingers like a puppeteer. "I can make a white man feel just what it's like to be a sorry negro in Mississippi with just a few licks of my guitar." He pointed at Huddie's head. "And that's power."

Huddie rolled his eyes. "He's selling magic," he said. "And I ain't buying."

"I think he might be on to something," Blind Lemon said with a smile and took a drink of his whiskey.

"Ah, hell," Huddie threw up his hands in frustration.

"I am," Charlie stated, paying no attention to Huddie. "And I need some partners."

"And that's us?" Lemon asked.

"Could be."

"Oh yeah?"

"Well, I can teach the music side of it. But that can't do it on its own. It's not just notes to play in a certain order. Quite the opposite, in fact. You gotta have it inside, you gotta have it deep inside." He pointed at his gut. "I can't say for sure exactly what it is, even. But you gotta have it. You gotta feel it so bad it hurts. Ain't no good otherwise."

"Oh yeah?"

"Yeah, and you two are the first I've found that've got it."

"Is that right?" Lemon said, smiling at the compliment.

"And I've been looking."

"Partners, huh?"

"Yeah, but I've got one requirement," Charlie said and put the notebook back into his pocket.

"I knew it," Huddie said.

"I'll give you full access to everything I know about music," he patted the notebook, "what I call the blues. But then there's the second part of the Blueprint, and, well, that's the revolution side of things. I need a commitment on the second before I let you study the first."

Blind Lemon contemplated for a long time. "That's a lot of wild talking you're doing tonight, Charlie Patton," Blind Lemon finally said with a smile. "And I like it. But I think we've gotta hear what's in this Blueprint thing before we tell you if we're up for joining a revolution." He smiled warmly.

"I ain't," Huddie stated. "I can tell you that right now."

Charlie paid no attention to Huddie as he thought over Lemon's proposal. "Fair enough," he finally replied with a shrug of his shoulders.

"You're actually gonna listen to this?" Huddie protested. "This is a bunch of madness, Lemon. Revolution? Risin' up?" He shook his head. "Just talking to this guy's likely to get us killed."

"You like being treated like a dog?" Charlie snapped and flashed his eyes to Huddie.

Huddie stopped what he was doing and turned and glared at Charlie. "Don't nobody treat me like a dog."

"Except for any white man that wants to," Charlie replied through clenched teeth.

"Take her easy, boys," Blind Lemon chimed in from the end of the bed. "Let's hear what he's got to say, Huddie. Ain't nothing but a little time drinking his whiskey anyhow." He held up the bottle and grinned.

Huddie grunted and lay down on the bed, "You're as crazy as he is, Lemon."

Blind Lemon grinned and held up the bottle. "On with your Blueprint, Mr. Charlie Patton."

Charlie couldn't help but grin at the bubbly blind man. He took up his guitar and opened the blue notebook to the first page. "This, boys, this is what I call the blues." His fingers came to motion and he played them the blues.

Both of their attentions were caught the moment he started playing. And for the next three hours, he read from his Blueprint and played his guitar and Blind Lemon sat on the end of the bed with his guitar in his hands and said things like "Oh, yeawwh," and "Yeeesss, boss," and would pick a riff when he really liked something he heard -- which was often.

Huddie, on the other hand, pretended to be only mildly impressed. He mostly just sat and listened with half an ear, cleaning the six-shot revolver he'd recently picked up in Dallas.

*

The next morning they all made a pact. Or Blind Lemon and Charlie did; Lemon was fully sold on the idea, and Huddie, as was customary, went along with Lemon. Together the three of them left the boarding house and set off into Texas. Charlie would come to call their alliance the Delta Triad, and for the next three months, he taught them all the intricacies of his Blueprint as they traveled throughout Texas, Louisiana, and Mississippi, playing shows in the evening followed by huddled, late-night soirees of drink, study, and discussion back at the boarding houses.

*

After a show that summer in Texas, they all left the juke joint and stumbled down the dirt road toward another late night at another boarding house. The moon was bright in the massive Texas sky and the breeze was cool and dry. They passed a whiskey bottle back and forth.

"Charlie's blues really gets people going, don't it?" Blind Lemon said with an excited smile. He held onto the arm of Huddie Ledbetter as they walked.

Huddie still wasn't fully convinced, but there wasn't much he could say. People really did seem to come under a spell when the three of them played Charlie's music.

"Tell me again, Huddie, about how Charlie played the guitar behind his head," Blind Lemon requested with a grin, referring to the tricks Charlie did with his guitar while he played. Charlie would rouse the crowd to the brink of explosion with wild guitar acrobatics, tossing it into the air and playing it behind his head or between his legs without missing a note.

Huddie rolled his eyes at Lemon's request and took a slug from the bottle. They continued down the road in high spirits, Blind

Lemon talking excitedly as Huddie and Charlie listened with grins.

"To the Delta Triad, boys!" Blind Lemon shouted with glee and raised the whiskey bottle to the sky. "Revolution!"

Charlie chuckled at Lemon. "Here, here," he said and took a slug from the bottle.

Then, from down the dirt road came the headlights of one of Henry Ford's new model T automobiles. The beams drew closer and the three men used their hands to block the bright headlights from their eyes. The vehicle slowed as it approached, its tires crunching over the gravel.

Before they noticed the large, white star on the side of the vehicle, it was too late. A sheriff jumped out of the Ford with a hand on the butt of his gun. "Don't even think about running," he ordered and stepped closer to them around the hood of his car. "What y'all doing out here?"

"We ain't doing nothing, sir," Charlie said. "Just heading home."

"Is that right?"

"It is."

The sheriff looked them all up and down. "Y'all look like y'all up to no good."

"No, sir. We're just heading home."

"Well, we'll see about that, won't we?" the cop said and ordered them against his car.

It didn't take long for him to find Huddie's gun. And when he did, he looked like a kid on Christmas.

Before Charlie could even explain to Lemon what was happening, they were alone on the road and the car's taillights were disappearing into the dust with Huddie Ledbetter in the backseat, arrested for possession of a firearm.

11

Clarksdale, Mississippi
2002

BY TWO a.m., when the band stopped playing, I was a mush from drink. It had all come on so quickly that I was a wreck before I knew it. I helped the band load up their equipment, but was little help. They were kind-hearted though and gave me simple tasks so as to keep my spirits up. I wrestled, to their amusement, with boxes of cords all gone a-tangle around my arms and body. My tongue was pressed out the corner of my mouth and I concentrated out of one squinted eye as I tried to make my way toward the trailer. Three quick steps forward, one and a half to the left, two back and a shuffle forward again and I had covered two feet.

"Looks like you dancing on stage," the old man chuckled at the huckleberry from a three-legged wooden stool discarded outside the back of the club. He grinned as he licked the glued edge of a freshly rolled cigarette.

"What the hell are we gonna do with him?" the huckleberry responded, leaning against the wall and watching my attempt to make it to the trailer with amused interest.

"You don't have to do anything," I attempted to interject, but tripped over a cord and nearly fell to the ground.

"He's right," the old man said as he lit his cigarette. "We're not going to do anything. He'll learn. He's got to. It's the road."

"Yeah, I suppose," the huckleberry said and nodded his head.

"I'll grab him a cup of coffee."

They hung around and made themselves busy while I drank one cup of coffee, and then another. But then, with no other excuse to wait any longer, and already running behind on a tight schedule, the band's patchy old tour bus clambered out of the parking lot and I was left wobbling alone behind the long-closed blues club adjacent to the glimmering, steel railroad tracks of Clarksdale, Mississippi.

While the coffee did help clear my head a little, it also gave me a jolt of energy that I knew would prevent any sleep even if I had a place to lie down. And the dark seemed a lot darker, and the quiet more foreboding, when I was alone.

I slumped to the ground to keep from having to stand. "*Trailersh fer sale er rent*," I sang loudly, breaking the quiet while I sat by myself in the middle of the dirt parking lot of the Ground Zero Blues Club in the pre-dawn hours of the Mississippi Delta.

I drunkenly swung my head one way and then the other, looking at my surroundings. I laughed out loud, my left arm rested on the rucksack that held all my earthly possessions. I laughed even louder.

"*No phooone no pewl no petsh*;" I yelled, then shouted at the top of my lungs, "*I AIN'T GOSH NO CIGARESH!!*" I laughed hysterically.

"I got some cigarettes, paly," came a hushed voice from behind me.

I swung my head around and tried to get to my feet, but my legs didn't cooperate.

"But you probably better be keeping that racket down," the voice continued.

I wobbled to my knees and saw a man cautiously stepping toward me from the streetlight shadows. I cursed the vile stuff that had put me in this state.

"Hmmm, on the skunk, ain't ya?"

I raised one foot to the ground and tried to stand again, but couldn't get off my knee. I tried to focus, I *willed* myself to focus, and like a newborn giraffe, I staggered to my feet and stumbled a few steps back and a couple to the left before I fully had my legs under me.

"Hey," was the best response I could muster after finally steadying my balance.

"Hey," came the reply.

I focused with all my effort on the man walking toward me. The fuzzy, double image wore a beat-up plantation hat and a worn tweed coat over brown work pants and an open-collared, old denim shirt; a red bandana hung loosely around his neck. The shadows still blotted out his face and half his body.

"You all right, young fella?"

I raised my arms to balance myself, set off kilter by the conscious effort to stay *on* kilter.

"Yup."

"I ain't here to give you a hard time," the man said as he came from the shadows. "Just wanted to be sure you're all right."

Once out of the shadows and closer, I could see that my visitor was just a little old man. His black skin was wrinkled and his eyes were squinted from overexposure to the sun. His battered boots looked to be two sizes too big for him and he couldn't have been more than five and a half feet tall. He smiled at me warmly from under a sparse white mustache, revealing worn teeth as well as a jovial spirit.

I staggered again, still coming to terms with my surroundings. The little man in front of me, a thin, frail body with a large, round head, looked at me in amusement. He came a little closer and reached into his pocket and I eyed him warily. The man pulled out a pack of cigarettes, taking out two and putting one in his mouth and holding the other out for me. "This ain't a great place to be hollering and calling attention to your person in the wee hours of the nighttime," he advised.

I grunted.

"You want this cigarette or what?" the old man asked, still holding the cigarette out toward me.

I noticed the cigarette and slurred: "Ackshually I got some," and reached into my pocket and pulled out my pack -- then reconsidered, "But yeah, I'll take a shigarette."

The old man chuckled and handed me the cigarette.

"Thanksh, I was jush shinging," I said between hiccups, wobbling a little as I took the cigarette.

"Haw," the old man chuckled, "I heard you, young brother, I heard you."

The old man snapped a match and lit his cigarette, holding the flame out for me.

I looked at him in that wide-eyed and dumfounded way one

looks while drunkenly trying to decipher fact from fiction and friend from foe in the haze of heavy intoxication. A task with which I was having mountains of trouble. The old man looked harmless enough, but there was also something about him that I couldn't put my finger on in my current state. He was looking at me funny.

I leaned down and cupped my hands around the match, accepting the light.

The old man took a long drag off of his cigarette and looked at me, and I took a long drag of my cigarette and looked at the little old man, and then wobbled a little.

"I wouldn'a pegged you to be old enough to be dipping into the spirits," the old man said. Then he leaned over and looked at the rucksack behind me. "And whatcha doing with that?"

I took a step in front of my bag and looked cautiously at the little old man.

"Heehee," the old man chuckled, "I ain't gonna rob you. Do I look like I could rob you?" he asked with a chuckle, then examined me and the condition I was in. "On second thought." The little old man started laughing and his tiny little body shook as he wheezed through his worn teeth.

"So what's your story, kid?" he asked with a smile once he'd recovered from his laughter.

I was still way too hazy and just shrugged my shoulders, puffing on my cigarette.

"Well, you must like the blues," the old man said, scratching his chin in thought, trying, I assume, to decode the young man swaying in front of him, "or else I figure you wouldn't be sitting in a blues club parking lot at witching hour, singing at volume ten. Do I got that right?"

I didn't say anything.

"Yeah, I suppose I do," the old man came to his conclusion. "Well, not a bad night for it. I like nights like these." He looked around at the night and sighed, then turned back to me with a smile. "I imagine you ain't from around here," he said.

I nodded confirmation, scratching my neck.

"And you damn sure ain't much for conversation," he said.

I did nothing but wobble.

He shook his head and chuckled. "You got a name at least?" he asked and flicked his cigarette butt into the dust.

I nodded.

"Well?" he prodded.

"I'm Frank, Franklyn O'Connor," I said and stuck out my hand.

He nodded slowly and screwed up his eyes as he looked me up and down, then stuck out his hand. "Furry, Furry Jenkins," he said as he shook my hand.

"Pleashed to meet you," I slurred.

"Yeah," he said. "You, too." He was still nodding as he took back his hand. Then he stuck out his lower lip. "And where did you say you were from?" he asked.

"I didn't," I replied.

"Indeed you didn't," he said with a chuckle. "So where are you from?"

"I'm from upstate New York."

"Is that right?"

"It is."

"Hmmm," the little old man grunted then looked me up and down again. Then he nodded and waved his arm. "Grab your bag kid, I'm gonna show you something."

"Huh?" I replied.

"Grab your bag," he instructed then shuffled back into the shadows. He emerged a moment later with a beat up guitar case and started to stride off to the right of me, looking back a moment later. "Well, you coming?"

I looked at the little old man standing in the parking lot and begged my brain to forge through the fires of whiskey to arrive at a prudent choice. No small task.

With a final, uncertain cock of the jaw, I reached down and grabbed my rucksack and swung it over my shoulder. Why not?

"Thatta boy," the old man said with a smile and waited for me, still wobbly on my feet, to catch up.

When I did, the little old man slapped me on the back. "Well, all right, Franklyn O'Connor, follow me," he said and started walking.

"Where are we going?"

"Ah, worry not," Furry Jenkins said with a smile. "We're gonna find you a place to get your sealegs under you."

I walked along with the little old man called Furry Jenkins.

12

Texas
1916

THE SUN was deathly hot and they could all hear the teasing sound of the river in the woods across the field.

"*Bring me a little water, Silvie,*" Huddie Ledbetter called out and swung his pick.

"*Bring me a little water now,*" came the response of the other twenty men in the chain gang.

"*Bring me a little water, Silvie!*"

"*Every little once in a while!*"

Picks swung into the rocky earth to the rhythm of the call. The other prisoners grinned at the wild, white-haired songster as the sweat dripped in steady streams from the tips of their noses down onto the arid soil. They had taken an immediate liking to Huddie Ledbetter when he arrived at their jail two months before. They all called him Lead Belly, because of the funny way he pronounced his last name in his Cajun accent: *Ledbehh.* And Lead Belly kept them entertained in the evenings with his twelve-string guitar and kept their spirits up during the day with his songs in the field.

The sun baked down and the guards fanned their faces and shielded their eyes, drops of sweat sizzling off their rifle barrels. From inside the car the boss waved his hand lazily out the window, permitting the men water in response to their chanted request.

Huddie felt like his heart was about to give out. The sun made his vision swim and the rhythmic swinging of his pick was all that kept him balanced. The sound of the river and its rush of cold water taunted him from across the field. Silvie finally approached with the water bucket and went first to Huddie at the end of the line. Huddie drank his spoonful in gulps and felt the water working down the dried cracks of his throat. Silvie allowed Huddie a second spoonful then moved to the next man. Huddie watched as he moved from man to man.

The last man took his spoonful and Silvie brought the bucket up to the truck and returned to his pick. Huddie watched as all the other men took up their picks and commenced to swinging.

There were four guards watching them, the boss and three underlings. Two of the guards leaned against the hood of the car the boss was resting in and the third was on horseback with the butt of his long rifle propped against his hip, the barrel pointed skyward. He was a mean bastard and walked his horse up and down the line no matter the heat, hoping for provocation. He stepped his horse slowly toward the other end of the line. Huddie looked through the rear window of the car and could see the top of the boss's hat rested against the headrest. Leaning on the hood on the other side of the car, the other two guards were discussing something, their hands swinging in demonstration.

Huddie looked at the rump of the horse halfway down the line and swung his pick down in a flash and sliced straight through the chain connecting his ankle to the man beside him. He couldn't believe it actually broke. He had been swinging at it every time the guard turned on his horse for the last hour. He grinned his mischievous grin and his eyes went wild. He quietly set down his pick and tip-toed across the road and started running madly across the freshly plowed field on the other side.

It wasn't until the mounted guard turned at the other end of the line that he saw Huddie fleeing across the field. He immediately raised his rifle and took two shots, both exploding into the loose soil behind Huddie.

Huddie ran with a wild smile on his face. His long arms pumped at his sides as he stumbled and rolled like a bowling ball across the ridges of the field.

The mounted guard dug his spurs into his horse's flanks and the black stallion took off like a bullet, its eyes going wide and spinning in its head as its neck shot out parallel to the ground, reaching full gallop within seconds. The horse and rider shot across the field and the guard fired from the saddle.

The bullets whizzed by Huddie and he could hear the pounding of the hooves getting closer and closer. He was almost to the forest and was laughing with adrenaline, his eyes wide and crazed as the bullets screamed past. He heard the rush of the river getting closer, then the whine of a bullet right by his ear. He felt a searing hot burn on the top of his shoulder from the glancing shot. He didn't slow a step and hit the forest with the horse so close behind him that he could feel the spray from its nostrils. He ran through the thick underbrush with branches and twigs snapping across his face. And then he leaped, his arms and legs flailing as he went airborne off the river bank. He flew through the air and landed with a splash in the center of the muddy water fifteen feel below.

The cold shock felt like a gift from heaven as he plunged into the current. He smiled as he held his breath under the swift-moving, turbid water, concealed by the torrent from the guard above. But his elation was short lived as his shoulder was driven into a log under the water. He screamed as the pain shot up and down his body. He lost all his air screaming and had to surface. His head breached and he took a deep breath of air and ducked under again..

The guard's horse reared as it reached the fifteen foot bank of the river. It kicked its front hooves in the air and screamed into the sky. The guard dropped the reins and was already firing into the muddy waters of the river before the horse's hooves even returned to the ground. The prisoner's white hair broke through the thick, brown current and dropped back below. The prisoner approached a bend in the river where he would go out of sight. The guard steadied his breathing atop the horse and calmly drew his sights across the water, waiting for the white hair of his target to surface one last time. And when it did, he exhaled, and squeezed the trigger.

13

Dockery Farms, Mississippi
1916

"OH YAAWWW, I like it," Blind Lemon said as they finished the song.

"That sure is some fine playing," Henry Sloan agreed and tapped on his guitar excitedly.

The three of them sat around Charlie's kitchen table in his home on Dockery Farm, all with guitars in hand. Lemon was in from Texas, and Henry had finished his work for the day.

Charlie nodded. "These blues will spread, boys, and our ideas will spread with it. Just like the boll weevil eating up fields of cotton. We'll infiltrate the fields of their minds." He tapped his head and grinned.

"You need to cool it with that kind of talk, boy," Henry Sloan said and shook his head. "The Klan's got enough reasons to wanna kill you, don't need to be giving them no more."

Charlie grunted and waved a hand at him.

"I'm serious," Henry said sternly.

"You're starting to sound like my father," Charlie replied with a roll of his eyes.

"Don't you get wise, boy," Henry warned and pointed his finger. It wouldn't be the first time he put a licking on Charlie. Henry had made it clear over the years that Charlie Patton didn't know how to shut his goddamn mouth sometimes -- and that could grow mighty irksome to certain folks.

Charlie chuckled at Henry and was just opening his mouth to speak when suddenly the front door of the house was flung open and a figure dove into the shack and rolled behind a chair.

The three men inside all jumped in shock and scrambled for defensive positions.

"What the hell was that!?" Blind Lemon yelled, unable to see what was going on. While Charlie and Henry jumped behind cover, Blind Lemon just sat at the table and covered his head with his hands.

From behind the chair in the corner of the room, the intruder poked his head up and grinned widely when he saw Charlie and Blind Lemon.

"You sonofabitch!" Charlie said with a smile and stood up from behind the couch.

"What the *hell* is going on!?" Blind Lemon demanded, still covering his head with his hands.

"I heard there's a big, blind Negro in here that needed an ass-whuppin'," the man said.

Lemon smiled widely and swung around in his chair. "Well, if it ain't Huddie Ledbetter," he said. "Come give me a hug, you white-haired devil."

Huddie Ledbetter stood and stepped around the chair and walked over and embraced his large, blind friend. Charlie could see that he was as dirty as a rat and still wearing his prison-issue black and white stripes. The left shoulder of the shirt was stained with blood and ripped, a fresh wound underneath.

"Jesus," Charlie said as he examined Huddie. But Huddie just chuckled with a big, crazy grin on his face.

"You smell like shit," Blind Lemon said and grimaced as he hugged Huddie. He leaned back, still grimacing and asked, "How the hell did they let you out so soon?" He, of course, could not see that Huddie was still in his prison stripes.

Charlie chuckled and Huddie smiled at his blind friend.

"Good behavior," Huddie said and winked at Charlie.

"What the hell happened to your shoulder?" Charlie asked.

"I got shot," Huddie said and grinned madly.

"You got shot!?" Lemon yelped. "Somebody tell me what the hell is going on!"

"Well, I mighta let *myself* out on good behavior."

"Ahhh," Lemon chuckled, "that's why you smell like shit."

Huddie grinned and looked over at Charlie.

"Huddie, this is Henry Sloan," Charlie introduced Henry who was watching the whole scene in astonishment, still partially hidden behind the half-wall of the kitchen. "Henry, Huddie Ledbetter."

"Decided I'm gonna go by the name Walter Boyd for a time now," Huddie said and shook hands with Henry Sloan, "but pleased to meet you all the same. Don't mention you saw me, though," he said with a smile but a clear tone that said he was serious.

"Don't gotta worry about Henry," Charlie said. "He's the original prophet of this thing we got, of the blues. The founding father of the Delta Triad, you could say." He nodded at Henry with a grin.

"Oh, no, no, no, I ain't got no part of this delusional mess you've got going on," Henry said and held up his hands. "Gonna get yourselves killed."

Charlie grinned at Henry then turned to Huddie. "So how the hell did you get here?" he asked Huddie.

"Well, I made a run for it, straight off, and made it, thanks be. Floated down a river for a ways to lose the dogs and such, then jumped a freighter in Flint over to the Yellow Dog, simple as that. You'd told me in your letter that y'all would be here at Dockery for a bit, so I jumped the Southern and come up. Got here this morning and watched from the woods till I saw y'all and followed you here."

Charlie raised his eyebrows at the thought of it all, and behind him Henry Sloan shook his head.

"Well, you came to the right place, brother," Charlie said and clapped Huddie on the back. "We can hide you here for as long as you'd like."

Huddie grinned at Charlie, and Henry shook his head again.

"Lemon's probably got some clothes that'll fit you," Charlie said, inspecting the filthy prison rags hanging off of Huddie, whose white hair was matted brown with dirt. "And you can get washed out back."

Huddie didn't move, instead he bugged his eyes wide. "No, no, no," he said with a wild grin. "We're gonna play some music."

Charlie and Lemon chuckled.

Once they had played some music and ate dinner and Huddie

had taken a bath and changed into some of Blind Lemon's clothes, the four bluesmen sat around the table and poured each other shots of whiskey.

"Good to have the Delta Triad back together, boys," Charlie said and raised his glass.

Huddie and Lemon cheered loudly and clinked their glasses, and Henry Sloan shook his head and grinned, slowly raising his own glass.

"So what's new?" Huddie asked Charlie and Lemon. "Nice place." He gestured to the home.

"Doing all right," Charlie said. Charlie's home was big compared to the other shacks at the Dockery Plantation. It was set back into the woods without any buildings around it. That was why Charlie had picked it. He was making good money playing all around the area, the people were really taken by his new style of music and the offers were pouring in. He wanted a place where they could play music into the night and not be bothered.

"That's right," Lemon said. "I got a little tour of Texas coming up in two weeks, got me a car and a driver to bring me anywhere I wanna go."

"You going with him?" Huddie asked Charlie.

"Nah, I'm gonna stick around here for a while, got a nice little circuit to play around the Delta when I want. Plus, I've been teaching some of the pups around here to play guitar."

"Well, I can't go back to Texas for a little while," Huddie said with a grin, "so I'll lay low here, if it's all the same."

"Sure is, I can get you gigs playing," Charlie offered. "Under your new name, of course; what was it, Walter Bold?"

"Walter Boyd," Huddie said with a grin, "and that'd be just fine." They all raised their glasses.

"To 'Walter'," Charlie said with a grin and took his shot.

There was a knock on the door and Huddie sat up with a start.

"Speaking of the pups," Charlie said and went to the door, patting Huddie on the shoulder as he passed.

When he opened the door three young men entered. They all looked to be in their mid to late teenage years and all carried guitars.

"Boys," he said to the three young men, "I'd like you to meet a very good friend of ours, Mr. Walter Boyd." He grinned at Huddie as he introduced him.

The three young men all nodded shyly at Huddie.

"This is Willie Brown, Tommy Johnson, and Cole Ricketts." He pointed to each boy as he said their names and Huddie nodded, not veiling his disinterest.

"I been teaching these boys how to play the blues," Charlie continued, obviously proud. "What say we give them a treat and show them how it's done, seeing as we're all here."

With that, the house shook with the sounds of the Delta blues late into the night.

14

Clarksdale, Mississippi
2002

THE LITTLE old man called Furry Jenkins sure could talk. He talked the whole time as he shuffled along in front of me. The beat-up guitar case -- which he carried like a box under his right arm -- was nearly as big as he was, but he kept right on walking and talking. He walked in that fast-paced determined way that old wildcats always seem to walk, forehead forward, his oversized suit coat bunched up over his shoulders.

I was too keenly concentrating on basic bi-pedal locomotion to hear much of what Furry had to say, but the little fella sure was excited about something.

After cutting down a long side-street and then an alley, and then a parking lot and another alley, we came out onto a sidewalk and Furry Jenkins stopped and turned around to me with a smile. A smile with such wisdom and sparkle that it could only be produced by an old, old man who had ridden the road long enough to know the bluest of blues.

"It's down this way," Furry croaked excitedly in his raspy voice.

The sky was just starting to brighten with the coming dawn and I was beginning to get my legs under me after the brisk walk following the little old man.

Furry speed-walked out in front of me, brimming with purpose, his little legs flipping back and forth effortlessly, though with a slightly awkward gait, evidently the effect of eighty years of life piled onto his boney knees. His legs picked up speed with each new block and I struggled to keep up.

"Where's the fire?" I yelled forward at him. I was not yet used to the heaviness of my pack and it weighed me down. The still of whiskey I had consumed earlier in the night wasn't helping my cause much either.

"C'mon," Furry commanded, looking back, "we ain't got much time."

I lumbered behind him, alcohol-laced sweat streaking down my forehead.

"Much time?" I asked and sucked in a gulp of air. "For what?" As my blood pumped with all the exercise and my mind began to clear, I started to wonder if coming along had been such a good idea. I was being led through dingy streets and alleys by a complete stranger in the pre-dawn hours of a broken-down Delta town with a head full of whiskey and *VULNERABLE* stamped across my entire being. The little old man seemed harmless enough, but...

"You're gonna like this," Furry said excitedly from in front, waving me along.

"Seriously, where are we going?" I asked sharply through gulps of air ten feet behind Furry, my impatience raising the pitch of my voice.

Furry slowed a step and eyed me openly. "You getting loud with me, boy?" he asked in a gruff tone and squinted one eye, raising the opposite eyebrow. His upper lip slowly rose on one side, part Elvis, part wolf.

He held this challenging pose for a moment then started spouting in raspy laughter. He slapped me on my back, and I slowed to rest, my chest heaving and whiskey-sweat pouring down my face. I shrugged my backpack down to the ground and put my arms over my head, taking deep breaths.

"Where the hell are we going?" I demanded.

The old man chuckled. "Where's your sense of adventure?"

"Where?" I spouted. "I got rid of it after it advised me to follow after you."

"Seem to be out of shape," Furry concluded matter-of-factly as he watched me gasping for air.

"Well, thanks for your goddamn input."

"Yep, outta shape," Furry mumbled with a grin and glanced

down at my bag. Then his eyes shot up behind me in terror. He pointed. "WHAT the--!"

I spun around, my adrenaline suddenly combusting.

At first I didn't see anything. The street was empty in the pre-dawn hours. Then I looked closer -- and still didn't see anything.

I heard a rustle and spun back around and the little old man called Furry Jenkins was running down the street with his guitar in one hand and my rucksack with all my worldly possessions in the other. The pack was swinging from his frail, little arm but the weight didn't seem to slow him a bit. I stood in stunned disbelief. This couldn't be happening again!

"Wha--?"

I rushed off in pursuit.

"GoddammitGoddammitGoddammit!" I muttered to myself as I sprinted after my assailant. The little old man was not as fast as the clepto-sprinter in the leather jacket and sweatpants in Chicago, but he was still shockingly swift considering he was about eighty years old and carrying a fully loaded rucksack and a guitar.

"GoddammitGoddammitGoddammit!" I fumbled ahead after the little devil.

Bit by bit, I was gaining ground. Unburdened by the weight of the backpack, I had an advantage. Not to mention the sixty years in age difference that should have been making much more of a difference than it was.

"Goddamn cigarettes," I mumbled through clenched teeth, staring at my bag bouncing ahead of me as Furry Jenkins balefully beat a rapid retreat, laughing into the night. But I was gaining, slowly, the gap closing with each step.

I finally caught up to within a few feet of him. But as Furry said, I was out of shape. Too many cigarettes, too much booze, not enough sleep. My arms lashed out at the back of Furry Jenkins but came up empty, inches from the collar of his coat. Furry's little legs pumped and pumped, his feet flinging out in front of him; and I could see the smile on his face as he ran for all his eighty-year-old body was worth, never dropping the bag or the guitar.

It started in my left leg. Suddenly it seemed to become jelly, like it wasn't there. My knee wobbled and I compensated and my right leg did the same. Momentum pushed me for two more shaky steps before it all let loose and I came crashing to a halt on the cold, broken concrete, rolling over myself, my dead legs trailing behind, my vision swimming. I couldn't breathe.

The little old man called Furry Jenkins ran off down the road laughing, his little legs kicking out in front of him in a bow-legged whirl, the eastern sky beyond glowing in its prelude to the coming dawn.

"Goddammit!" I coughed through gasping breaths, the sweat pouring off of me. "Fuck!"

I quickly gulped a couple of deep breaths and took off running again. He was an eighty year-old man, for Christ's sake!

"GoddammitGoddammitGoddammit!" I ran for all I was worth, my very survival at stake. Everything I had was is that bag. My breath wheezed and my legs wobbled, but I kept on, lumbering down the street, head down, watching my feet toppling to the concrete in front of me, sweat cascading off the tip of my nose.

15

Dockery Farms, Mississippi
1918

"THE RED Sox beat the Cubs in the World Series," Charlie yelled out to Blind Lemon Jefferson and Huddie Ledbetter. He was reading the newspaper at the table inside while Blind Lemon and Huddie sat on two wooden chairs on the porch. Blind Lemon was humming a tune and picking at his guitar and Huddie was just listening.

Huddie yelled back to Charlie, "They're good, and they're gonna stay good, boy," he point up with one finger. "That kid, what's his name, Babe something?"

"Babe Ruth," Blind Lemon said.

"Babe Ruth! He's the real deal, boy. I bet he gets the Sox a few more."

Charlie muttered something and kept reading and Huddie rested his head back against the chair. They both listened to Blind Lemon pick a tune, relaxing as the sun dropped over the cotton.

Charlie walked out onto the porch as the bottom of the sun just touched the horizon.

"I ain't seen this sight in some time," Huddie said to Charlie.

"MMM-huh," Lemon agreed. "It's nice to be back. Tell me what it's like, Huddie. Are the colors amazing?"

"They are, Lemon, they are."

They all smiled and looked out at the sunset. For the past two years Blind Lemon had been mostly touring Texas and Huddie had been playing throughout Mississippi and Louisiana under his assumed name, Walter Boyd. They would swing through Dockery every couple of months to bring progress reports to Charlie, but it had been nearly four months since they last came by and they were both happy to be back.

Charlie had been making a good living playing in the Delta towns and plantations around Dockery while also teaching his music to the aspiring musicians around the area. He never exposed the true purpose of the music he taught, though, and Huddie, Lemon and Henry Sloan were still the only ones who had laid eyes on his Blueprint. But still, people could now hear variations of his blues music in nearly every juke joint across the south, and they ate it up.

"I'm gonna bring Willie Brown and Tommy Johnson in on the Triad," Charlie said abruptly as they watched the sun settle.

Huddie turned and looked at Charlie in wonder. "What!?"

"I'm gonna bring Willie Brown and Tommy Johnson in on the Triad," Charlie repeated.

Huddie was shocked. "It ain't really a Triad when you got five people," Huddie said and shook his head.

Charlie stared at him and then burst out laughing. Of all the arguments he thought he might get for further exposing their clandestine operation, that was one he hadn't expected.

Hudie shrugged and Charlie smiled and took a sip from his whiskey.

"Well, I've been teaching them guitar for a couple years now and I think they're ready," Charlie said. "And I think we're ready. I think it may be smart to expand a little. Just in case."

Huddie raised his eyebrows and started to speak, then sat back into his chair. "You're the boss, boss."

"How about Cole Ricketts?" Blind Lemon asked.

Charlie sipped his whiskey. "Not Cole Ricketts," he answered, "I don't think he can be trusted."

*

On the side of Charlie's house, Cole Ricketts squatted against the wall and listened to the conversation. He cringed. He was fascinated by the three musicians on the porch -- to the point of hero-worship. He would often sneak through the woods to Charlie's house when the other men were in town. He would listen to them talk and play guitar all night. He knew Charlie would kill him if he ever found out that he had been sneaking around, but it didn't matter.

"We'll bring them in tomorrow night," he heard Charlie say from the front porch, "give them a little initiation. Then I'll start teaching them the Blueprint."

Cole was furious that Willie and Tommy were being let in and he wasn't. He had been learning with them just the same. And now he was being thrown out. He kicked the dirt. He wanted to know what was in this goddamn 'Blueprint'. He had heard Charlie and the other two talk about it often while he was eavesdropping. He didn't know exactly what it was, but from what he gathered, it held all the secrets to the blues, among other things.

"I want to do it now," Charlie continued, "since you guys will be around for a few weeks. Get them taught right before we leave for the Texas tour, so they can practice while we're away."

Cole Ricketts peered around the corner of the house and saw Huddie suddenly sit up and hold his finger up in the air. "Let's beat them with broom handles for initiation," Huddie said and nodded his head expectantly.

"Heehee," Blind Lemon chuckled from his rocking chair.

16

Clarksdale, Mississippi
2002

AT ONE particular moment, while I watched my feet pound to the concrete as I ran after the fleeing Furry Jenkins, I saw a familiar sight out of the corner of my eye, familiar colors.

I spun my head to the right. This couldn't be.

My legs almost gave out again as I tried to stop, my momentum carrying me forward. I was at a sleepy intersection. And sitting on a bench beside it was the little old man called Furry Jenkins -- with my rucksack on the ground beside him.

Furry had his guitar out on his knee and he looked at me with a mischievous grin. I was furious, scowling at the little old man -- but also barely able to breathe.

"Take a seat," the old man said with a smile and patted the bench next to him. "You look like you could use it."

He was right, I could hardly stand. But even so, I walked as sternly as I could over to my bag and slung it up onto my shoulder to leave. But I couldn't even carry my own weight, let alone the weight of my bag. So, despite my best effort, I slumped down onto the bench beside the little old man called Furry Jenkins.

Furry looked over at me with a twinkle in his eye and a grin parting his eighty-year-old teeth. "Yep, outta shape."

"Fuck off," I mumbled, my energy sapped.

The little old man just grinned wider.

I glared at him and snatched up the strap of my backpack to leave, whether I could walk or not.

"You ever seen sunrise at the Crossroads," he asked and strummed a chord on his guitar.

"What?" I sat up and looked at the intersection in front of me. Sure enough, Mississippi Highways 61 and 49. A historical marker on the corner read, simply: *The Crossroads*. I turned and looked at Furry Jenkins in amazement, and he pointed wordlessly out across the intersection.

At that moment, directly behind a distant, old wooden church steeple, the very top curve of the sun peered over the cotton fields to the east, pouring its first morning rays over the Mississippi Delta as a synchronized swirl of a host of hundreds of sparrows danced forth from the trees in front of the fiery golden sliver of the rising sun.

I was awestruck. I turned to Furry. "Is this why you--"

Furry raised his hand gently to interrupt me and pointed at the sunrise.

He was right; now was *not* the time for talking.

I nodded my understanding and turned my head and we both sat idly on the bench at the Crossroads as the sun rose over the lip of the Mississippi sky. And then Furry began to play his guitar.

I gazed in wonder out at the world in front of me being painted by solar pastels, my mind rocking in a cradle of ease as the little old man called Furry Jenkins strummed his strings and sang with a Mother River rasp that drew the sparrows to the telephone wire to stare down at God's own creation sitting with the toes of his too-big, beat-up boots pointing inward and his knees pressed together to prop up his old six-string guitar. His eyes were closed and his arthritic hands moved effortlessly up and down the fret-board, the tips of his calloused fingers blindly finding every note and squeaking intimately off the strings with each shift of position.

I did nothing but stare at the Mississippi sun crawling up from its underworld and over the Crossroads. I didn't think about my father, I didn't think about my friends, I didn't think about the girl named Blue or my plans. The world as it was and the world as it will be did not exist. Money, sustenance, shelter and creed amounted to naught on that stirring Delta daybreak. I said nothing to Furry and Furry said nothing to me, he just played the blues.

Part Three

17

Texas
1918

A YOUNG man watched Charlie, Lemon, and Huddie carefully from across the room of the smoky Texas juke joint. The three musicians were leaning on the bar, chatting with the owner. They'd put on a hell of a show that night, and the place had been packed to the gills. But now there was only a handful of drunken stragglers remaining.

The young man watched the trio carefully, and for a long time, nervously making sure none of them were paying attention to him. With three shallow breaths and his jaw clenched tight, he took off across the room and shuffled by the chairs that held the musicians' jackets and guitars. As he moved past, he deftly slid his hand into Charlie's jacket and pulled out his room key and slipped it into his pocket. Without glancing back, he ducked out the front door and into the night.

*

Half an hour later the three musicians walked down the dirt road toward their boarding house. All three were in good spirits and a full moon shone bright over their heads.

"Give me a little whiskey, Charlie; give me a little whiskey now," Huddie Ledbetter sang with a smile and reached to snatch the whiskey

bottle from Charlie.

"Go fuck yourself, Huddie; go fuck yourself, now," Charlie sang back and guarded the whiskey bottle with a grin.

Huddie chuckled and grabbed at the whiskey again.

And, again, Charlie sang, *"Go fuck yourself, Huddie; go fuck yourself, now."*

Huddie stopped smiling and a coldness drew across his face. "Give me the fucking whiskey, Charlie," he said with a tone that had lost the element of joking.

"Fuck you," Charlie said with a grinning snarl. He was drunk and enjoying the rise he was getting out of Huddie.

"Fuck *me*?" Huddie shouted. "You sonofabitch!" He lunged at Charlie, but Lemon held him back by the arm.

"Whoa now," Blind Lemon said, trying to keep the sparks from igniting.

"You little fucking runt," Huddie yelled at Charlie.

"Go fuck yourself, Huddie; go fuck yourself now," Charlie sang again and laughed menacingly in Huddie's face.

"Just give him some whiskey," Lemon pleaded. He didn't like it when Charlie got like this.

"Look at these two," Charlie said, drunkenly waving his hand as if he were talking to a crowd, "a retard leading a blind man." He cackled. "Where they end up, nobody knows."

"C'mon, Charlie," Lemon pleaded.

"Baahhh," Charlie spat, "the poor imbeciles can't take a little joking?"

"Just stop, Charlie, give him some whiskey," Lemon said, his patience wearing thin.

"Fuck you, Lemon, you big, blind moron."

Huddie Ledbetter's face contorted into a snarl and he growled like a wolf and tore himself free of Lemon's grasp and grabbed Charlie by the front of the shirt and punched him square in the face. "Not Lemon, you sonofabitch!" he screamed. "Not Lemon!" He punched Charlie again in the face. "You ain't nothing but a goddamn sonofabitch!" He punched Charlie again.

Lemon followed the sounds of the scuffle and found Huddie on top of Charlie. He grabbed Huddie and pulled him off. "Okay, all right," he said. "Okay, now, let's just relax here, boys." He held Huddie from behind in a bear hug. Huddie was a big man, but Lemon was bigger, and stronger.

"You're just a fucking bully," Huddie shouted at Charlie with tears running down his face. "You ain't never gonna be half the man Lemon is," he yelled. "You ain't nothing but a sonofabitch."

"Is that all you got, you big retard," Charlie said as he wiped the blood from the corner of his mouth. He reached down and picked up the whiskey bottle that lay on its side and took a long drink. "You two are perfect for each other."

"I'm warning you, Charlie," Huddie said with rage in his voice. "You apologize to Lemon right now or, so help me God, I'll fucking kill you with these bare hands."

"Fuck you," Charlie said, "and fuck him."

Huddie growled and tried to go after him, but Lemon held him tight. "It's okay, Huddie," Lemon said, "he don't mean it. He's just drunk."

"Like hell he don't," Huddie snarled, emotion lacing every word. "He ain't nothing but a sonofabitch that thinks he's better than everyone."

Charlie just watched with a drunken smirk on his face and took a drink from the whiskey bottle.

"No he ain't," Lemon said, trying to calm Huddie down. "He don't mean what he says sometimes." Lemon turned to Charlie. "Just give him some whiskey, Charlie," he said.

Charlie shook his head and rolled his eyes, but, after taking a swig, he held out the whiskey bottle to Huddie.

Huddie snatched the bottle and Lemon let him go.

"Okay, now," Lemon said in a calming tone. "We're all friends here."

Huddie took a long slug from the bottle and glared at Charlie. But he obeyed Lemon's wishes and didn't go after him. He took another drink and turned with a snort and started marching toward their boarding house, slowing just enough for Blind Lemon to find the crook of his arm.

Five minutes later, Charlie, Huddie, and Lemon approached their boarding house in silence. Huddie was still fuming, and marching ahead. Charlie lagged behind, stewing in his own distemper.

As they neared the boarding house, the door to Charlie's room suddenly swung opened and a figure slunk out, his face covered by a large hat.

"What the--" Charlie yelped. In the intruder's hand was the blue notebook.

"HEY!" Huddie yelled and immediately sprung after the figure.

The intruder looked up in shock then darted off down the road.

The sudden eruption of activity came as a great surprise to Lemon. "What the hell is going on?" he yelled, his arms flailing.

Charlie grabbed him by the arm and led him quickly to the bench in front of the boarding house. "Somebody just stole the Blueprint!" he explained in a shrill voice. "Stay here. I gotta go." Charlie didn't wait for a response but took off after Huddie and the thief.

Up ahead, Huddie was gaining. Charlie could see the glint of Huddie's knife in his right hand, reflecting from the street lamps. As they approached an intersection, the thief tried to turn left around the corner, but Huddie cut the angle and tackled him to the ground, driving his knife into the thief's side as they crashed to the ground.

The man screamed out in pain as he went down and the knife plunged in. It was a horrifying sound, inhuman. Huddie flipped the thief over onto his back and raised his knife to drive it once again into the man's chest. Then, suddenly, he stopped.

Charlie was fifteen feet away and watched as Huddie dropped his knife and looked down at young Cole Ricketts. Cole was trying to talk, but all that came out of his mouth was blood. Charlie stopped dead in his tracks. He couldn't believe his eyes. Was it really Cole Ricketts? What the hell was Cole Ricketts doing here in Texas? And why was he trying to steal the Blueprint?

He stood in shock. So much so that he barely noticed when Huddie suddenly looked straight forward and flung his hands in the air. It took a moment for this action to register within Charlie's spinning mind. But it all became clear when a second later a policeman came into view from around the corner in the direction Huddie was looking. The cop had his revolver trained on Huddie. He carefully stepped forward and his eyes glanced up at Charlie. He was as surprised to see Charlie as Charlie was to see him.

"Don't move!" he yelled and swung the gun toward Charlie then back to Huddie. His eyes and his gun moved back and forth nervously from one man to the other.

In the split second he had to decide, Charlie gambled that he was out of accurate pistol range. He glanced at Huddie, who was on his knees with his hands raised, the Blueprint in his left hand.

Huddie's eyes were apologetic and sad as he looked back at Charlie. Charlie nodded at his friend, and in a flash, he turned and ran. The cop swung his revolver and let loose two shots that flashed off the brick wall to the right of Charlie. The cop couldn't leave Huddie to chase Charlie and had to watch him go, swinging his gun back down to Huddie. On the ground in front of Huddie, Cole Ricketts expelled his last dying breath and his lifeless eyes stared up at the full moon.

A few minutes later, Charlie reached Blind Lemon still sitting on the bench in front of the boarding house. "Huddie just killed Cole Ricketts and the police have got him!" he yelled, out of breath. "We gotta scram!"

"Wha--?" Blind Lemon stuttered as Charlie pulled him up from the bench. They ran into the room and grabbed what they could and fled out into the night.

18

The Crossroads
2002

FOR NEARLY an hour I received a private performance of world-class blues with sunrise at the legendary Crossroads as the stage and amphitheater. My eyes were becoming heavy in my relaxed state; it had been nearly twenty-four hours since I last slept. My feet rested out on my pack like it was an ottoman. The sun warmed my face and further relaxed my sore muscles. I pulled my jacket tighter around myself and yawned deeply, settling into a glorious, toasted comfort on the wooden bench.

"Up! Up and at 'em!" Furry was suddenly yelling, pouncing to his feet.

"What?"

"Get up."

"Why?"

"Get up. I'm gonna show you something."

"Oh no, I learned my lesson, I'm not chasing off after you anymore."

"Really? Didn't turn out okay last time?" He motioned to the Crossroads and the beautiful sunrise.

I lifted my eyebrows and shrugged, conceding the point.

"And by the looks of you last night, you could use the exercise."

"Exercise? Christ. I need sleep is what I need."

"Can't sleep. Not in the daytime if you're sleeping outdoors. Don't you know anything about hoboing? That's a perfect way to get shot or beat up by gangs of school kids -- or arrested, of course. And you don't want any of those options."

"What? Gangs of school kids? What the--?"

"I said: you come out on the road, you *better* know how to GO. It ain't all flower petals up your ass."

"Flower petals--?"

"Gotta know how to press through."

"--up my ass?"

"Get the fuck up, boy."

"What the hell are you--?"

"UP!"

"Nah, I'm just gonna nod off for a few."

"And I'll rap you in the goddamn head with my goddamn shoe. How's that? Which'll be a hell of a lot better than what the Mississippi fuzz'll do to you. You hear me, boy? Ever been woke up by the bite of a Taser?"

"Eeee," I said. The thought was terrifying.

"Fuckin' right, boy."

"Hmmm…"

"Well? What the hell else-a shit-bag like you got on the fire for today?"

"I dunno."

"So come on with me, I'll work some meat off your bones."

I cocked my head at Furry.

"Don't be crass," Furry responded.

"I don't really want the meat to be worked off my bones."

"You lazy ol' cocksucker. Get up!"

"'Lazy old cocksucker'? Why, that's offensive, Furry," I said and grinned at the worked up old man.

"Arghhhhh! Get up off your ass, boy!" He was reduced to angry spoutings. "Goddamn generation of sloth. Spineless, wiseass, pussy kids, goddamn…" he trailed off, mumbling his disgust.

I raised my eyebrows, egging him on. "I won't hesitate to smack an old man in the mouth, Furry."

"I guarantee *YOU*," little Furry Jenkins snapped around with a twitch in his eye, "that there would be the last dumb-ass decision you ever made." He shook his little arms out at his side. "You wanna take a poke at Furry Jenkins?"

"Don't come at me with that garbage, Furry."

"I ain't bringing garbage, boy, you can bet your dundies on that. And there's a pile of Korean slants that'll attest to that fact from a shallow grave just north of the thirty-eighth."

"The thirty-eighth?"

Furry scoffed and glared down at me. "The thirty-eighth fucking parallel, you goddamn idiot. Did you sleep through your goddamn history classes as well? Fucking kids! No respect. Get up off your ass boy!"

"All right, all right." Slowly I grabbed my pack and rose to my feet, sluggishly swinging the pack onto my shoulders. "Where are we goi--?"

BAM! Once I was standing in front of him, Furry flashed out a stiff left jab square into my jaw.

"Jesus, Furry!" I yelped, and the strike made me slump back down into the seat.

"You threaten Furry Jenkins you better be ready to back up your flub."

"My flub? What?" I rubbed my jaw where Furry had hit me and then slowly stood up. "Fuck, man."

Furry spun and strode off. "Let's go, we got about twenty miles."

I stopped in my tracks. "Twenty miles!?"

"Yeah but it's flat," Furry called back smiling, already pacing across the intersection. "Right straight through to Money Road!"

I stood and watched Furry hop onto the curb on the other side of the road. He turned back to me, still stepping backwards.

"I'm not walking twenty miles, no way in hell," I yelled across the intersection.

"All right, little boy," he said and waved his hand. "No problem with me. You don't want to see Robert Johnson's grave."

This perked my ears, as much as I didn't want it to.

"That's right," Furry called out from across the intersection. "You just go to sleep there, boy."

His tone was annoying. But, in the end, fuck it. What the hell else did I have to do? "Wait up. I'm coming, I'm coming."

Across the street Furry was waiting for me.

"Don't they have a bus or something?" I asked when I reached him.

"Nope, no busses." Furry spun and took off, his head down, striding forward with purpose, his guitar bunched under his left arm.

"Well, can we get a cup of coffee at least?" I said as I scrambled to catch up to the little old man.

"I know a perfect place," he said.

*

The rusted old sign read: Hopson Plantation.

The small buildings surrounding the large, main barn appeared to be nothing but rundown shacks and outbuildings. But, then we got closer.

Furry walked along with his head down and the arm that wasn't holding his guitar swinging widely in step to his expeditious gait. He cut diagonally between two shacks.

From between the cabins, Furry made way across a dirt farm road to a gap between two other buildings. It didn't take a genius to notice the furtive way he crossed the open area. I looked both ways and darted out behind him, uneasy and unsure of why we were darting, but figuring to err on the side of caution.

We reached the buildings across the way and Furry moved quickly down the gap without a pause. At the back of the shacks, strewn with rusted, old farm equipment, Furry turned to the right and stepped rapidly, keeping close to the wall.

I trotted to catch up to him behind the shack, catching him as he slowed behind an old tractor to scan the area. "Hey," I whispered, still not sure why we were being so stealthy. "You don't happen to know a white blues guitarist that goes by the same name as me, do you? Franklyn O'Connor. He'd be about fifty-five." It was a strange time to bring it up, I know.

Furry stopped scanning and turned to me. He looked at me for a long moment, then held his finger up to his lips. "Shhh."

"I'm just asking," I whispered.

"Why do you want to know?"

"He's my dad and I'm looking for him."

"And now is when you ask?"

I shrugged my shoulders. "Seemed as good a time as any," I whispered. It wasn't.

Furry shook his head. "No, I don't. Now shush," he said and

put his finger to his lips.

Furry stepped out from behind the tractor and continued along the back of the line of shacks. As we snuck along, I looked in one of the shack windows and could see that the shacks were in fact not shacks at all. In fact, they were plush and comfortable cabins, hotel rooms dressed to look like run-down plantation shacks. Curious.

Approaching the back of the big barn, Furry shuffled quickly up to a plain, metal door, and I was right behind. He turned and handed me his guitar case, then, without a word or hesitation, he pulled open the unmarked metal door and stepped inside, startling a dishwasher plying his trade in the back of a large, fancy kitchen. It was a restaurant kitchen and Furry tipped his cap to the dishwasher and walked straight to the coffee pots on the left. The dishwasher watched Furry, then turned to me. I shrugged my shoulders. I didn't know what was going on either.

At the coffee pots, Furry methodically filled up two mugs with coffee, slowly pouring cream from a stainless steel pitcher into one, and then the other, and then another splash in the first. Then he grabbed some packets of sugar, shook them a few times, tore the tops off and poured two sugars into each coffee mug before walking confidently back to the door. The dishwasher stared at him the whole time, unsure of what to do. At the door, Furry gave one mug to me, raised his in a 'cheers' to the dishwasher, who continued to stare, and then stepped out the back door.

Furry and I retraced our steps back out to the road, drinking delicious, hot coffee out of warm china mugs. At the road, we turned right and started plodding down the dusty strip of macadam that stretched off in a straight line through a seemingly endless sea of cotton toward Greenwood, Mississippi -- the final resting place of Robert Johnson.

"There's a pretty nice saloon restaurant in that big barn back there," Furry mentioned and thumbed back as we walked down the road. "I used to play it quite a bit."

"Is that right?"

"It is," he said and looked over at me out of the corner of his eye. "Lotta good memories there."

I nodded and looked back at the barn. "Just looks like a plantation from the outside."

"It does. And it was," he said, pointing to the cotton fields of the Hopson Plantation. "And Pinetop Perkins worked the fields right here back in the day, before he went and got famous tickling the ivory."

"No kidding," I said and looked off at the fields.

"Yessir," Furry confirmed with a smile. "And you ever hear of the International Harvester?"

"It rings a bell."

"Of course you wouldn't know."

"All right."

"It's a mechanical cotton picker. It caused the Great Migration."

"The Great Migration?"

"You're a fucking idiot."

"All right."

"That's right."

"All right."

"What's in Harlem?"

"Harlem?"

"You heard me, what's in Harlem?"

"I don't know."

"Of course you don't, you're just a dumb-ass white kid. You know what's in Harlem?"

"No, Furry, for fuck's sake, tell me what's in Harlem."

"You getting loud with me, boy?"

"Jesus Christ!"

"You wanna know what's in Harlem?"

"Yes I fucking do. I wanna know what's in Harlem."

"Do you?"

I growled.

"Black folks." Furry grinned. "Black folks is in Harlem, that's what's in Harlem."

"Black folks?"

"Yeah, black folks."

"That's the grand knowledge you wanted to enlighten me with: 'black folks is in Harlem'?"

"That's right."

"Brilliant, Furry."

"Reason so many black folks is in Harlem, and Chicago, and other northern cities, is because of the International Harvester, you filthy cod, invented right here at the Hopson Plantation." He cupped his hand and gestured grandly toward the fields of cotton.

"Really?"

"Yessir, it did the work of twenty negros in half the time. Six million folks left the south shortly after it was invented, Mississippi mostly, and fled for the northern cities in search of work to feed their families."

"Damn."

"Enslaved, freed, indentured, fired, and driven away."

"Damn," I said and shook my head.

"You said it, kid. They call it the blues."

The fields flowed nearly to the horizon, row after endless row of chest-high cotton plants. It didn't take much imagination to picture the slaves in those fields of a hundred-fifty years ago. Throughout the Delta the Antebellum plantation mansions still rose above the cotton blooms, perched atop the only elevated pieces of land around, so as to keep an eye on the whole slave-powered, blood-money machine surrounding them -- and to serve as a constant reminder to every slave in the field that the Boss was *always* watching.

To me though, the mansions resembled big, fancy prisons, surrounded and confined by moats of their own depravity. The way these spectacles rose from the flat tides of cotton flowing below them drew the image of the rock of Alcatraz rising out of the San Francisco Bay. How the 'masters' could have slept on their knoll at night with the seething red energy from the souls of those viciously abused engulfing the plantation house with such levels of disdain for their constant, hell-bindingly inhuman sin, I could not say. It's like a rapist cozying up for a nap while surrounded by his victims, all day, every day. It takes an entirely other level of evil.

And to make matters worse, nowadays the Red-Cross-donating, inbred descendants of this cotton-gentry celebrate these atrocities with 'Antebellum Tours' and plantation mansions converted into Bed and Breakfasts. They smile warmly from below gaudy feathered hats and welcome the paying tourists to gaze at the beauty of their mansions as if they and their homes are a part of our American history we should smile fondly upon instead of the pitiful and shameful monuments to the very worst of human wickedness that they are in reality. To my mind, the mansions should be museums on the order of the holocaust museums of the Nazi concentration camps, and the heirs of these sin-fed fortunes should be shot and tilled into the fields as fertilizer. So shall it be.

I looked over at Furry striding along beside me. The lines of the old man's face were deep crevasses running in every direction. His white hair poked out from below his hat. I had no doubt that Furry had seen those same strands of wickedness many times over in his seventy-something years as a black man in the Deep South. I could almost feel the blues emanating from the tiny old man marching along beside me. That man no doubt knew blues that I could never know, blues that seared effortlessly through the hardest of jaded hearts and sank souls to the darkest depths; the very blues that stabbed so deep as to allow the creation of the most remarkably beautiful and moving of music: the blues, an oddly potent refinement of the worst sludge at the bottom of the wickedness barrel into the most heavenly and healing of sonic libations.

19

Dockery Farms, Mississippi
1925

"I'LL CRACK your damn *head*, Charlie!" came an exclamation from outside.

The preacher, Eddie 'Son' House, was sweeping the floor of his church, watching carefully for any donations that may have fallen out of the hat, when he heard the commotion outside.

He dropped the broom and ran to the door. Before him, all the beauty of God's natural palette was laid bare. It was that time of a summer's afternoon when the symphony crescendoed, when the ancient oak trees spread like mountains, with animated leaves casting a flittering shade on the rich grass below, the flowing white tangles of beard lichen swaying in the breeze, hanging like scrolls of wisdom from the static, gnarled limbs.

But amongst all this, Charlie Patton, in bare feet and bare chest, was being chased down the street by his third wife, Minnie Franklin, who was swinging a pitchfork with deadly intent. Charlie, in his own right, was swinging his guitar right back, in no more civil of a manner, though maybe at least partially to fend off her blows.

"You're a rotten goddamn drunken fornicator!" Minnie yelled and swung the pitchfork. "I give you a hundred second chances, and this is what I get?" She swung the fork down like a sickle, narrowly missing Charlie's knees.

Charlie jumped to miss the blow and ran before she could

reload, turning after ten feet to brace for the next attack.

"But, baby, you know--" Charlie started.

"Don't call me baby!"

"But, baby--"

"I know what you're going to say, and don't you even think about it!"

"But, baby."

"You're just a drunken asshole, Charlie. That's all there is to it. I can see behind your stupid little eyes you trying to figure a way you can blame this on what happened with Huddie and that boy. Just like always! I can see it right now, right there behind those stupid, little, drunken, liar eyes." She swung the pitchfork and missed narrowly.

"But, baby--"

"One doesn't have a damn thing to do with the other, Charlie!" she continued her rant. "You can feel guilty and be a goddamn mess for a long time, and you can even keep using it as an excuse for a long time after that even. But not seven damn years, Charlie! It's just a goddamn excuse!"

Charlie didn't say anything. And Minnie didn't swing the fork this time. She exhaled, and hesitated, a moment of empathy for the skinny little man crouching in front of her. But this was a mistake. Charlie saw his opening and leapt from his crouch and swung his guitar down like a sledge over the head of his wife. The guitar rang out and Minnie Franklin slumped to the ground in a heap.

The preacher Eddie 'Son' House was running across the lawn toward the couple when Charlie let her have it with the side of his guitar. He couldn't help but stop and cover his mouth.

"Good-NESS, Charlie," he yelled. "What the heck are you doing?"

"She was trying to kill me," Charlie said drunkenly, staring down at Minnie who was now moaning on the ground as she came to.

The preacher Son House shook his head. "Get inside, Charlie."

*

Half-an-hour later, after the preacher Son House had returned Minnie to her house and made sure she was looked after, he returned to his church. There on a pew, sprawled out, shirtless, and with his head resting on his guitar, was Charlie Patton, asleep, loudly.

Son House shook his head and went back to sweeping the church.

Charlie came to about an hour later, shaking his head and rubbing his eyes. Son House was sitting down the pew, looking out the window at the willow tree. It was a hot day, and the tiny, one-room church felt like an oven. Son House was fanning himself with his hat.

"What the hell?" Charlie said.

Son House turned to him. "You start cussing right off the bat?"

"Ah shit, Son," Charlie responded. "I don't want to hear it."

"You're lucky you ain't beat to nothing right now, boy. That girl's father was looking to take it out of you."

"Boy?"

"Lay off it, Charlie. Go splash some water in your face."

Charlie just frowned and yawned, looking around at the church.

"This place makes me nervous," he said.

"There's a reason for that," Son House responded.

Charlie rolled his eyes and stretched his arms above his head.

"What are you doing, Charlie?" Son asked.

"I don't want to hear it."

"Well, I'm sick of saying it, too."

Charlie rubbed a spot on his forehead as if he just remembered he had a smudge of dirt there and it had to come off that very instant.

"I don't know why the heck you seem to keep ending up here to talk about it," Son House said. "But you do. And then you ridicule me when I try to help."

"Ah, hell, Son," Charlie said, looking up with a smile. 'Well now you make me feel bad. I don't mean nothing by it."

Son grunted and waved him away. He stood up and grabbed the broom and began sweeping again.

"Minnie's right, Charlie," the preacher continued as he swept. "You're just using it as an excuse. You know you didn't kill him, Charlie, and you didn't tell Huddie to either. So get over it already and stop using it as an excuse." Son House kept sweeping nervously and didn't dare turn around and look at Charlie. It took all the courage he could muster just to utter those words.

Chalie's eyes dropped and he sat there staring at the wood grains on the pew in front of him for a long moment.

Son House immediately regretted his gruffness. He was not very good at being stern. He was a small man, prone to smiling. And Charlie Patton made him nervous. But the Preacher had learned that Charlie would respond to nothing but the coarsest approach. And then he would crumble, for a short time, and begin building himself back up again. It was a gruesome cycle Son House had been watching for too long now.

"You didn't kill him, Charlie," Son House said and put a hand on Charlie's shoulder and sat down..

"Yeah, but Huddie did. And he's spending the rest of his life in prison for it. And for what? A stupid notebook?"

"Well, from what you've told me," Son House said, "this Blueprint, whatever it is, was meant for good. You can't blame yourself that Cole went crazy and tried to steal it."

Charlie shrugged his shoulders. "It doesn't matter now," he said, "he's dead and Huddie's in prison and there ain't a damn thing come of it."

Son House shook his head and tapped the top of the bench they sat on. The stagnant heat inside the church was oppressive and his attempt to bring peace to Charlie Patton was completely futile. But he tried nonetheless.

"It's brought happiness to a lot of people, Charlie," he said, "and it's certainly done some great things for Lemon Jefferson."

Blind Lemon had been getting rich playing the blues all over the country. For the first few years after Huddie went to prison, Blind Lemon would come by Dockery regularly to see Charlie or meet him out on the road. But Charlie was mostly a mess, drinking like a fish and fighting with anyone who looked at him wrong. He still played the blues, and played it better than anyone, but now it was just a job; he had lost all purpose. He tried to find solitude at the bottom of a bottle and in the embrace of any loose woman he could find. But that only made it worse. He stopped caring about anything. In time, the visits from Blind Lemon became less and less frequent, and eventually, about two years ago, he'd stopped visiting altogether.

The mention of Blind Lemon only upset Charlie more.

Son House shook his head. "The Good Lord works in mysterious ways," he said in a weak attempt at comfort.

"The Good Lord? Jesus, Son, this doesn't have anything to do with the Good fucking Lord."

Son House threw his hands up in exasperation. "Well, if that's true, why the heck do you keep coming to me to talk about it?"

"I don't know," Charlie said and shook his head and slumped his shoulders.

"Listen, Charlie," Son continued, "you've done great things. The music you created has brought great happiness to folks in their darkest times; I've seen it with my very own eyes. I suggest you recognize that, and let it lift you up."

"Don't get all queer about it, House. Jesus. My music ain't done shit and I was a goddamn idiot to ever think it would. And Huddie and Lemon were even dumber than me for believing my bullshit."

Son House just shook his head. After the Blueprint was lost that night in Texas, Charlie had never attempted to write a new one or to carry on with its agenda. In fact, Son House knew, he tried like hell to forget about the thing altogether.

Son House suddenly stood up. "C'mon, Charlie, let's mosey on over to Henry's and play some guitar," he suggested. He waved Charlie to follow him.

Charlie grunted and stayed put.

"It'll be good for you."

Charlie rolled his eyes.

"Come, now, what the matter is: the blues got you."

He waved his hand.

"Yessir, the blues got you," Son House said again, "Come, now," he waved him toward the door, "play some blues, the blues got you."

"Hummph," Charlie grumbled.

"Come, now, what the matter is: the blues got you. Gotta play some blues."

"Gotta play the blues, huh?"

"Gotta play the blues."

"You gonna play the blues too?"

"I'll play the blues."

"You'll play the blues?"

"Yeah," Son House nodded his head. "What the matter is: the blues got you. Gotta play the blues. Come, now."

"And you'll play the blues, huh?"

"I'll play the blues."

Charlie looked up at him and a smile cracked his face. "I thought you burst into flames for playing the blues," he said, his smile growing wider.

Son House chuckled. "I just might," he said with a smirk, "but them blues just feel so good," he grinned at his downtrodden friend, "and the blues got you, so I gotta help."

"Well, my my," Charlie chuckled, "I guess the Good Lord *does* work in mysterious ways, Mister House."

"I guess he does."

"I guess he does. But He might just strike you down with lightning before you get the chance."

"He just might," a grin spread across Son's face. "But that's better than listening to your whining all day." He smirked at the bluesman.

Charlie chuckled and stood up and hung his arm around the young preacher. "When you gonna give up this worthless preaching and come over to the blues for real?" he asked. "Lord knows you ain't no good at the preaching."

"You got the Devil in you, Charlie Patton," Son said with a smile.

"You know," Charlie said as they walked out of the church and into the sunlight, "people been telling me that my whole life. And I think they just might be right."

Son House grinned at his friend. He thought they might be right too.

*

Charlie Patton and Son House walked down the dirt road toward Henry Sloan's house and a train whistle shrieked in the distance.

"I like the sound of that," Charlie muttered as he reached with his toe to kick a stone from their path.

Son House nodded his head and glanced over and they continued down the dusty road, kicking stones and listening to the train.

They reached Willie Brown's shack and Charlie hopped up onto the porch. "Willie!" he yelled through the screen door, "Come on over to Henry's and play some music."

Willie Brown opened the door, wiping his hands on a dirty rag. "Hell yeah, boss," he said, then noticed Son House, "Sorry, preacher," he said with a wink.

Son House chuckled at Willie. They had been friends for quite some time and Willie liked to josh him about his chosen profession.

"Just grab your guitar and let's go," House said and smiled.

Willie raised his eyebrows, "My, my," he said and tossed the rag aside as he went inside to grab his guitar.

Charlie smiled. Willie Brown always made him feel better. "You seen Tommy?" Charlie asked him, referring to Tommy Johnson.

"Saw him about an hour ago," Willie hollered out from inside his shack. "He was drunk as a skunk already, stumbling on down the road."

Charlie shook his head. Tommy had turned out to be a pitiful drunk. He could sure play the guitar, but otherwise he did little but get drunk and into trouble. Charlie often wondered if he had made the wrong choice in choosing to bring Tommy Johnson into the Triad instead of Cole Ricketts. Cole would still be alive and Huddie would be free if he had made a different decision. It kept him up many nights.

*

At Henry's house, Charlie, Willie, Henry and Son House sat around and played guitar and passed bottles of bootleg corn liquor back and forth. Within a few songs, and after a few swigs, Charlie was back in top spirits. For the next two hours, they all laughed and drank and played the blues and the evils of the world were all forgotten.

During a break in the singing there was a knock on the door.

"Come in," Henry yelled.

The door opened and the sixteen year-old, Booker T. Washington White, better known as simply 'Bukka', stood in the frame. "Mistah Charlie," he said, embarrassed to be interrupting the men.

"What's up, Bukka?" Charlie asked. Bukka White was one of the only bright spots in Charlie's life right now. Willie Brown and he had been teaching Bukka guitar for a few years and the boy's youthful exuberance was infectious.

"There's a man down at your house looking for you," Bukka said shyly.

"A man?" Charlie asked.

"Yeah," Bukka drawled.

"Well, what kind of man, Bukka? White man? Black man?"

"Black fella, sir," Bukka White said. "Didn't give no name."

Charlie thought for a moment. "Well, send him over then."

The caller piqued the interest of all the musicians and they all made their way out to Henry's porch.

A few minutes later, the man came walking down the drive. He wore a pressed black suit with a pure white shirt and dark sunglasses, and he carried a guitar. He was chewing on a long blade of grass. Charlie saw him and nearly fainted. He had to grab onto the railing to keep from toppling over. He would recognize that dome of white hair anywhere. He walked out to Huddie Ledbetter and hugged him for the first time in seven years.

He held Huddie for a long time, then stopped and grabbed his arm. "Let's get you inside and out of sight," he said and pulled him toward the shack.

Huddie grabbed onto Charlie's shoulders and looked him directly in the eyes. "No need to do that, boss," he said in his Cajun accent. "It works, Charlie, it really works."

"It works? What works?"

"This," Huddie held up the blue notebook.

Charlie almost toppled over again. He was sure he would never see the book again. "How the hell do you still have that?"

Huddie grinned. "I told them it was my songbook night I got arrested. And they bought it."

Charlie's mouth hung open.

Huddie got very serious and looked Charlie deep in the eyes. "I studied this for the whole seven years I was in there, Charlie," he said, emotion cracking his voice. "It was all I had to do." He looked at the notebook for a long moment. "You know I wasn't much of a believer before, but I tell you, Charlie, this really works."

Charlie smiled. He was just happy to have Huddie back. He didn't yet know how he felt about the notebook. "Come in, Huddie Ledbetter, tell me all about it."

*

Inside Henry's shack, after Huddie had been fed and everyone had been introduced, they all sat around, impatiently waiting for Huddie to tell the story of how he came to be sitting there with them.

"Well, like I told Charlie," he started once he was comfortable, "I spent the whole time in there studying this Blueprint and testing it out on the guards and such. And wouldn't you know, before long I had privileges that no other prisoner enjoyed."

"Privledges?" Charlie asked.

"Yeah, I guess. They took it easy on me, best work jobs and such, and all I had to do was play the blues. And I did, for the whole place, guards, warden and lowly old prisoners alike."

"Play the blues, huh?"

"'*Play me your blues, Mister Lead Belly*,' them guards would say, with the Mister and all."

"Mister Lead Belly," Charlie chuckled. "Ain't that something."

"It is. And it went like that for a while, me playing the blues for the whole place. Then, round about a year ago, I find out that Governor Pat Neff's gonna be visiting our very prison. Taking a tour of the joint and so on."

"The governor?"

"That's right," Huddie said. "Governor Pat Neff. Ran on the platform that he'd never pardon a single prisoner. A real hard-ass on criminals and such. Nobody cared much for him. Well, then he come and I find out he's heard about me, about lowly old Lead Belly, nothing to nobody and rotten besides. He's heard about me and he wants to hear me play my blues."

"He did not."

"He did."

"So, what did you do?"

"I played him the blues, is what I did. I'd been studying that Blueprint and I just played him the most low down blues I've ever played and right there for him like the rest of the world wasn't even out there."

"And what did he do?"

"He didn't say nothing but just look. Like he was seeing his dead grandma in her dundies. I didn't know what to make of it. Here I was, a nigger in Texas in prison murder, and him there, the governor. I didn't know what to do, so I just kept playing this here twelve-string till I looked up and he was gone."

"And then what?"

"Now, I thought that was the end of it. Like I said, he'd run for office on the platform that he'd never pardon a single prisoner, no matter how little the crime. And like I said, I was a nigger in Texas, in prison for murder. I forgot all about it and went back to what you do in prison: wait and waste time, wait and waste time. You get good at wasting time in prison. Too good. But lo and behold, Charlie, on the governor's last day in office, one week ago today, the guards come by my cell and told me I was a free man, just like that, my sins wiped clean by the good governor, Pat Neff."

Charlie Patton stood speechless.

"Yessir," Huddie said. "A full pardon."

"That's not really how it went?" Charlie asked.

"On my soul," Huddie said. "It was the Blueprint, Charlie, it really works."

"You're bullshittin'."

"I ain't doing that."

"Come, now."

"I ain't," Huddie said with a grin. "On my soul."

"Come, now."

"Ain't, Charlie."

"My God," Charlie said and shook his head. He still couldn't believe it: a black man in prison for murder?...in Texas?...set free? Just like that? He looked up at Huddie with a smile. "Play me that pardon song, Huddie Ledbetter, I gotta hear it."

And Huddie did. He played it just like he had played it for the good governor, Pat Neff. And it was some mighty low-down blues.

When he was finished, Charlie smiled. "Well, I would've pardoned you too," he said and clapped his friend on the back. Then he picked up the blue notebook and stared at it, falling silent.

Charlie looked up at Huddie. "Huddie Ledbetter," he stated simply and couldn't believe that he was sitting in the chair across from him.

Huddie grinned across the table. "Charlie Patton," he said.

They sat like that for a while. Then Charlie suddenly jumped up. "We gotta get hold of Lemon," he said.

"You know where he is?" Huddie asked.

Charlie frowned. "We ain't been in touch for some time now."

"Is that right?"

"It is," Charlie said, then smiled again. "But I think I can find him."

"Yeah?"

"I think so."

"Well then, what the hell are you waiting for?"

Charlie grinned. "The Delta Triad is back in business!" he yelled and stomped his foot.

*

Three days later, driven by his chauffeur, Blind Lemon Jefferson arrived at Dockery with all the fanfare of a visiting foreign dignitary. The party that ensued was the stuff of legends. They played music and drank bootleg whiskey and chased the gaggles of questionable women mingling amongst them until late into the night for three days on end.

As the sun started to lighten the eastern sky on the morning of the third night, Charlie, Huddie, Henry, Blind Lemon, Son House and Willie Brown were all sprawled across the furniture of Charlie's shack.

Charlie and Blind Lemon sat at the table and picked their guitars together softly and the other men listened and drank from their jugs of whiskey.

"I've missed you, Charlie," Blind Lemon said during a break between songs.

"I missed you too, Lemon," Charlie said with an apologetic tone.

And Lemon nodded. "You been all right?" he asked.

"I've been all right," Charlie answered, "but I'm a hell of a lot better now." He looked to Huddie, Lemon and the Blueprint. Three things that just days before, he thought he would never see again.

"It's good to see you," Blind Lemon said. Then he added, "Kind of," and pointed to his blind eyes.

Charlie chuckled and Blind Lemon smiled and took a drink from the whiskey bottle that was sitting on the table between them.

"Lead Belly!" Blind Lemon suddenly shouted with a slight slur as he raised the whiskey bottle. "Play me your pardon song again," he demanded with a smile. "And tell me again what that

Governor's face looked like when he was listening. Boy, I wish I could see just to have seen that."

Huddie grunted joyfully and tried to stand up from the chair he was lying across, but immediately fell over drunk, crashing to the ground. All the men laughed as he rolled over with great effort. He smiled and belched before taking a long drink from his jug. He didn't even attempt to rise from the floor again. "Ayee don' think ayee can make it, Lemon," he slurred.

"You'll play it for me tomorrow?"

"Ayee will do that," Huddie said with a smile and pointed his finger in the air and tipped his jug of whiskey back.

Charlie chuckled at the white-haired maniac and grabbed the bottle of whiskey off the table. "So tell me what's going on with you, Lemon," he asked, turning to Blind Lemon and taking a slug from the bottle.

"Ahh, you know, this and that," Blind Lemon replied.

"Yeah?"

"Yeah. Got me a recording session set up in Chicago in a few weeks. Gonna be my first time in a studio. Should be fun."

"Is that right?" Charlie asked, happy for his friend.

"Yessir," Blind Lemon said. "The Windy City. I hear things are good up there, that the speakeasies are jumping, and Al Capone doesn't let anyone mess with the musicians."

"I heard what he did for Louis Armstrong," Charlie said.

Blind Lemon nodded. "Got him his trumpet back. And far as I know, nobody's messed with him since."

"Good guy to have on your side."

"I guess. How about you?" Lemon asked.

"I'm lining some stuff up myself with a guy named H.C. Speir," Charlie said.

"I heard of him," Lemon said, "I hear he's good."

"Yeah, me too."

"That's good, Charlie," Blind Lemon said with a smile, "That's good."

"It is," Charlie replied and nodded his head.

They sat in silence for a moment, both lost in thought, then Lemon sighed and turned to Charlie, his face serious. "I know you been down for a while, Charlie," he said, "but we gotta keep going with this. The blues is really starting to take hold. It'd be a shame to stop now."

Charlie looked at Lemon and thought for a moment, then opened his mouth to speak.

"Hear, hear!" Son House drunkenly hollered from across the room before Charlie could reply. With much effort, the preacher rose to his feet and tottered over to the table. He stumbled to a stop in front of Charlie and leaned in and tried to focus his eyes, his face comically serious. "Ayee want in, Charlie Patton."

Charlie chuckled at the drunken preacher. "You want in on what, Son?"

Son House hiccupped and shuffled backward, dramatically attempting to express his shock at the question. "Ayee want in on the *Triad*, Charlie Patton. Ayee wanna know the secrets of the blues." He held one finger to the sky. "Ayee wanna be a *bluesman*!"

"Oh you do, do you?" Charlie asked with a grin.

Son House hiccupped and nodded his head. "Ayee do."

"And the preaching?"

House grinned and tipped back his jug.

Charlie clapped him on the shoulder and laughed. "Well, preacher-man, if you feel the same in the morning, I'd be happy to have you," he said with a chuckle.

Son House smiled widely and raised his jug of whiskey and took a long pull. "Now play me some fucking blues!" he yelled and stumbled backwards.

Blind Lemon chuckled and swayed his head. He hadn't been this happy in a long time. He tapped his guitar four times and then he and Charlie Patton fulfilled Son House's request.

The blues moaned from Charlie Patton's small home in the woods of the Mississippi Delta until long after sunrise.

20

Mississippi
2002

THE WALK to Money Road took forever. Furry's pace nearly killed me. He was right: I was out of shape. But, I wouldn't be for long if I kept up in this manner with the little old man called Furry Jenkins.

Aside from the strain, the walk was pleasant. The sun shone through sparse, floating, marshmallow clouds and a gentle, cooling breeze brushed over the sprawling cotton fields.

Furry never showed signs of fatigue and talked at nearly the same pace as he walked, yarning-on in extravagantly illustrative accounts of his many escapades. The accuracy of which made little matter, as far as I could tell.

At noon, we stopped under a large oak tree and Furry strummed his guitar and we watched cars periodically pass on the dusty, rural highway.

"So, tell me your story, kid. What are you really doing around here?" Furry asked as he mindlessly plucked his guitar strings between songs.

I smiled at the little old man. There I was, sitting under the umbrella of an ancient oak tree beside a lonely southern highway in a land previously relegated to the realm of abstraction in my mind while a wrinkled old bluesman strummed his guitar beside me. It made me chuckle. "I'm looking for my old man, like I said before," I answered.

"And why do you want to find him?"

I chewed on it for a while and lit a cigarette. "I want to tell him he's an asshole."

Furry raised his eyebrows. "That's it?"

"Pretty much," I answered.

"It's none of my business, I know," Furry said, "so you don't need to answer, but why *is* he such an asshole?"

"He ran out on my mother when I was five," I answered. "Left her with three kids and nothing else."

Furry took a breath to speak, but stopped before anything came out and dropped his head and plucked a lick on his guitar, then looked off up the road.

"He just left one night," I continued. "We lived in Texas at the time and he was playing a show that night. Left for the show like any other night. My mom waited up all night, and for three days after, and he never came back. Left us with nothing, *nothing*. My poor mother, God bless her, had to beg for bus fare to get us back to upstate New York where her parents lived."

"That's terrible," Furry said, shifting uncomfortably. "But maybe it's not that simple."

I snapped toward Furry, my jaw clenched. "I don't give a damn how goddamn simple it is or isn't. The fucker left, and that's it."

Furry held up his hands. "I'm sorry, I'm sorry, I didn't mean anything by it. I shouldn't have said anything."

"Goddamn right you shouldn't have," I snarled.

Furry squinted his eyes. "Don't push it, boy."

I grunted and waved him away.

Furry shook his head and played a lick. "Do you remember much about him?" he asked after a moment.

"Not really. My brother and sister are both older than me, three and four years, so they remember him some. But he's just a vague recollection for me. Just glimpses of a memory, you know?"

"And what makes you think he's around here?" Furry asked, mindlessly plucking a lick on his guitar.

"Well," I said, and sighed as I remembered, "we get an envelope every year around Christmas. It never has a note or anything else, just a thousand dollars in cash and a guitar pick." I shook my head and threw a rock into the dirt. "The lousy bastard can't even call on the telephone. He just sends a thousand freaking dollars once a year. What a jerk. Like a little money once a year will repair what he's done."

Furry pinched his cigarette in his fingers, a look of sadness crossing his face.

"Well, anyway," I continued, "the postmark on the envelope is always from Clarksdale, Mississippi. So, I assume he must live around here."

"Yeah," Furry said absently and snubbed out his cigarette. "Have you had a bad life?" he asked, suddenly looking me in the eyes.

I was a little surprised by the question. "No," I answered. "I've had a fine life. Thanks to my mother."

"So it turned out all right, then? Even though your old man was gone."

"I guess," I answered, annoyance creeping into my voice. "Like I said: thanks to my mom."

"Your mother sounds like quite a lady," he said after a moment.

"She's an angel. A goddamn angel. She never felt sorry for herself for a second. She raised us kids and made sure we never wanted for nothing. She's a saint."

"And yet you're out here," Furry said as he gazed up the road, sending just a glance my way. "Looking for your long lost father."

I stopped what I was doing and glared at Furry.

He looked back silently until I dropped my head and kicked at the dirt.

"I'm just saying," Furry said, "if you think he ran out on you, why the hell do you want to find him? You've got a good mother, a good brother and sister, why not be happy with that?"

"Cause I want him to know that I hate him. I want him to see me and know that I hate him."

"Life is too short for hate, young brother," Furry said, looking me directly in the eyes. "If you learn anything from the blues, it's that. You can waste your life running around chasing hate, and it won't get you nowhere. I'll tell you this, boy," he continued, "and it's the most important thing I'll ever tell you or anybody else: don't you ever lose sight of the value of having folks back home that care about you."

"No, I know," I said and waved my hand dismissively.

"No, now you listen," Furry cut me off, "a man is only as good as the people he's got awaiting his return from wherever he's venturing. This little adventure you're off on, it's only as good as the folks that give a damn that you're gone. Your story -- any story -- is only as good as the people that give a damn that it happened. You lose sight of that and you'll be lost. Be thankful, boy, be thankful you've got what you've got, be thankful you've got *who* you've got. You remember that, boy. Maybe you know what your old man did and why he did it, maybe you don't. But whatever he did, he left you in good hands. Be thankful for that. Life is way too short to waste time on hate."

I didn't know whether to be angry or appreciative of the advice. In the end I just nodded my head and thought about my family. A truck rolled over the rise and past us with a grumble of downshifting gears and Furry and I sat silently smoking our cigarettes with our backs against that ancient oak tree along that dusty Mississippi highway.

21

Clarksdale, Mississippi
1928

SON HOUSE sat on a stump beside Big D's Blues Club in Clarksdale, Mississippi. The small juke joint was packed with people inside and out. Son House was on the bill for the evening and was tuning his guitar as he listened to the conversation of the other men. Huddie Ledbetter, Henry Sloan and Willie Brown stood with Blind Lemon Jefferson and Charlie Patton.

"I'm heading out Wednesday to record with H.C. Speir," Charlie Patton said and tapped Blind Lemon on the arm.

Blind Lemon smiled and swayed his head. "Things are going well here then?" he said.

"Well, I been kicked off a number of plantations for inciting the field workers," Charlie laughed, "Including Dockery a couple of times. So, the Blueprint seems to be working."

Blind Lemon chuckled. He seemed happy to be back with the gang. He had been mostly in and around Chicago for the last couple years, coming down through the Delta when he could.

"I think it's been more for his wandering pecker than anything to do with the Blueprint," Huddie Ledbetter said with a grin.

Willie Brown bugged his eyes and nodded his head in agreement.

Henry Sloan stood beside Charlie, shaking his head with an exasperated smiled curling the corners of his mouth. "All I know is that I'm getting too old for all this messin' around, is all I know," he said.

Blind Lemon raised his eyebrows in mock seriousness. "Is that's what's been going on down here while I been working myself to the bone up in Chicago? A bunch of messin' around?"

"Bahh," Charlie chuckled and patted Blind Lemon's growing belly. "You don't look like you've been working nothing to the bone."

Lemon laughed. "Well, I never said I was missing any meals," he replied and rubbed his stomach.

"Doesn't appear you have," Huddie chimed in with a grin.

Son House sat on the stump beside them, smiling as he tuned his guitar. He was trying to remember the lyrics to a song he wrote the night before and was humming to himself as he looked at the trees. The sky was painted with the colors of the sun that had just dropped below the horizon and a train whistle called out in the distance. While Son House hummed, he noticed a white man walking down the road toward the club. Something about the man seemed off. Not only was he a white man approaching a juke joint with mostly all black folks, but there was something about his eyes. He was scanning the crowd, in and around the place, his eyes darting back and forth. Something definitely seemed off about him.

Son House watched as the man reached into his jacket and then suddenly ripped out a hand gun and began firing indiscriminately into the crowd. The quiet, peaceful scene erupted into mayhem. People screamed and scattered in all directions and the gunman let loose one shot after another. It all happened so fast. One second the place was quiet and the birds sang, and the next it was an exploding war zone. Son watched in shock as the gunman took sight at a young girl running away. Before even thinking, Son House jumped into motion and rushed the man.

The gunman saw House coming out of the corner of his eye and swung the pistol toward him, firing twice. The second shot caught House in the leg and he stumbled. But House's momentum carried him into the man and he tackled him with his shoulder.

The two men went to the ground in a puff of dust and the pistol went flying. They wrestled for a few seconds before the much smaller Son House battled to the top and wrapped his hands firmly around the larger man's throat. The gunman flailed and tried to hit House but House's grip didn't weaken. The former preacher squeezed as hard as he could and the man's face turned red and his eyes bulged and he kicked and swung his arms in a desperate attempt to remove House's grip. But Son House had him and wouldn't let go.

The man's struggle became more frantic and his face turned a ghastly shade of blue and he opened his mouth to scream but nothing came out but silence. The only sound was Son House's snarl as he squeezed ever tighter. The blood vessels in the gunman's eyes were bursting and the whites became filled with blood as he looked at Son House squeezing the life from him. The man flailed twice more and his mouth opened like a fish out of water and he looked into Son House's eyes, then went limp.

When the police arrived a moment later, Son House still held his hands around the lifeless gunman's neck. The rest of the crowd was frozen, watching in stunned disbelief. The thunderous booming of the gunshots had given way to an eerie silence but for the voice of Blind Lemon yelling at Huddie to tell him what was happening. Son House looked back at the group with blank eyes as he stood up and raised his hands into the air. Not a word was said.

*

Later that night, Charlie, Huddie, Henry, Blind Lemon and Willie Brown sat in shock at Charlie's house. Nobody played music that night. They all waited in anticipation as Charlie hung up the phone and turned toward them.

"What're they gonna do with House?" Willie asked.

Charlie sighed. "They're taking him on the Parchman Train in the morning," he answered and shook his head, referring the train that brought prisoners to the Parchman Farm prison facility in Parchman, Mississippi. Son House had been arrested and was being forced to plead guilty to assault to avoid being charged with murder.

"How in the hell can they do that?" Willie asked angrily.

"Cause he's a nigger in Mississippi that killed a white man."

"The guy was gunning down woman and children in cold blood!"

"Don't gotta tell us," Charlie said.

"Who the hell was the shooter? Anybody know?" Huddie

asked.

"No idea," Charlie answered, "a fucking crazy."

"Actually Charlie," Blind Lemon said from his chair at the table, his demeanor very somber. He had been quite somber since the incident, as if he were weighing something in his mind. "About that," he paused, "I don't know if this means anything, but I heard from a pretty reliable source that the Klan's been taking a keen interest in the blues."

"I knew it!" Henry yelled from the other side of the room. "What'd I tell you, Charlie, what'd I tell you all these years about the Klan?" He had fear written all over his face. "And now--now, Charlie, this ain't just small potatoes no more, you all are actually becoming known. And they damn sure don't like seeing a bunch of niggers getting paid and power and 'inciting folks', as you put it. I tell you--I tell all of you," he waved his arm to all of them, "you keep up with this shit and singing about the things you been singing about and trying to incite folks and such, and you're all bound to get yourselves killed."

"You think that's what happened here?" Charlie asked Lemon.

Lemon shrugged his shoulders. "Didn't say that, boss; I'm just saying."

Charlie scratched his chin in thought. "Well, either way, I think Henry's right," he concluded. "We gotta be smarter. Gotta be smarter about what we say flat out. Gotta disguise our purpose a little more. Understand? We want people to *feel* our blues, not just hear the words were saying. You got a song about a yard boss, call him your woman. '*My baby's been so mean to me*', and so on. Okay? People'll still get the point, but they won't know nothing but we're playing music. It's the subconscious we're after, boys; and we gotta sneak in like burglars in the night. Got it?"

"Burglars in the night?" Huddie said with a grin and raised his eyebrow.

Charlie didn't pay him any mind. "But, with that said," he continued, "only the Lord knows what happened tonight. That guy was probably just some crazy."

"I don't know," Willie Brown said from the corner.

"Regardless, we all know the Klan'll be on us no matter what. As long as we're doing well, they're gonna want to snuff us out. You all knew that before you signed up and it's just something we're gonna have to deal with. Got it?"

They all nodded.
Henry shook his head. “Not exactly what I had in mind.”

22

Greenwood, Mississippi
2002

WE HAD been at the cemetery for about an hour when the cop arrived. He was a rotund caricature of a good ol' boy with chaw-spit dribbling out his rotten teeth and down his layered chin. Furry's demeanor turned to arctic ice as soon as the cop pulled himself out of his cruiser, pausing to spat a stream of tobacco juice before putting his stiff-brimmed hat over his buzzed head.

"What y'all doing out here?" he drawled as he adjusted his gun-belt.

Furry glared at him from squinted eyes and didn't say a word. The cop, evidently noticing the unspoken hostility, zeroed in on Furry.

"I asked you a question, boy," he said and spat, never taking his eyes off Furry. He didn't pay much attention to me.

Furry didn't move and the cop stepped around his car and started toward us, walking leisurely with his hand resting on the butt of his gun, never taking his eyes off Furry.

The cemetery was beside a dilapidating one-room church called the Little Zion Baptist Church. It lay on Money Road, a nearly deserted country track in Greenwood, Mississippi. The cemetery and the church beside it were old and over-grown. The wooden headstones, adorned with hand-written names and dates sloppily painted on their weathered fronts, were listing in all directions at the head of sunken depressions in the ground: body-length, shallow sink-holes created by the deterioration of the pine caskets that lay six feet below.

At the back of the small cemetery, nearly to the tree-line, was the grave we had come to see. Below the squat granite head-stone, littered with the offerings of previous seekers, lay the remains of none other than Robert Johnson, put to rest at the young age of twenty-seven, the Devil coming to collect his debt in the form of a jealous husband with a vial of poison. On that stormy night, at a tiny juke joint just up the road, Robert Johnson sipped his drink onstage then played his last song on earth, dropping dead in the middle of *Cross Road Blues*.

"We're not doing anything, just checking out the grave," I said to the cop with a forced smile as he approached, a bad feeling working up my spine.

The cop turned his glare toward me and his eyes narrowed. "You don't sound like you're from around here, boy," he said in a menacing growl and scanned me from head to toe, pausing to study the rucksack on the ground beside me, his eyes resting on the Amtrak tag.

I eyed the cop warily.

"You sound like you're a long way from home, in fact," he continued, threat lacing his tone. He spat at my feet and grinned.

I took a nervous step back.

The cop smiled at my uneasiness, revealing rotten teeth. "You in the woods now, ain'cha?" he said, then turned to Furry. "And for some reason hanging around with this dirty old nigger."

Furry didn't flinch, but instead jutted out his wrinkled jaw. "A dirty old nigger that fucked your toothless mother last night," Furry said calmly and without hesitation, his expression turning to a challenging grin.

Did he just say that? My eyes went wide and I swung my head slowly toward Furry. Did I just hear what I thought I heard? He couldn't have said that! Not to a cop. Not to *this* cop.

Oh shit.

"Eww-eee, you got some kind-a nigger mouth on you, boy," the cop said with a menacing chuckle as he spat directly on Furry's boot. "Keep talking like that and I'll knock your nigger teeth straight through your skull." The cop clasped his hand around the handle of his billy-club and grinned threateningly at Furry.

Furry turned to me and handed me his guitar.

"Now now," he said. "But, I'm just an old man." He winked at me.

And, with that, this little journey completely changed.

I took the guitar without a thought and looked up just as Furry spun around like a cat and cracked the cop with a vicious right hook. The cop never had a chance to react and went down like a sack of potatoes. Evidently, Furry had not been boasting when he said you don't threaten him without being ready to back it up.

Furry calmly turned to me -- I was absolutely astounded, naturally -- and grabbed his guitar. "Probably don't wanna stick around here too long."

"You think!?" I squeaked.

"Let's just say goodbye to R.J. and skedaddle."

"You can't just knock out a cop!"

Furry smiled. "Yeah, I got him good, didn't I?"

"Jesus, man!"

"You don't know southern cops, boy," Furry said, turning serious. "You don't know *this* cop. He'd-a ate you up. They just love greenhorn yankee drifters around here."

"Well great! What do you think they'll do to me now that we just knocked out one of their own!?"

"We, huh? Pretty sure I did most of the heavy lifting there, if my memory serves."

"What do you think they'll do, Furry? Huh? What do you think they'll do to me now?"

Furry thought for a moment. "Probably won't be too kind," he said. "And that's why I believe we should skedaddle."

I shook my head. What the fuck had I gotten into? Frustration and exhaustion hung heavily from my shoulders.

"You know Furry, you keep sucker-punching people and you're bound to get knocked on your ass."

Furry didn't take kindly to that statement.

"That sounds a bit like a threat, boy," he said.

"Don't get started, Furry, you hear me?"

Furry's eyes narrowed.

"I'm serious, Furry. I'll hit you back this time."

"No you ain't."

"Furry."

"No you ain't."

"Son of a bitch!" I yelped in frustration. I looked down at the cop sprawled out on the cemetery ground. "Let's get the fuck out of here, man!" I slung my rucksack over my shoulder and started off toward the road. But Furry held up a hand before I passed.

"Don't wanna go that way, chief," he said, nodding toward the road. "There's a chance the cops'll be looking for us."

"And why would that be?"

"Yep," he said, disregarding my sarcasm, "I think we're gonna have to take the back way home." He nodded toward the swampy tract behind the burial ground. The forest was lush and marshy, taking advantage of the fertile flood plain of the Mississippi Delta.

"I'm so glad I met you."

23

Chicago
1929

"YOU SHOULD hear the madness going on up here," Blind Lemon said into the telephone. "Investors are throwing themselves out their office windows. The banks are boarded up. People are whipping themselves into a frenzy talking about the end of the world."

"I heard," Charlie said at the other end of the line. "And ain't that a shame. The pigs lost their fortunes, and just the thought of having to work for their meals is sending them swan-diving off the buildings. They ain't worth the cracks they're making in the sidewalk."

"Jesus, Charlie," Blind Lemon said, taken aback. "Ain't you a ray of sunshine."

"I call it how I see it, Lemon."

"I suppose you do," Lemon replied, "I suppose you do. So, how's things down there?"

"Doing all right. I just got good news on my record."

"That right?"

"Yessir."

"Well, congratulation, my friend," Lemon said. "The fruits of our labors, eh?"

"You said it, Lemon. Taking the world by the tits."

Lemon laughed into the phone.

"Got me some new recordings set up too," Charlie continued. "House is getting released from Parchman next week and I've been talking with a guy in Wisconsin. Gonna head up there with Willie and Son this summer, I suppose. You should try to come along."

"I'll try, boss, I'll try. They been keeping me pretty busy up here though."

Charlie chuckled. "Busy chasing tail."

"Me?" Lemon said in mock surprise, "No suh, no way. I'm a one woman man, Charlie Patton."

"Yeah, and I'm president of these United States, Mr. Lemon."

"Maybe someday."

"Maybe someday you'll be a one woman man."

"Hell, I *am* a one woman man," Lemon said defensively, then added, "at a time, that is."

Charlie chuckled. "That sounds about right."

"Speaking of," Lemon said wryly, "I better get hoofin'."

Charlie chuckled. "Good to talk to you, Lemon. Take care of yourself."

"You know I will," Lemon replied, "And you take care of yourself too, Charlie Patton."

"You know I will."

Blind Lemon hung up the phone with a smile and picked up his guitar case off the floor. He felt the wall to orient himself as he stepped out of the phone booth and back into the club.

"Great show tonight, Lemon," the bartender said.

"Thanks, Slim," Lemon replied and waved to the voice he knew so well. Slim had been good to Lemon. His club was one of the first Lemon had played at regularly when he was new to Chicago. Slim believed in him before others would even give him the time of day, and Lemon never forgot it.

"Want me to walk you back to your hotel?" Slim asked.

Lemon raised his head in mock shock. "I'm blind, Slim, not stupid," he said with a grin as he wrapped his thick scarf around his neck and buttoned up his heavy overcoat.

Slim smiled at the jovial blind man. "All right then, Lemon, you take care, you hear."

Blind Lemon waved and stepped out the door into the cold air of Chicago. He stopped when he got outside and took a deep breath. The air was frigid, but it felt wonderful in his lungs after being cooped up in the packed, smoky club for the past six hours.

He took another deep breath and smelled the fresh snow in the city. He could feel the snow falling on his face. It was coming down lightly now but Lemon guessed there were at least a few inches on the sidewalk beneath his feet. Something about Chicago in the winter always touched his spot. The noises seemed muffled and the smells were fantastic.

He stood with his face to the sky for a long time and let the snow fall on his closed eyelids and forehead, smiling at the tiny cold tickle of each flake as it landed. The wind moaned through the towers of downtown and Lemon could feel the icy grains it kicked up off the roofs, ledges, and road. He could hear the flags of his hotel next door snapping against the howl, and feel the cold grip of the air slithering up his socks and under his cuffs. He tried to imagine what it looked like right then. People had told him that the snow was pure and beautiful, that it looked like the city had been covered in a white cotton blanket. Of all the many sights in the world, if he could have five minutes of vision, Blind Lemon would want to use it to see a fresh snowfall on the streetlamps, trees, and awnings of Chicago. Or at least that would be a close second to a supple-bosomed lady in negligée. He chuckled as he weighed the two options in his mind. And the thought reminded him, as if he needed a reminder, that there happened to be a supple-bosomed lady waiting for him at his hotel right now. And hopefully in negligée.

"Hey mister, you got a light?"

The voice startled Lemon. He hadn't heard the footsteps in the fluffy snow. He reached into his pocket for his matches and turned toward the voice. "Sure," he said and smiled, "Sorry, you startl--" The last thing he felt was a sudden flash of heat on the back of his skull, then everything went black.

*

When Lemon came to, his head was throbbing. He moved to reach his hands up to it, but couldn't. He couldn't move at all. And he was freezing cold. He was seated with his legs straight out in front of him and the icy wetness below him told him that he was seated on top of snow. His arms were behind him, wrapped around a cold, square piece of what felt like stone. His hands were bound with rope on the other side. His head hurt so bad. He tried to speak but his mouth was gagged with some kind of cloth.

As his mind cleared, he began to panic and thrash, but his wrists were tied tight around the stone. He could feel the snow falling on his face.

Then he heard movement beside him. Footsteps. Then more. He thrashed and grunted, trying to call out. The steps were moving all around him; he heard at least two distinguishable pairs of footsteps. They stopped moving and he could sense the two figures standing over him. He thrashed and grunted but the two beings didn't respond. Then they moved. He heard the crunch of the snow as the two people walked away. He thrashed madly, nearly pulling his arms out of socket, but the steps just faded away into the cold night, never saying a word.

*

Three hours later the two figures returned. They stood at the gate of the cemetery and watched the snow fall over the man they had tied to the gravestone. The snow now covered his legs and was working its way up his torso.

"Think we can untie him now?" one figure asked the other.

24

Greenwood, Mississippi
2002

OFFICER RON Tweed woke up choking on his plug of tobacco beside Robert Johnson's grave marker at the Little Zion Baptist Church on Money Road in Greenwood, Mississippi. He coughed and spat and hocked out the lump. But only half of it came out, the rest he inadvertently swallowed. He could feel the spongy mass sliding down his esophagus, the tingle travelling all the way to his stomach, but there was nothing he could do to stop it.

"Ugghh," he groaned, resting on one elbow. He put his fingers up to his eye, which was throbbing with the first signs of bruising.

"Rrrrggh." He angrily rose to his feet and the rush of blood leaving his brain made him woozy and he took a moment to find his balance.

Once steadied, he immediately bent over and retched, right at the base of Robert Johnson's headstone. He grabbed the top of the headstone for support and spat out the remnants of his now tobacco-laced lunch from the back of his mouth.

As he retched, his eye caught the familiar outline of boot-prints in the spongy soil. The trail of his attackers led past the headstone and straight back to the forest. Ron Tweed studied the mossy ground for a moment then turned and picked his hat up off the ground and staggered back to his patrol car, retching on another grave before reaching the road. At the road, he scrambled up to his car, a disheveled mess. He jumped in and immediately grabbed his phone.

"Goddamn NIGGER!" he yelled to himself as he pressed a button for speed-dial. The call rang twice before it clicked to life on the other end.

"Get the fucking boys together," Ron Tweed shouted without waiting for a hello. "Meet me at the Pit Stop in half-an-hour and bring the fucking guns!"

He then retched loudly out the open door of his cruiser.

"Good Lord," came the drowsy reaction to the disgusting sound. "Slow down, hoss, what the hell's going on?"

"Just get them together and meet me at the Pit Stop in half-an-hour!" Ron Tweed shouted. "We got some fucking hunting to do." He snapped the phone shut and stuck his head out the door, retching onto Money Road.

25

Wortham, Texas
1929

THE WHISTLE of the evening train drone in the distance and a hard-pounding rain cascaded off the eaves and down the darkened windows of the home. A roll of thunder took hold and drowned out the train, sharpening into an acute crack that rattled the frames on the walls of the warm room.

Inside the room, it seemed to Charlie that of all the multitudes of people crammed into the home there were at least seven different women who considered themselves *the* current girlfriend of Blind Lemon Jefferson. Charlie chuckled at the thought of it.

"That ol' dog," he muttered to himself and watched the women. They were all veiled in black and held kerchiefs to their eyes as they cried hysterically over Blind Lemon's ashen face lying peacefully inside the jet-black coffin.

"What'd you say, boss?" Son House asked, leaning closer to Charlie.

"Oh, nothing," Charlie replied and smiled at him.

Another rumble of thunder lingered outside and the flicker of lightning continued to lighten the rain-splattered windows every few seconds.

"He's looking down on us with eyes that see," Willie Brown said solemnly.

"Indeed," Henry Sloan agreed.

The bluesmen were all in a circle in the back corner of the room, talking quietly and telling light jokes about their deceased friend. Now and then, an uncontrolled hiccup of hearty laughter rose out of their group and above the dull din of the rest of the room.

Son House shook his head. "I just can't believe it. How the hell does he get lost when he's only half a block from his hotel?"

"I guess it was a really snowy night," Willie Brown offered, trying to make sense of it. "He must have gotten turned around."

"Turned around?" Son House responded defiantly. "That old hound could find his way better than a damn -- well......*hound*."

Willie Brown shook his head at House.

Huddie Ledbetter unfolded himself next to them and everyone stopped talking. He was inconsolable. Blind Lemon Jefferson was his best friend. He mumbled something unintelligible.

Nobody asked him any questions.

Charlie turned and patted Huddie on the back without a word. The giant now looked like a shriveled old man. His white head hung low to his chest and his guitar case dragged along the ground as he walked away and out the door and into the black night and the cold cascade of rain that washed down outside the funeral home.

PART FOUR

26

Greenwood, Mississippi
2002

THE LAST remnants of dusk were blotted from the sky and a heavy darkness set in as Furry and I moved through the swampy forest. Furry never seemed to tire and I kept up simply from the forced rush of fear. The forest around us screeched in a cacophony of angrily disturbed insects and animals. The stagnant waters of the shrouded wetlands threatened from feet away, seemingly salivating at the prospects of consuming we two beings that dare trespass into its lair. My eyes darted about and fought to distinguish reality from phantasm, my mind playing vicious tricks.

Furry had not spoken in nearly an hour. He marched ahead on the narrow trail with his eyes never wavering from straight forward, never startling when animals moved out in the forest or scattered from the trail. But despite his outwardly stoic demeanor, Furry's very quietness betrayed the instinctual fear he felt, the same fear as me, a fear built into human DNA over thousands of years of evolution. The sense that you are in immediate danger, someone or something is watching, waiting for the right time to strike. Right now, our brains were telling us to flee, screaming into our inner ears. And our instincts were right.

The air was heavy and damp, and the temperature had not dropped after dark. Through the canopy of the forest we could see a starry sky -- or at least I could, because I was glancing around furtively; Furry just kept plodding along, eyes forward.

Then I noticed the first hitch in Furry's step. It came when the low rumble of a distant clap of thunder passed over us. Furry's reaction was barely noticeable, but it was there: a slight hitch in his stride and a nearly imperceptible turn of his head. Without a word he hastened his gait in front of me, again barely noticeable.

I had the bad feeling that Furry was trying very hard to hide his fear from me, almost as if he worried I would freak out if I knew the full extent of our danger. And I probably would have. I tried to think of something to ask Furry, *Where are we going? What are we doing?* But we had already discussed those plans. I couldn't think of anything. I wanted to hear that we were almost out of this god-awful swamp. That we would be safe and comfortable in no time. But I knew there was no question to ask that would provide that truthful answer.

27

Louisiana
1930

HUDDIE 'LEAD BELLY' Ledbetter wailed to the rafters and hammered his guitar strings with an open hand. His whole being was practically oozing with the blues and the crowd stomped their feet and flailed their arms in a collective attempt to dance away all the many horrors in the world. Huddie was still deep in mourning for his fallen friend. Even now, months later, he could barely play a tune without thinking of Blind Lemon's jolly voice and hearty laugh. Blind Lemon Jefferson was all that was good about this world. Why had God taken such a kind soul as Lemon? He thought about it day and night. Why not him? He hammered a chord and sang out.

After finishing the show, Huddie gathered his things and made his way out of the club. He had never been the most approachable person in the world, but since Lemon's death, he carried himself with such a volatile sadness that the crowds all but parted around him as if he had the plague. Wordlessly, he received his pay from the owner of the club and left. Outside, the many intoxicated patrons who had enjoyed their Saturday night were spread about the property, carrying on in all forms of jubilation.

Huddie sulked away from the juke joint and into the dark of night. The air was cool and fresh and smelled of the rich soil of Louisiana. The lingering light of the club dispersed and soon

Huddie was engulfed in blackness. He took two deep breaths to choke back the tears that were starting to well. He could practically feel Blind Lemon's hand pulling on the crook of his arm, as it had so many nights. He had always led the blind man through the world, and yet it was Blind Lemon Jefferson who had led him through life. Symbiotic friends, one lost without the other. Blind Lemon had gotten lost. And now Huddie was, too.

He succumbed to the tears and wept as he stumbled along. He could feel the pull of Lemon on his arm and it just made him cry harder. He cursed God and Jesus and anything else that could be held responsible for bringing so much harm to such an inherently kind soul. What kind of God creates such a wonderful person only to knock him down at every turn? Blindness was not enough? And for what? Why not him? He didn't possess a sliver of the goodness of Lemon Jefferson, and yet here he was, living. What kind of sick creator would dictate this sort of senselessness?

Huddie kicked the dirt road. He should have been there to lead Lemon home that night in Chicago. That was his job, a fractional remittance for the great gift of Lemon's wise leadership and kind friendship -- and he had failed. He failed his friend. When Lemon needed him, he wasn't there. Huddie wailed into the forest and wished for a tree to fall on his head and end it, the outburst sending slumbering birds erupting into the darkness all around him. He was filled with pure, red, self-loathing as he thought about the last moments of his greatest friend sitting alone in a snowstorm. Freezing to death. To death! He screamed. He screamed louder and fell to his knees and pounded his fists into the dirt road. He screamed at the ground with hate and rage, and his head went faint, and his eyes felt like they would burst, and then he screamed louder and louder and wailed to turn his insides out. But no force could eject the leaden weight in his gut. He hadn't been there for his friend. He began to sob and held his head in his hands. He longed to hear Lemon's voice, he longed to feel his hand on his arm -- and he almost did. But he never again would. The Devil had won. Blind Lemon Jefferson was dead and God is a complete Asshole. Huddie vowed never to call His name again.

With the combined effort of every fiber in his being, Huddie Ledbetter composed himself and rose to his feet. He wanted to lie down and die, but God had seen fit to instill an instinct for continuance in the human psyche that made one press forward down this demented gauntlet of life so that further pain could be inflicted.

Huddie continued down the road and took some deep breaths. Blind Lemon wouldn't want him thinking this way. He drew in another deep breath and exhaled heavily, wiping his eyes.

He didn't see the figures that moved through the bushes in front of him.

28

Greenwood, Mississippi
2002

"DAMN, YOU look like shit, hoss."

"Don't fucking start with me, Bobby Ray," Officer Ron Tweed snarled at Bobby Ray Sheills. He could still feel the sharp pangs of poison from the tobacco plug in his stomach and his eye had swollen nearly shut.

Four old pick-up trucks were parked in a line at the Pit Stop Gas Station, all with some form of the Confederate flag displayed prominently. Ten men stood around the back of Bobby Ray's Dodge Ram, on the window of which was a decal of a little boy pissing on the letters M.L.K.

"Y'all know where you're going, right?" Tweed asked as he wiped the sweat from his forehead, his stomach still upturned from the ingested plug of tobacco. "They gotta come out at one of the trails and y'all better be ready." He looked around at all the faces surrounding him. "Where's Jimmy?"

"He ain't coming, hoss," Bobby Ray said. "Said he ain't gonna be coming no more, not to meetings or nothing." He shook his head.

"Why the fuck?"

"Guess his broad's been trying to convince him the spooks ain't savages," Bobby Ray chuckled and picked a long string of snot out of his nose.

"Well, fuck him, he'll see for himself," Ron Tweed said. "All right, well, we'll hea--" Suddenly, his eyes bulged and he raised his hands to his mouth. He searched desperately around himself then bumbled to the front of Bobby's truck and retched into a garbage can along the side of the convenience store, just as a woman carrying a baby walked by.

The woman jumped back, aghast.

"Move the fuck along, woman," Officer Ron Tweed yelled to her, between heaves.

"Eeee," Bobby Ray flinched as he heard Tweed. He jogged over and helped the shocked lady along. "Sorry, ma'am, he ain't feeling well."

The woman looked in disgust at Officer Tweed vomiting violently in the garbage can. "Is he drunk!?" she asked angrily. "While on duty?"

"Oh, no no, ma'am," Bobby Ray said and tried to calm the lady, he was perspiring through his cut-off shirt.

Ron Tweed suddenly pulled his head out of the garbage can and spun around, standing up straight and glaring at the lady.

"Get the fuck on!" he seethed. "And I'm not fucking drunk." He held fast for a moment, then he spun back to the garbage can and retched, breaking wind loudly at the same time.

The woman stepped back in terror, covering her mouth and fleeing for her car, shielding her baby as she ran.

With a passably solemn look on his face, Bobby Ray watched her leave then turned back to his friend and patted him on the back. "Get it out, buddy."

Ron Tweed slapped Bobby's hand off his shoulder and glared up at him from the opening of the garbage can.

"Go to your *fucking* positions."

"All right, hoss," Bobby Ray said and raised his hands defensively. He turned and pointed to the guys all standing around watching, silently signaling them to saddle-up.

As the trucks roared to life and peeled out of the parking lot, a white-haired husband and wife stepped out of the convenience store and slowly shuffled toward their car, rounding the corner to see Officer Ron Tweed bent over in front of them with his head in the garbage can. At just that moment, he broke wind repulsively as he heaved into the receptacle. The wife halted in fright and the husband shook his head and led his wife quickly around the spectacle.

*

Some time later, Officer Ron Tweed spat into the garbage can and then stood erect, wiping his mouth with the back of his sleeve. Each time his stomach twinged, his anger rose. By now, he was a seething, red beast with hell-fire stoking his engines. His uniform ragged about him, half-untucked and stained with toxic sweat. His boots wore splatters of his regurgitation. But his stomach finally felt steady, steadier. He paid no mind to composing himself and saw but one thing ahead of him: a bloody red X over the face of the little old man called Furry Jenkins.

Seconds later, his police cruiser squealed out of the parking lot, sending sparks flying from its undercarriage. Officer Tweed punched the gas hard against the floor and his speedometer shot around its orbit, quickly reaching one hundred on the dark, country highway.

As he turned right onto Jones Road, the rain washed over his cruiser, coming down in torrents. The rain didn't slow him a bit though as he stomped on the accelerator, racing the front edge of the wave of water.

29

Louisiana
1930

"DO IT. Put me out of my fucking misery."

The man removed the white hood from his head and looked down at Huddie, mildly confused. "Oh, so you're gonna be easy huh?" he said.

"Fuck you, just do it."

Huddie was on his knees in the graveyard, a forty-four revolver pointed between his eyes. The two Klansmen had been waiting for him along the side of the road.

"Well, this ain't no fun at all," the Klansman said with disappointment as he cocked his head, looking at Huddie.

"Just pull the trigger."

"Well, damn, I don't know if I want to now."

"Just off the nigger," his partner said from a few steps away. He, too, held a revolver on Huddie.

"Boy, Joe, I just thought we was gonna have some fun tonight," he said, turning to his partner. "I thought for sure he'd be more difficult than his blind friend."

At this, Huddie looked up and his eyes narrowed and filled with molten lava.

The Klansman chuckled. "Ahh, now *that* got your attention, didn't it? Didn't think we knew about your little group up there at Dockery, did you?" he said, glad to be getting a rise out of Huddie.

"I don' know what the fuck you're talking about," Huddie said.

"Yeah, sure you don't," the Klansman laughed. "We know you niggers are up to something."

"You don't know shit," Huddie said with hate slurring his voice.

The Klansman smiled. "I know one thing, I know your blind friend cried for his momma like a little baby."

Huddie growled.

The Klansman laughed in his face. "Pissed hisself too. Can you believe that? Even a flea-ridden dog is housebroke." He laughed, then added, "But not that dumb nigger!"

"I'm gonna kill you," Huddie said through clenched teeth.

"Well, now, that's the spirit!" The Klansman smiled and clapped his hands. "Did you know we had to carry that big ol' nigger ten blocks just to get him to that cemetery where we left him? And he was a heavy ol' coon." The Klansman laughed and spittle flew out of his mouth. "I think I might've even throw'd out my back." He began to cackle then spat on the ground, looking at his partner, who was laughing as well. "Had to have Joe here tie him up for me cause I couldn't even bend over to reach." He continued laughing and Huddie glared. "Don't worry about me though," he said with a sneer. "I took his money to pay my doctor bills. Turns out the dirty ol' nigger actually had a bit of cash on him." He grinned with his yellow teeth. "Nice of him to bequeath it to us, don't you think?" The two Klansmen looked at each other and burst out laughing.

As the men laughed with each other, Huddie's hand dropped slowly toward his boot. He slid up his pant leg and in a flash, tore a boot-knife from its sheath and lunged at the man in front of him, burying the knife into his stomach before he could even raise his hands in defense. The whole act took only fractions of a second and then Huddie was off like a whip into the graveyard.

The stuck Klansman yelped like a pig as he slumped to his knees on the cemetery floor. He looked down at the blood spewing out of his mid-section and tried to cover the hole with his hands.

The second Klansman seemed to be in shock for a long moment, frozen in time. He must have barely seen the flurry that had left his partner gutted. And now there was blood everywhere. He didn't appear to comprehend what was happening, staring at the lengthening streaks of red running down his friend's white robe. But his surprise quickly waned and turned to rage. He screamed as tears of hate welled in his eyes, then he raised his pistol and started firing.

The bullets came in quick succession and ricocheted off the granite headstones on each side of Lead Belly as he ran away, spraying him with chunks of tombstone dust. He darted back and forth through the graves, stumbling and running like mad for the other end of the cemetery through a hail of pistol shot.

When the second Klansman's hammer fell on an empty chamber, he reached down, his face a grotesque, red mix of sweat and froth, and took his partner's gun and ran after Huddie, tears of rage and hate streaming down his face.

Huddie dove over the wrought-iron fence at the border of the cemetery and rolled and came to his feet sprinting for the road and the town beyond.

A moment later, spinning around a street corner, a police car appeared and came racing down the street toward him. The car was coming on fast, apparently alerted to the gunshots. With nowhere else to run, Huddie ran out into the road and flagged down the cop. "Help!" he yelled, "they're trying to kill me!"

The car skidded to a stop and the cop jumped out just as the second Klansman clambered over the fence of the cemetery, running toward them with his gun still in his hand and his white robes flowing in the wind.

As the cop jumped out of the car, he drew his weapon and swung it level as the Klansman approached. The cop was young and his hand shook as he raised the pistol.

Huddie watched as the barrel of the gun swung straight toward his chest. "Put your hands up!" the cop yelled at Huddie.

Huddie shook his head, but raised his hands. "They were going to execute me," he pleaded.

The Klansman arrived at the car out of breath, sweat soaking through his white robes. "That nigger stabbed my cousin," he yelled to the cop.

The cop cautiously approached Huddie and shoved him against the car.

30

Greenwood, Mississippi
2002

AFTER HOURS of marching through the swamp, Furry and I finally reached the edge of the forest. Despite the dark, moonless night, we could see that a hundred yards ahead, the trail opened up into a field, and Furry said a road lay just beyond.

Our plan was to follow the road back to Clarksdale, walking in the cotton fields that lined it, allowing us to spot and take cover from any approaching vehicles as we move along.

But as we drew within fifty yards of the opening to the field, Furry stopped dead in his tracks and grabbed my arm.

"What are--?" I started, but Furry smacked me in the back of the head to shut me up. He was always doing that kind of stuff. Furry's knees were bent slightly as his old eyes peered out the open end of the tunnel of foliage.

My heart jumped into my throat when I saw the sudden panic that washed over Furry. I followed Furry's gaze, at first seeing nothing in the impenetrable darkness.

Then I saw it: a barely perceptible change in the tone of black, fifty yards out into the field, the unmistakable silhouette of a pick-up truck.

"What is that?" I asked and bent to one knee.

"Pick-up truck."

"Probably just a farm truck right? It wouldn't have anything to do with us, right?"

"Dunno," Furry offered with a shrug. "But I don't suggest we go waltzing out into that field without taking a closer look."

And Furry was right.

We crept up through the foliage twenty yards left of the trail. The swamp had partially given way to drier ground before the field, but it was still wet. I tried to silence the buckles of my pack as we slithered through the underbrush, crawling into position at the tree line.

Both Furry and I peered through tiny gaps in the swampy growth. The clouds had moved in to cloak the stars but they reflected just enough light for us to see three men in and around the truck.

Furry tapped my arm and pointed at the guy at the front of the truck. It was clear to see, even in the darkness, that he was wearing night-vision goggles. Equally clear were the two rifles and the shotgun in the three respective pairs of hands of the watchmen.

"Damn, I'd rather it were the cops," Furry mumbled, thinking out loud.

"Who are they?" I whispered to Furry.

"Some half-ass band of the Ku Klux Klan," Furry whispered back, never taking his eyes off the truck.

"Ku Klux Klan!" I choked as I tried to keep my voice to a whisper.

Furry looked over at me and raised his wrinkled, old eyebrow. "You ain't spent much time in the South, have you?"

"No, I said, "but---the fucking *KLAN*!? It's the twenty-first goddamn century! They're still around?"

Furry chuckled and shook his head at me, "Well, mostly it's just bunches of inbreds that don't do much more than get drunk and talk shit about niggers. But," he gestured to the truck, "as you can see, they're still just as dumb, armed and vicious as ever."

"What do we do?" I asked, then thought for a moment about the question that was really on my mind: "What'll they do to *us*!?" I yelped.

Furry peered out at the three Klan members. "Probably won't be too kind," was all he said.

Without even realizing it, I found myself rubbing the cross that hung from a chain under my shirt. Now I was truly scared. A lynch-mob wasn't what I had in mind when I'd boarded the train in my hometown to shove-off in search of my stupid father. In my mind it would just be a series of great adventures, and the adventures would be things like traveling from town to town and hitchhiking with friendly strangers and playing harmonica around a campfire with four hobos singing *a-cappella* blues songs in perfect pitch and harmony, accented by my harmonica -- which I didn't actually know how to play. Then we would all laugh and high-five and life would be merry and grand and I would be on to my next playful adventure, not a worry or responsibility in the world.

In the books I read, the trials and tribulations of the protagonists seemed so glorious and were always quickly followed by heroic acts and self-satisfaction. The world seemed so wonderful when boiled down to a dime-novel where the good guy always gets his girl, and my mind had conveniently disregarded any interpolation of the realities of life between those lines of prose. But I now found myself in the flesh and blood world -- and this world was different than the books. The swamp was actually wet in real life, and my pack uncomfortable and heavy. My legs and feet actually hurt in real life, with nothing glorious in the pain. And the guns in the hands of the men before me certainly shot real bullets in real life. Death, I was coming to understand, was a very real part of real life.

I wouldn't know until years into the future how pivotal these few moments at the edge of a Delta swamp would be in my life and in my understanding of the world in which we live. I *did* know, at the moment Furry punched that cop in the graveyard, that we would be in hot water with the authorities if we were caught: a fine, some time, or at the very least, a major pain in the ass. But facing a cross-eyed band of the Ku Klux Klan, armed and snarling with blood-lust in their veins, left hundreds of possibilities for a frightened young mind to conjure, none of which was glorious.

Furry continued to study the situation in the field as I held at the verge of hyperventilation. We could see that the three men were taking turns using the night-vision goggles, arguing about who would get them next.

After what seemed like hours, but was probably only a few minutes, Furry turned to me. "How's your throwing arm?"

"My throwing arm?"

"Yup, can you throw a rock?"

"A fucking rock!?" I looked at him with wide-eyed panic.

"Your plan is to attack them with fucking rocks!? How the hell did you make it to a hundred-and-fifty years old being so goddamn stupid?"

Furry cocked his head and glared at me with the same stank-eye I had come to recognize as Furry getting riled up. Then, BAM! Lying on his stomach, he flashed out a left jab into my jaw. The strike stunned me for a moment, then the shock turned to anger and I reached out to grab the little old man who had gotten me into this mess. While both of us were still on our stomachs, we swatted each other and wrestled, clutching at collars and arms until we both stopped dead at the sound of a stick breaking below us.

The sound seemed so loud. We froze and looked at each other, Furry shooting daggers with his eyes. Then he flashed out one final left jab to my jaw. It was a classless thing to do, in my opinion. And it stung. But I was too scared to move. Slowly, we both turned our heads toward the pickup to see if we had been heard. The three bigots milled about, scanning the forest and spatting out char-spit, not showing any signs of hearing a thing.

As we watched with arrested breaths, I could hear a growing rumble of thunder coming from the west.

Furry's ears also perked at the sound. He turned back to me, annoyance still painted on his face. He picked up a rock the size of a baseball and shoved it into my hand. "I didn't plan on *attacking* them with rocks, you filthy rube," he snarled. "Now take that and follow me." He turned back to the field and held steady, watching the three men.

Within a couple of minutes the Klansmen started arguing again about who should get to use the night-vision. They huddled up on the other side of the truck and began yelling and pointing fingers at each other, all three grabbing at the goggles. In an instant, Furry darted out of the underbrush and across the open dirt farm track at the back of the cotton field. I glanced once, saw that the Klansmen were still arguing amongst themselves, and took off after Furry. In the opening, I felt the first heavy plop of a rain drop on my shoulder.

As I approached, Furry waited, squatting between two rows of cotton. He grabbed my shoulder and pulled my ear close when I tumbled up to him. "Now throw that rock as far as you can that way." He pointed toward the forest-line on the other side of the truck.

Then I understood what the rock was for. Just a few years before, I'd played J.V. baseball for my high school team and had a decent arm. *J.V. baseball,* I suddenly thought with wonder. It brought up a flash of strange memories of what seemed to be a different life altogether. My mom? My friends? My brother and sister? What the hell? Had I really been there, at my *home,* my home…? Had I really been there at my home just two days before? What an abstract dream that place seemed to be. My life; the memories inside my head; J.V. baseball? Jesus. It was a swirl. Surreal.

The sight through the cotton plants of the three Klansmen made me snap out of my momentary reverie. All three heads were turned away from me and the goggles were being played tug-of-war with.

I set my pack on the ground and quickly sprung to my feet and reached back and heaved the rock along the line of trees. It was a decent throw for having a cold arm, and the rock sailed over the trail opening and thirty yards further, lightning flashing as it arched through the air, landing with a sufficient crash on the edge of the forest.

The sound snapped all the Klansmen's heads toward the forest and they all raised their weapons. Within two seconds of the rock landing, all three guns exploded to life, firing into the forest in the direction of the sound.

The sudden eruption of gunfire surprised even Furry, who gawked in horror at the seriousness of the enemy standing fifty yards away from us. His surprise lasted for only a second and he turned and started running hell-bent down the row of cotton toward the road.

The three Klansmen moved toward the rock's landing position with their backs to us, their gunfire reverberating through the air and mixing with the sharp crash of thunder from the approaching storm, the lightning-strikes stomping down like bright, skeletal legs marching across the cotton fields to the west.

The distraction with the rock was all Furry and I needed and we were half-way across the field by the time the gunfire slowed. I could hear the Klansmen shouting to each other as they searched for their quarry. "There ain't nuthin here!" I heard one yell between cracks of thunder.

They would no doubt scan the fields when they couldn't find

the cause of the sound. Furry and I were now three quarters of the way to the road. The three Klansmen would be coming back our way any second now, and the cotton plants only concealed us to the waist as we ran upright, choosing speed over stealth. We needed to get over the road. I could feel the hair rise on the nape of my neck as the wave of rain hit from the west, blown in as a sheet, turning the ground to mud.

31

Dockery Farms, Mississippi
1930

"*THAT'S EEEEEVILLLL, eeevilll is going on wrong,*" Chester Arthur Burnett sang out on Charlie Patton's front porch; "*That's eeeviiilll, evil is going on wrong; I got to warn you brother, you better watch that happy home.*"

Chester Arthur Burnett was a large, twenty-year-old man with a bull-like head and a mean slant to his eyes. His voice was a booming, raspy growl that had recently earned him the nickname, Howlin' Wolf. He snarled, only partially joking, in the face of the other young songster seated next to him.

This other young man had exaggerated, bulbous features and a funny-looking, ducktail haircut -- and, at the time, he was grinning at Howlin' Wolf's taunt. He seemed to be used to it; and he waited patiently for his own chance to sing. His name was McKinley Morganfield, but his mother had taken to calling him Muddy since birth. Of late, he had branded himself Muddy Waters, and he rolled his eyes at Howlin' Wolf.

"You about done squawking about nonsense?" he said.

"Nonsense?" Wolf snapped and stopped playing.

"That's what I said," Muddy replied lazily.

"I tell you, boy," Howlin' Wolf growled, "that's what the blues is all about: that *Eeevvviiil.* And you better watch it."

"Not only do you sound like a rabid animal, but you're as dumb as one too," said Muddy Waters as he leaned back. "The blues is about them ladies, boy."

Howlin' Wolf grinned. "Same thing, ain't it?"

Muddy grinned back, conceding the point.

Charlie Patton was leaning against the door frame, listening to the two pups bicker.

"The blues is about them women, man," Muddy Waters said again, and then added, "And maybe some whiskey, gambling, and reefer, too." He turned to Charlie Patton. "Ain't that right?"

Charlie looked at the two boys. "Is that what you think the blues is about?"

"It is, ain't it?" Muddy replied.

Charlie shook his head. "My God, you two are a couple of the dumbest sonsa--"

"I know what the blues is about, Mister Patton," came a voice from the bushes beside the shack. Eighteen-year-old Robert Johnson stepped out into the open.

"Ahh hell, where the fuck did you come from?" Howlin' Wolf hollered at the boy.

Robert paid him no mind, keeping his eyes fixed on his hero, Charlie Patton. "I know what the blues is about, Mister Patton," he repeated eagerly.

Charlie looked down at the boy and scowled. "Get the hell on, boy!" he yelled and shooed him away. "Stop your goddamn lurking around my place."

Young Robert Johnson dropped his eyes and sulked away, dejected.

"That boy gives me the goddamn creeps," Howlin' Wolf said and shivered.

"Get the hell on!" Charlie yelled and shooed him away again when young Robert turned back to look.

Robert Johnson flinched and shuffled into the woods, guitar in hand.

Willie Brown stepped out of the shack to see what the commotion was all about.

"Take it easy," he said as he saw the sad look on Robert Johnson's face as he disappeared into the woods. He put a hand on Charlie's shoulder.

Charlie turned to him and grinned.

"Give the kid a break," Willie implored with a roll of his eyes. "He just wants to learn."

"Learn? Shit, I'll tell you one thing: that boy is the worst guitarist I've ever heard."

"He ain't *that* bad," Willie said without much confidence.

Both Muddy and Wolf raised their eyebrows silently, their expressions saying all that needed to be said. Willie looked expectantly at Bukka White, who had been sitting quietly on a bucket beside Muddy Waters, and Bukka cocked his head and turned away, unable to agree with Willie.

Willie shrugged his shoulders, conceding the point. "But he really wants it, gotta give him that," Willie pleaded. "I hear that Tommy Johnson once told him that he had learned to play the blues by going to the Crossroads at midnight and selling his soul to the Devil. And since then, that boy Robert Johnson has been going to the Crossroads near every night, trying to make himself the same deal."

"No way," Charlie said, amused.

"What I hear."

"Wouldn't surprise me none," Howlin' Wolf chimed in. "That boy's as crazy as a loon."

Willie Brown shrugged his shoulders. "I think he's just ambitious."

"Well, it's damn sure either ambition or craziness makes him think he'll ever be able to play that guitar," Charlie said with a grin.

Bukka, Muddy and Wolf all grinned and Willie shook his head and waved his hand at the four of them.

The phone rang inside the shack and Charlie set down his whiskey and stretched his back and sighed before he lazed inside and across the room toward the phone. The three youngsters went back to playing and Willie stood in the doorway and listened.

Inside the shack Charlie picked up the phone. "Hello," he said into the receiver.

"Charlie?" the voice on the line asked.

"Huddie?" Charlie said into the phone and smiled. "What's happening, my man?"

"Charlie, listen, you're in danger!"

"What?"

"You're all in danger."

"What do you mean, Huddie?"

"The Klan knows, Charlie."

"What?"

"I don' know how much they know, but they know about the

Triad, and they're fixing to take us all out."

"What? Wait, wait, slow down. What's going on?"

"The Klan."

"What do you mean? What the hell is going on?"

"Listen, Charlie! They killed Lemon."

Charlie stopped and went silent.

"They killed Lemon, Charlie, they told me, clear as day, just before they tried to kill me."

"What, Huddie? What the hell is going on?"

"I'm in jail, Charlie. They got me on attempted murder for stabbing one of them while I was getting away."

"You're in jail?"

"Yeah, Charlie, I'm headed to Angola."

Charlie was silent.

"Don't worry about me," Huddie said, hearing the worry in the silence, "just watch your back."

"You're sure it was the Klan that killed Lemon?"

"They told me, Charlie, flat out. They tied him up and left him to freeze to death in that boneyard in Chicago---the mother fuckers."

"Mother *fuckers*!" Charlie said with gritted teeth.

"My times up, Charlie, I gotta go. Watch your back, boss, they coming."

"Don't worry about me, Huddie. Just hold tight, I'm-a get you out of there."

"G'bye, boss."

Charlie was silent until he heard the click of the line disconnecting. He hung up the phone and stared at the wall. He felt like his head was filled with brick mortar. He stared at the wall for a long time then smashed his fist into the wood and yanked the telephone box off the wall and smashed it onto the ground.

Willie Brown came running in from outside at the sound. What he saw in front of him was a wild animal.

Charlie threw the remaining piece of the phone across the room and stormed over to his cabinet. He threw open the door and grabbed the whiskey bottle inside. He pulled the cork out with his teeth and spit it onto the floor. He pointed Willie to a chair at his table. "Sit," he ordered.

Willie took the seat cautiously, watching Charlie as he pulled from the neck of the whiskey bottle and then slammed the bottle onto the table and pushed it toward Willie. Willie took a long pull from the bottle.

"Bukka!" Charlie yelled.

A second later, Bukka White scurried in the front door.

"Go get Henry and House," Charlie barked.

Bukka paused, not sure if there would be further instruction.

"NOW!" Charlie yelled. "And the rest of you get the fuck out of here."

*

When Henry Sloan and Son House arrived with Bukka, Charlie dismissed Bukka and then stood in front of Henry Sloan, Son House, and Willie Brown and told them what the phone call had been about.

"We need recruits," Charlie said when he finished recounting what Huddie had told him, "and they need to be able to defend themselves."

Henry frowned and Willie Brown thought about it for a second then nodded his head. "I got three in mind," he said and pointed his thumb toward the front porch where Bukka White, Muddy Waters, and Howlin' Wolf had sat earlier.

Charlie took another long swig from the bottle and slammed it down again. "Fucking mother *fuckers*!" he seethed, his mind unable to think past the revelation that Blind Lemon had been murdered by the Klan and Huddie Ledbetter was going to be in jail for a really long time.

"Ain't nothin' we can do about what's already been done," reasoned Son House, who had just recently been released from the Parchman Farm prison facility.

Henry Sloan stared at the floor, drawn and tired as Charlie took another pull from the whiskey bottle.

"How about Robert Johnson?" Willie Brown asked cautiously.

Charlie shot him a cold glance.

"There's something about him," Willie said defensively. "He wants it bad."

"And you think we should try to teach him just because he wants us to?" Charlie asked.

"I don't know. I feel bad for the kid."

"You feel bad for him, huh?"

"Yeah, I guess. I mean, Christ, Charlie, the kid goes to the Crossroads every night and sits there waiting for the Devil to come teach him how to play guitar in exchange for his soul. I can't see how somebody could want it much worse than that."

"Sounds goddamn crazy to me."

"What part of life ain't?" Willie said and shrugged his shoulders.

Charlie sighed.

"Just give him a chance."

Charlie looked at Henry and House and then took a drink and thought for a moment. "Well, we need recruits," he said and shook his head, "so, if you think so, I suppose I could go up there and have a chat with him one of these nights."

Willie nodded a Thank You.

Then Henry's head suddenly rose. "All you're doing is just signing a death warrant for these boys," he said, fixing his eyes on Charlie.

All three bluesmen looked at the aging legend.

"That's all you're doing, Charlie" he continued. "You talk about that boy Robert being crazy. *You're* the one's crazy. You can see what is happening right in front of you, plain as day, yet you're just closing your eyes on it."

"Pipe down, Henry," Charlie said with a dismissive sneer.

"Pipe down!?" Henry snarled. "You tell me to pipe down! Look how the times change," he said and shook his head. "You sell a couple records and think you got the world all figured out, huh? And you talk to me in this way, with this kind of disrespect?"

Charlie glared back at him. He was not in the mood to be lectured.

Henry Sloan, the *true* father of the Delta blues, kicked the chair back and rose to his feet, his guitar rested under his arm. He took a breath as if he would launch into a tirade, but he stopped himself and just shook his head tiredly.

"I'm taking my family to Arkansas," he said. "I ain't risking my family's lives on your goddamn delusions."

Without another word from anybody, Henry Sloan turned and walked out the front door, never to return. Son House and Willie Brown watched in shock. Charlie looked after his lifelong mentor with a cold squint to his eyes, the rest of his face remaining frozen and emotionless. He continued to stare long after the door closed, his mind turning but his body remaining still. Then he cocked his head to the side and gave the closed door one, final, long glare before turning to the rest of the men.

As he turned, so did the page, and he was on to the next. "Bring Bukka, Muddy, and Wolf here tonight. I'll go meet Robert tonight at the Crossroads. You said he goes there at midnight, Willie?"

"What I hear."

Charlie shook his head. "All right," he said, "I'll meet him at midnight and we'll be back here by one. Be here. Got it?"

Willie and House nodded their heads in silent obedience.

32

Greenwood, Mississippi
2002

FURRY AND I neared the edge of the field at a full sprint through the rain. The road was elevated four feet above the fields flanking it, totally exposed. We had seconds to cross before the three Klansmen who had been probing the forest where I had thrown the rock turned their attention. Lightning exploded above us, turning the night to day. If the Klansmen were looking our way at all, there would be no chance of concealment, the lightning providing nearly non-stop light.

Crouched by the road, Furry glanced back to check on the Klansmen. They were still searching out into the forest where the rock landed. But that wouldn't keep them occupied for much longer.

The rain pounded over us in sheets. We had only a tiny window to make a dash over the highway. I didn't have time to think or regret or assess my situation beyond the immediacy of staying alive. Thunder boomed and rattled the ground.

Thinking we were in the clear, Furry jumped up and took off toward the road. He vaulted onto the blacktop and skittered to his feet.

But at that same instant, a pair of headlights suddenly appeared from over a small rise in the road to the west. Furry froze for a split-second, but was already out in the open and had to make a run for it, crossing the road and diving into the row of cotton beyond.

I hesitated, knowing I didn't have time to wait for the car to pass, but worrying that whoever was driving might see us and report us to the police. Or worse, alert the sentries in the field.

I decided to chance it, hoping for an oblivious motorist more concerned with the pounding rain than the figures crossing the road ahead. I rose to my feet -- but just as I did, another light came on just up and to the right of the approaching headlights on the car. A spotlight! I dove back to the ground as the car lurched forward with a roar of its motor, its spotlight searching the field where Furry entered on the other side of the road. The car flew up and screeched to a halt right in front of me. I could see the red lights on the roof and the lettering: SHERIFF, on the side.

Then, in a flash of lightning, I saw my worst fear as the police car slid to a stop in front of me: the cop, *the* cop, the one Furry had knocked out in the graveyard. I dropped my head to the ground and hid, trying to lay as flat as possible -- until I heard the thunderous report of the cop's rifle out the window of the police cruiser. I looked up and could see in the space between the cruiser's undercarriage and the road the figure of Furry Jenkins running for his life in the opposite field. I could just see the top of the cop's head as he took aim with his rifle.

With the first crack of gunfire the three watchmen by the forest turned and started running toward the road. Another report from the rifle boomed. I could see Furry still sprinting down the row of cotton, halfway across, with nowhere to hide, fenced in by the row of cotton itself. Despite the gunfire, he still carried his guitar case, unwilling to drop it, as if it held a treasure. I looked up at the cop working the bolt action on his rifle. I had to do something; Furry was a sitting duck. I popped my head up and stole a glance back at the three Klansman running across the field behind me, almost half-way, and with guns in hand. They would be on me in no time.

Without a second to weigh decisions, I sprang up and darted toward the back of the police car. I slid in behind the bumper just as another shot rang out from the rifle.

Knowing I had but a second while the bolt was worked, I sprang from behind the car toward the barrel that was sticking out the driver-side window. I reached for the gun and my hands clenched around the hot steel at just the moment the cop jammed the bolt back into firing position. My sudden appearance startled him and I used the surprise to rip the gun from his hands and smash the butt back into his face, exploding his nose in a geyser of blood.

But the big hillbilly didn't go down like he had in the graveyard, the strike stunned him and he took a few seconds to recover, but he immediately went for his side-arm, blood gushing like a sieve out of both nostrils and down his tobacco-stained chin.

I had the rifle in my hands, locked and loaded, and had time to shoot the stunned officer if I wanted to. I twirled and pulled the gun around to firing position and even pointed it at the cop who was clutching at his nose and reaching for his pistol.

But I couldn't do it.

The cop looked me directly in the eyes from behind a bloodied face as he finally pulled the police issued nine millimeter from its holster. He even smirked as I failed to pull the trigger on the rifle. I spun and ran like hell down the row of cotton, Furry nearly to the woods in the same row ahead of me.

Through the roar of the rain, I could hear the shouting of the other three Klansmen nearly to the cruiser, then the distinct *Chh-Chhut* of the cop racking his pistol. The shot came a second later, a cotton plant to my left exploding as the hollow-point projectile tore apart upon impact. Two more shots came in rapid succession and I fell to the ground. I wasn't hit, but my internal defenses had shut down my legs, forcing me to take cover. But this time my instincts were wrong. This was beyond the realm of instinct. The row of cotton was like a bowling lane, and the pissed-off killer behind me had a clear line of sight straight down the alley at a single pin scrambling frantically. I jumped immediately to my feet as two more shots peppered the ground behind me and then ran as fast as my legs could carry me away. I was halfway across the field when something suddenly twisted me down to the ground. A split second later, the thunderous report of a high-powered hunting rifle identified what had pushed me down.

But I didn't hurt; and in pure flight defense I didn't even think about it as I staggered to my feet and continued down the path. One by one the three watchmen all reached the cruiser and started firing their weapons, the bullets singing past on all sides. Twice more I was tugged to the ground and twice more I scrambled to my feet and continued on. As a rifle-shot zipped past my left ear, close enough to feel the heat brush along my cheek, I finally reached the woods and Furry, who was waiting for me, taking cover behind a tree. I dove to the ground ten feet into the forest as more shots splintered the trees at the edge of the field. I didn't even realize I was still carrying the cop's rifle.

The slats of the spotlight penetrated through the branches of the trees, pinning us down as they fired exploratory shots into the forest around us. Without a word, Furry grabbed the rifle out of my hands and spun around onto his stomach, raising the sights toward the police cruiser on the road.

I watched him do it and said nothing. I wanted to tell him to stop, to not cross that line that can never be uncrossed, but I just watched. I watched as he took aim. I watched as he checked the safety. I watched as he took the slack out of the trigger and exhaled slowly. I just watched. I never said a word or moved a muscle -- as if I had become a spectator to reality, watching myself just watch as my accomplice steadied to gun-down an officer of the law.

And then the sound of the blast ripped through my ears, bringing me crashing back into body. The muzzle flash blinded spots in my vision and the gravity of that pull of the trigger plunged ice-water through my veins. The sound seemed to ring for hours.

Then, *POP!* The spotlight on the cruiser exploded, smashed into a million pieces from the thirty-caliber round.

The shot and muzzle-flash drew a wave of gunfire into the trees and we both held our heads to the ground as saw-dust fell around us with the pounding rain. After the initial flurry the guns went silent but for sporadic bursts.

Furry raised his head and reached to his left and grabbed a stick off the ground. Wordlessly he snapped the two branches on the stick down to about three inches in length and jammed the other end into the ground to make a support with the Y of the stick. He then took the rifle and laid its barrel into the Y, digging the butt into the ground so the gun pointed over the heads of the gang at the road.

"You have any string or thread or anything?" Furry whispered as he made final adjustments, placing a rock at the back of the rifle to hold it in place and jamming a straight, eight-inch stick into the ground alongside the butt of the rifle.

"I've got a little spool of sewing thread my mother gave me," I answered.

"Perfect, give it here." Furry held out his hand.

I shimmied out of my pack, still lying face-down in the forest, and pulled the pack up in front of me.

Then I stopped dead.

I saw for the first time the three bullet holes that had pierced my pack.

"Where's that threa--," Furry paused in mid-sentence as he saw what I was looking at. His eyes slowly shifted to mine.

"I owe you a big one," he said.

I couldn't speak. I reached a trembling hand into the front pocket of my rucksack and pulled out a small spool of dark blue thread.

"Perfect," Furry said as I handed him the spool.

Furry quickly tied the end around the trigger and ran the thread loosely back three feet and cut it with his teeth. He then pulled the top of a three-foot-tall pine sapling and tied the end of the string to its very top and then tied another piece of string to the sapling and tied the second string to an exposed root, holding the sapling bent over. He then pulled out a cigarette and lit it, cupping it in his hands to block its glowing tip. He tore a large leaf off a plant to his right and used it as an umbrella as he moved the burning cigarette down beside the second string.

I raised my eyebrows and shrugged.

"We gotta move out and get as far over as we can before that cigarette burns down," he said and started crawling diagonally to the right, away from the open field and the fused gun. "That oughta keep them from coming across that field for a little while yet," he said, grinning back at me as I followed him.

Once we had crawled thirty yards into the woods away from the fused gun we rose to our feet and crept through the forest, traveling as fast as possible without making any loud noises. The rain was no longer a thunderous downpour to swallow all sounds, but it was still steady enough that we didn't have to worry too much; and as a result, we'd made a good distance when we heard the report of our rifle. We knew it was ours and not another of the shots we had been hearing sporadically from the Klansmen, because directly after the shot, the four guns of the Ku Klux Klan erupted into a blending cacophony of hell-fire that lasted a full two minutes.

Immediately at the outset of the barrage, Furry turned slightly left and shifted into a full sprint and I followed behind. With the roaring clatter of the battery, we didn't need to be worried at all about making noise, and we took full advantage of that fact, running madly through the forest. By the time the peppering had ceased we were well into the ink-black woods, far beyond ear-shot and long gone from rifle range.

Furry stopped to rest and looked back into the blend of trees in the direction of the field as he took a deep breath and wiped the rain and sweat off his forehead. "Nearly shit myself there," he said, then slowly grinned at me.

"Holy shit we fucking made it!" I sputtered in muted rejoice between gulps for breath as I stumbled to a halt behind him. "We fucking made it!"

Furry jammed his hands into his hips as he looked off. "Doesn't look like that cop's just gonna let bygones be bygones, does it?"

"You think?" I snipped as I raised my hands over my head and gulped for breath. "I mean really, how the fuck *have* you made it to be so goddamn old."

Furry's demeanor changed and he gave me the look.

"Don't even start with that shit, Furry."

"I'm-a let you go with that 'cause you might've just saved my life. But…" He nodded his head at me to be sure I got the point.

"Oh shut the fuck up, Furry." I wasn't in the mood.

He turned and glared.

But then: *BAM!* I flung out a straight left jab into his jaw. A preemptive strike. Not a hard shot, but a little payback.

"Ha, beat you to it, you sneaky old fuck," I taunted as I smiled in triumph and held my fists up in front of me, ready for a retaliation.

Furry stepped back and rubbed his jaw. "So, your sister taught you to punch, huh?"

"Oh, shut up."

"No really, did she?"

"I didn't want to break an ancient artifact."

"I been hit harder by a fart."

"Good for you."

"It was like I was brushed by the wings of an angel. A girl

angel."

"You're gonna get brushed by a goddamn tree-limb if you keep it up."

"Dusted by Tinkerbell's feather duster."

"You know, Furry, you're a bad fucking influence."

33

Dallas, Texas
1931

"GIVE YOUR mother a kiss!" Bess Lomax demanded sternly from her son who had just dashed down the stairs and was about to go out the front door.

Alan Lomax sheepishly trotted back into the living room and kissed his mother on the cheek. It was a chilly evening in Dallas, and he was leaving to go camping with a friend.

"Now, you have fun and catch lots of fish," Bess said and touched his face. She couldn't believe her boy was almost seventeen. She brushed a lock of his scraggly brown hair from his face and cupped his chin in her hands.

"I will, Momma. And I'll be back tomorrow afternoon to help you with the garden."

"Did you bring enough blankets?" she asked. "It's supposed to get mighty cold tonight."

Alan rolled his eyes. "I'll be fine, Momma."

"All right. Run along," she dismissed him.

"See you tomorrow," he yelled back and dashed out of the house.

John Lomax just grunted and nodded his head from the living room, more occupied by the attempt to fix his bowtie in the mantle mirror. Bess watched her son out the front door then closed it and turned to her husband. She had a playfully sad look on her face and she huffed her chest and sighed dramatically as she pouted at her husband, brushing a lock of strawberry blond hair from her eyes.

"Oh, he'll be fine," John said chuckling. He hadn't even looked over at his wife but read everything he needed to know by the sound of the sigh.

"Hhummphh," she huffed again.

John turned to her and smiled. "You're a nut," he said in affectionate mockery.

Bess smiled and wiped the single tear from her cheek and danced over to her husband. "Seems like just yesterday he was learning to walk," she said as she took hold of her husband's tie and pulled it straight, fluttering her beautiful blue eyes. When it was centered she pressed her palm tenderly against his chest and leaned into the nook of his arm. John pulled her close and she looked up at him with doe-eyes full of motherly worry.

John smiled down at his wife. "He'll be fine, love," he said and kissed her firmly on the lips.

Bess moaned and then pushed herself away and grinned mockingly at John. "You, sir, have a speech to give." She said and wagged her finger.

John grinned at his wife and she pulled herself closer and began straightening his tie again.

"Listen John," she said, her demeanor turning serious, "you know I don't ask for much."

He cocked his head. "You don't?"

She punched him on the chest. "I'm serious, John."

"Okay, darling," John replied and bowed his head in apology. "Continue, my love."

"I just---I really think you shouldn't talk about the stuff...the Negro stuff, at the Society meeting tonight. I already hear they're calling you all sorts of ugly names around town."

"Arghh," John grunted and threw up his hands, "I just like the goddamn music. And for Christ's sake, shouldn't some of it be recorded for history? We *are* a goddamn Folk Society! That *is* what we're supposed to do!"

"I know, John. You know I know. But just don't push it," she suggested with a heavy tone. "Some of these guys take this stuff pretty seriously."

"They're a bunch of goddamn--" John started, but then stopped as they both noticed Walter standing in the living room doorway. The seven year-old black child stood there with the sadly defiant look that they had grown accustomed to in the year since they had taken him in.

John looked at his beloved wife and words were not needed. They both knew what he was really fighting for. He kissed her strongly on the lips and then said goodbye and took Walter by the hand and left the house.

Out on the street, John and Walter strolled down the sidewalk toward the reception hall.

"Maybe afterwards we can go to the store and listen to music," John said to Walter.

The boy's eyes momentarily lost their melancholy and he smiled up at John. He loved John's record store. John had learned that the only time the boy seemed happy was when they were listening to, or talking about music. And John was more than happy to oblige. They talked about music the rest of the way to the reception hall, Walter skipping and kicking stones down the street.

*

At the reception hall, John Lomax stood tall behind the podium in the front of the room and prepared to give his speech.

In the back corner, Walter had snuck in and was watching from the shadows of an empty closet doorframe.

"Gentlemen," John addressed the other members of the Texas Folklore Society, "we are at a great precipice in the evolution of music and folk history. There is a new sound that echoes from the hills of Mississippi, all across the land. We--"

"Argghhh, the *nigger* music!" yelled someone in the crowd.

"Quit with the nigger talk, John! We don't want to hear it," another shouted.

"I knew it!" yelled another.

As each new voice erupted, the simple act of its eruption gave four others the courage to erupt. The effect snowballed around the room. The tenor of the shouts was that of hate. Unencumbered hate, boiling to the surface from its ulcerous home and moving like a flowing plasma over the crowd.

From where John stood, up on the stage, he had a good view of the crowd. He could see the red, shouting faces with bulging veins and dribbles of spittle quite well. Beside each of these faces were faces of indecision, incapable of independent thought. These folks looked around and thought: *Everybody else is yelling, might as well yell.* And they did. And John Lomax looked back at the crowd and couldn't keep from smiling in pity. Deep down, he had expected nothing less. These people didn't know what they were even yelling about. They just knew somebody said *nigger*, and that makes for a nice opportunity to do some hate-letting.

John didn't move but to cock his head and raise his eyebrows at the onslaught. He had almost managed three sentences. He picked up the remaining pages of his speech and tapped them calmly on the podium to straighten the leaves. After one last look of pity at the crowd -- the Society he had founded -- he chuckled and shook his head and turned and strolled to the edge of the stage. He stepped down the steps and walked to the back of the hall to a ringing of boos. He never turned his head or showed any sign of the rage he was feeling inside.

As he neared the back of the hall, he saw Walter dart out of a dark doorway and out a back door. Seeing the young black child brought a frightening reality to the surreal swirl of the rest of the room. He forgot about the speech and the crowd's reaction and hurried off toward the exit.

He pushed through the door and stepped from the hot, rancid, mugginess of the reception hall into the cool, dry air of the Texas evening. As the door closed behind him, he scanned the area desperately for Walter. After a moment, John saw a small face poke out from behind a parked car. The child's wide eyes betrayed his fear.

John stepped quickly over to Walter and hurried him along. As they walked away from the hall, John reached down and wanted to place a hand on Walter's shoulder, but shame and embarrassment stopped him. He knew the boy should never have seen that. Not after what he had seen that night one year before. And he was right. The boy was in shock, and John could only imagine the horrible memories dug up in the boy by the sights and sounds of the hall.

He started to speak, but looked down at Walter and didn't know how to make any sensible explanation for what made the world and its people the way they are. Instead, he put his hands in his pockets and they walked down the street in silence.

*

It took nearly an hour to reach John's music store, and in that time, he hadn't thought of anything positive to say to the boy. There was no way to spin it. No way to make it anything but exactly what it was: hate. Unreasonable, unfounded, unproductive, and unending. There is no way to explain that to a child. But he watched in wonder as Walter skipped into the store. Walter had regained his spirit not long after they had started walking. That fact alone made John sick: to see the child so easily move on after what he had seen at the hall and the memories that must have been dug up with it. No child should be so acclimated to that kind of hate to be able to move on so quickly. John shook his head in shame as he watched the boy moving rapidly around the record store, picking his favorite records. John sighed and closed the door behind him.

"What do you want to listen to first?" he asked Walter as he hung his hat onto the hat-rack.

"Charlie Patton," the boy answered excitedly.

It was always Charlie Patton when the boy had his choice. Charlie Patton or Blind Lemon Jefferson, John's personal favorite. The boy had not been around to meet Blind Lemon when John knew him. But he loved the music anyway.

Walter came to the counter with his arms full of records. John raised his eyebrows and smiled. "Do you plan to listen to all of those, sir?" he asked the child.

"Yep," Walter said with a grin and a nod of the head.

"Well, all right," John said and nodded back. He took Charlie Patton's album off the top and set it carefully onto the disc of the record player. He flipped the switch and the record began to turn and he carefully set the needle into the outer groove. Like a bull, Charlie Patton's voice erupted out of the phonograph. Walter smiled from ear to ear and was instantly mesmerized as he watched the steady revolutions of the record. He could sit in front of that machine for hours, watching the records go round and round.

John watched the boy, and in that instant he knew there was nothing he could say that would help, nothing he could do. Everything the boy needed to hear was right there in the notes of those songs coming from the phonograph. He and Walter would never talk about what happened that night, or the night one year before, and that was all right. The boy had his own way, and his smile at that moment was the truest thing in the world.

John chuckled. Walter's head was entirely inside the phonograph and his arms were wrapped around the sides like he was hugging it. John leaned back in his chair and clasped his fingers behind his head. He smiled and stared at the ceiling as the mournfully bright sounds of Charlie Patton danced throughout the darkened store.

They stayed at the music store listening to blues records until long after midnight.

As they walked home, Walter chatted on and on about the music they had listened to. He compared the different musicians and their styles, and pointed out the slightest nuance within each of the songs. John just smiled and listened to the happily chatting boy. The boy sure did like to talk about music.

They walked along and kicked stones down the road and could smell a drift of wood smoke in the cool Texas air. The smell of a campfire always made John smile, reminding him of younger years. Tonight it made him think of his son Alan, out camping with a friend, probably around a campfire at that very minute. What a night, he thought, what a night. He looked down and smiled at Walter, who kept on talking, seemingly without taking breaths. John chuckled and patted the child on the head as a train whistle called out in the distance. John drew in the sweet smell of the wood-smoke and listened to the train announce itself to the world behind the child's excited chatter. It was times like these that he had hope for the world.

The train's whistle grew more faint and eventually dissipated into the night behind them and the only sound again became the voice of young Walter talking about the blues.

As they walked along, the smell of wood-smoke grew stronger and slightly more acrid, and the smoke became like a fog. It was a slight hint of gasoline that made John suddenly stop and smell the air deeply. A look of terror came across his face and he started to run.

When they reached the house it was already engulfed, and in the lawn stood a tall burning cross.

John screamed into the night and ran toward the inferno.

34

Dockery Farms, Mississippi
1931

CHARLIE PATTON sat at his kitchen table and read the newspaper. He could hear Muddy Waters and Howlin' Wolf arguing on the front porch. Inside his house, Willie Brown and Son House were on the sofa with guitars in hand, trading licks back and forth. Twenty-one year-old Bukka White sat on a chair and read intently from the blue notebook and a young boy by the name of John Lee Hooker sat across the table from Charlie, practicing the simple chords Charlie had just taught him.

Charlie pulled his newspaper to the side. "Hey, what's the name of that white guy in Texas Lemon used to always talk about?" he asked in the direction of Willie and House.

"The folk guy?" Willie Brown asked in response. "John something I think."

"John Lomax?" Charlie offered.

"That's it. Why do you ask?" Willie asked and both he and Son House turned to look at Charlie.

Charlie looked down at the article about the tragic fire at the Lomax house in Dallas and shook his head sadly. He read about how the charred remains of Lomax's wife were found hugging the melted frame of the family photograph. And about the burning cross planted in the lawn. Of course, there had been no arrests. The thought of it made the bile rise in the back of Charlie's throat.

He felt a familiar needle of murderous rage in his chest.

"What do you think about recruiting a white man?" he asked Willie and House when he looked up.

"Lomax?"

*

One week later, a train slowed into the Dallas station and let loose its whistle to announce its arrival. Charlie stepped off the train and looked around at the sun-bleached platform. It was a nice day.

It took him twenty minutes to walk to the music store. When he entered he didn't see a soul. He scanned the interior and was startled as he noticed a black boy staring at him motionless from behind a rack of records. The boy had the look of a deer in headlights. He stood stiff as a board, his eyes like saucers, gawking at Charlie.

"Would you be able to tell me if John Lomax is in?" Charlie asked the boy.

The child didn't move or make a sound.

"Can you hear me, boy?" Charlie asked and looked oddly at the frozen child. Then he heard movement in the back of the store and a pale, drawn, white man stepped out of the back.

"How can I help you," John Lomax muttered without emotion as he dragged himself behind the counter. When he looked up, he seemed to recognize who he was talking to. But his look was that of mild surprise, completely devoid of care.

"My name is Charlie Patton and I wondered if I could talk with you for a few."

John Lomax looked at him for a moment, then waved him back into his office, as if he didn't have the energy to do anything but agree, as if just coming out of the office had used up a week's worth of effort.

In the office, Charlie sat down on a chair and didn't know what to say. He didn't know if he should offer his condolences, or not bring up the fire and stick to business. He couldn't decide so he sat there for a long minute and silently watched as John Lomax rolled himself a loose, wet, cigarette then slid the end into his mouth lethargically, not bothering to remove the stray strands of shredded tobacco that hung out the end. John poured himself a heavy shot of whiskey into a dirty glass, then, as an afterthought, poured another into another dirty glass for Charlie. John never raised his head from slumped over and never raised his eyes beyond the end of his empty desk. John lit the crooked cigarette hanging out of his mouth and blew the smoke straight down into the whiskey glass resting on the table in front of him before emptying the glass in one drink. He offered neither the slightest bit of conversation nor an ounce of interest for why the legendary Charlie Patton was sitting in his office right then.

35

Ruleville, Mississippi
2002

FOR NEARLY two hours Furry and I stayed mainly to the forest, skirting around fields and properties and darting across the two small roads we had to cross. While we walked, Furry kept right on with his extravagant stories of his past, and I didn't believe much of it. In fact I listened very little. I was grumpy, to say the least. My legs were killing me, my back was crippled, and my shoulders were raw from the pack's straps. But it was my feet that hurt the worst; they had been wet, like the rest of me, since we entered the swamp behind the graveyard at sunset. It was now midnight. Each step sent bursts of discomfort up my legs.

But all the pain combined didn't amount to the all-encompassing discomfort of fatigue. I'd been awake since I woke up with the beautifully mysterious Blue Deveaux on my shoulder at sunrise of the day before, riding a train bound for the Delta. I did the math. That made forty-one hours straight without sleep and nearly thirty miles of walking, the last ten of which had been through swamps and forests while evading capture and death. I no longer gave a damn about finding my father. I just wanted sleep.

In front of me, Furry suddenly went quiet and slowed his step. I heard it too. It was faint, but distinct. At first, I thought it was thunder again, but then it became clear that it was a tractor-trailer downshifting in the distance.

"We're getting close to it, seems," Furry said with his hand cupped behind his ear. The *'it'* he spoke of was Mississippi Highway Forty-Nine, the road we had strolled down earlier in the day, happily trekking to the final resting place of Robert Johnson. Since the melee at the graveyard, we had been trying to avoid it, staying as far into the backcountry as we could. But now we had to face the dreadful highway.

I had been following Furry, and Furry had done well keeping us to the shadows. So I trusted him when he said that we were approaching a town and would have to cross the road. He seemed to know exactly where he was going and why. All I could do was hope he knew the land as well as he claimed. But, I couldn't figure if Furry was an insane homeless fiend or a wise old man.

Insane homeless fiend seemed more right to me.

The truck downshifted again; we were getting close.

Furry cocked his head a little. "That's strange."

"What's strange?" I asked. "Are we lost?"

"No, I know exactly where we are," Furry said with a snarl, "and that's why I'm wondering why that truck is downshifting so much."

"What?"

"The truck, it shouldn't be slowing down out here," Furry explained. "Remember from earlier, just south of Ruleville, it's a straight burn through the cotton fields -- open road and fifty-five mile-an-hour speed limit."

"Maybe he's slowing as he gets to town."

"Nah, we should still be five miles south of town."

"Should be?"

"We gotta be," Furry said, scratching his chin.

"You don't have a fucking clue where we are!" I yelped and threw up my hands. "What the fuck am I doing? I'm out here following some goddamn delusional lunatic through the fucking swamps of Mississippi! Getting shot at and--"

"Shut up your fucking whining and let me listen!"

The truck downshifted for a third time, this one long and low, there was no doubt the truck was slowing to a stop.

Before we even reached the edge of the forest we could see why the truck was stopping. Flashing, blood-red lights danced through the trees, reflecting off the vegetation to create a hellish, flickering scene growing brighter with each tentative step through the underbrush. I felt like Dante approaching the Gate, the strobing redness engulfing us as we crawled to the edge of the forest.

The police cars came into view across the field to the southwest as we moved the brush aside at the edge of the field. The officers were outside with their flashlights, sweeping each car that passed.

"Fuck," said Furry.

"Think it's for us?"

Furry just raised his eyebrows and continued to stare at the roadblock.

"So what does this mean?"

"Means it's official, for one. Which is good *and* bad."

"Good?" I said.

"Well, it may make it a bit harder to get away. But, also, it should mean they're not going to be trying to kill us anymore, just arrest us. But, of course then they'll try to make it look like we assaulted and shot at a cop."

I raised my eyebrows and cocked my head, looking dumbfoundedly over at Furry. "That is pretty much *exactly* what we did. What *YOU* did."

"Ahh, fuckin-eh, you know what I mean, it wasn't like that."

"No, it was pretty much *exactly* like that! I saw it with my own fucking eyes. Plus, I think your three-hundred-year-old ass actually missed the cop and just played it off like you were really shooting for the spotlight."

Furry scowled at me, his tone cold as ice. "I ain't missed in sixty years."

"Sure thing, Clint Eastwood. Either way, we're fried if they catch us."

"They ain't gonna catch us."

"But if they do, we're fucked. You realize that, right?" I was getting nervous. What had I gotten myself into?

Furry cocked his head and looked out at the cops. "That'd probably be accurate."

"Holy fuck, man!" My temperature was rising. I felt like I was hyperventilating. I *was* hyperventilating.

"Just relax," Furry said, eyeing me warily.

"Just fucking relax?" I screeched. "Are you kidding me? Just fucking relax? They're gonna burn us like regular cop-killers, Furry. They're gonna drag our bloody fucking entrails through the streets, man! Can you hear me!? They're gonna feed our fucking eyeballs to their dogs! To their fucking dogs--!" I gasped for breath that wasn't there. "--one by fucking one. You hear me?" My vision was swimming. "One by one, so we have to witness the beasts popping through the first eyeball before they come to dig out the second!" I clasped my hands together and ground my teeth, my chest heaving rapidly. "Goddamnit, man! They're gonna skin us alive with rusty fucking lawn equipment! Do you realize this!?" Sweat poured down my face. I felt like I would burst. The exertion was getting on top of me. I started to tip. "They're gonna tack us to the fucking courthouse with dock-spikes." I tried to catch my breath and my voice rose in pitch as it receded in volume, the energy emptying quickly. "Through the fucking sternum--" I was getting woozy. My body slumped as if weighed down, my voice reduced to a whisper. "--so we can hang there like a couple of blue fucking ribbons." I slumped further to the ground. "The birds--" I slumped further, the sound only a whisper. "Good God, what the fuck is happening?"

"Jesus, man," Furry muttered and leaned back. "You've gone straight out your head talking like that."

I slumped further, my head nearly on the ground. "Oh God."

Furry didn't move. He just stared at me. "You having a heart attack, boy?"

"Yes."

Furry rolled his eyes. "Get it together, man!"

"All is lost."

"Jesus Christ. You know something, something flipped in your little fucking brain. You got it? You're talking crazy talk, boy. The cops ain't gonna do shit to us cause they ain't gonna catch us, okay? 'Less you keep ranting and raving like a wild fucking Indian out here. Jesus, Mary and Joseph, get it together, boy!"

"Fuck off," I said and sat back against a tree, finally receiving some breath from my seized lungs.

"You okay now?" Furry asked sarcastically.

"I'm okay," I replied, catching my breath.

Furry shook his head. "Glad to have you back. How were your travels?"

"Fuck off."

"You mentioned that."

"How the hell are you getting us out of this bullshit, Furry?" I demanded.

"Well I'd tell you if you'd strap your balls back on and stop acting like a goddamn little schoolgirl."

"Watch you're fucking mouth, Furry, I'm not in the mood."

"I can see that," he said, looking down at the disheveled mess before him.

"So what's your fucking plan, man!?" I yelled.

"I'll smack you so goddamn hard, boy."

"I will eat your liver raw, old man! Tell me what your fucking plan is! Right now!!"

Furry shook his head with exaggerated disappointment. But he moved on. "Well, unfortunately for the future of your little goddamn escapade, it looks like you're gonna have to skedaddle from the Delta for a while." He nodded his head at the cop cars with their swirling red lights. "You agree?"

I glanced over at the roadblock across the cotton field. Furry was right. I couldn't take the chance. The hillbilly cop could no doubt identify me and the call had obviously gone out around the area. I would have to flee.

"What about you?"

"Oh, they can't fuck with ol' Furry around here," he said and revealed a toothy grin.

I was too tired to care what he meant. "Okay, so…where does that leave me?"

"You're leaving on a freight train."

"A freight train?"

"Yessir, I got a guy," Furry nodded his head.

"Ahh, Jesus."

"Well, you can't just go in and buy a ticket for a passenger train. That'll be the first place they look. You saw that cop eye-ball your bag and that Amtrak tag back at the cemetery. They'll be at every train station, airport and bus depot from here to Natchez."

"You think so?"

"I do," Furry nodded his head and grinned. "And that's why you, my friend, you get to see a little piece of blues history."

"Blues history?"

"Pea Vine, brother. Pea Vine."

PART FIVE

36

Ruleville, Mississippi
2002

"PEA VINE?" I asked. "What the hell does that mean?"

Furry raised his eyebrows. "I thought you were a fan of the blues?"

"I'm a fan of watching you die a slow death, is what I am."

"I'll put you over my knee, boy! I won't even hesitate."

But neither of us had any energy for a scrape and Furry just shook his head and continued.

"I'll tell you all about it on the way," he said. "For now, we need to get across this road. Once over, we'll head due west." He pointed west and his mind seemed to wander as he looked over the road. "To Dockery," he said in nearly a whisper, to himself as much as to me.

"Dockery?"

Furry just shook his head and continued. "You see that plantation house over there." He pointed across the road to the north-west.

"Yeah."

"From the shacks in the back of the field behind it there's a trail that leads to Dockery Farms, only about ten miles. Field workers would use it back in the day to go listen to the blues on Saturday nights. Kept them off the roads and out of the eyes of the KKK and such."

I looked over at Furry, and he sighed.

"So, how do we get over there?" I asked after a moment.

He pointed north up the tree-line we stood along. "We can go a little further north as long as we stay south of route four-forty-two," he said, looking back at me. "It'll get us away from that roadblock a little bit. Then we'll just have to cross forty-nine and we should be in good shape. We can meet the trail in the back."

A few minutes later, we scuttled along between the rows of cotton plants in the moonlight, north of our previous position. The storm had passed, and the stars had come back out, but the ground was still soaked with rainwater, and the plants provide little cover and none above waist level, so we were forced into a grueling crawl across the muddy field.

We were getting very near the road. The highway had steady traffic and the cars coming north through the roadblock were staggered just enough that there weren't gaps long enough for us to safely make a break over the road. And the southbound traffic was getting backed-up with cars waiting to be passed through the roadblock.

Further north, I could see a line of about ten cars moving south toward our position. With ten more cars in line the stopped traffic would be backed up to us. We'd be sitting ducks if anybody glanced down our row of cotton. Even now the cars passed slowly as they braked coming into the line of cars at the roadblock. We had been lucky as yet that no one had looked over -- but it was only a matter of time.

Furry could see the same predicament, and he turned back to me. "We gotta just make a run for it before those cars get here," he said and pointed to the line of headlights to the north, "and hope for the best."

I just nodded my head nervously and glanced down the highway.

Furry took a deep breath, crossed himself and made a run for it just after one of the cars coming north from the roadblock passed. The car behind it was already through the roadblock and accelerating toward us. An alert driver would see us, without a doubt. But there were no other choices. I followed Furry and we scurried up and over the road. There was no way to run that would make us inconspicuous, no cover. Speed was all that mattered, and a boat-load of luck.

We dove into the row of cotton on the other side and froze.

The moment of truth.

The headlights approached, and I couldn't tell if they were slowing down. The beams came closer and closer, and I held my breath. The swirling red lights of the police cruisers at the roadblock were making me nauseated.

The outline of the car appeared behind the headlights and rolled toward our position. Crouched beside me, Furry couldn't even watch. He had his head down, his chin to his chest.

The car came closer, and closer, and then abreast----without slowing down.

I could see a middle-aged, red-haired, librarian-type driving the Subaru as she passed. She looked like every PTA mom across the country: a do-gooder with thick glasses and her hands at ten and two. She was looking intently in the rear-view mirror. And I soon found out why. Turns out, she was looking so intently in the mirror because she was checking to make sure the coast was clear. As she drove by, while she was right in front of us, she opened her window and her hand suddenly darted out of view and a split-second later, she launched a crumpled piece of garbage out her window and onto the side of the highway.

Littering! My God!

I didn't know if I was more shocked that we were not seen, or by the littering. I couldn't believe it. I could just see that same lady with balled-fists jammed into her plump hips looking down her nose at a teenager who had done the same thing. I had been on the receiving end of plenty such occurrences, and it made me question every one. *Mrs. Branigan from chemistry,* I thought. I could see the patented look she gave. Did she have a secret littering life as well? What was in her closet? Had she been seen at cock fights? Maybe she killed people?

"Hey!" Furry whispered back sternly, already ten yards down the row of cotton. "What the fuck, man? Snap out of it!" He squinted his eyes as he studied me. "What the hell are you doing?"

I shook my head and followed after Furry. I needed sleep.

*

"Yessir, would you believe me if I told you I once beat up Huddie Ledbetter right in the back of the old meeting house of the

Dockery Plantation," Furry said as he walked along beside me on the trail that had originated behind an immense Antebellum Mansion. And then passed the slave shacks as contrast.

I rolled my eyes at Furry. "No, I wouldn't."

"And he was a big ol' buck," Furry continued, "and mean as a wolverine when he got mad."

"Lead Belly?" I asked skeptically. "You're claiming you beat up Lead Belly?" The guy sure could talk.

"That's him," Furry confirmed. "Mean ol' bastard. I loved him like an uncle, and he could play the blues to make you cry, but he was mean, twice incarcerated for murder, that ol' cottonhead. And that's just the ones they caught him on." He chuckled at the thought. "And you know the best part?"

"No, what?" I asked, half-listening.

"Both times he was pardoned after singing pleas for pardon to the governors. You believe that?"

I had heard something like that before about Lead Belly. I couldn't remember the specifics, and it was tough to distinguish fact from fiction when listening to the little old man called Furry Jenkins. "Really?"

"Yep."

"No bullshit?"

"No bullshit, and that's a fact," Furry said. "In 1925 and 1933."

"No shit," I said.

Furry glanced over at me and shrugged and a grin spread across his face. He looked at me silently for a while, his mind turning behind his eyes.

"What?"

Furry just continued to stare, his eyes squinting smaller and smaller.

"What, Furry?" I asked again.

Furry finally nodded his head and raised his finger into the air. "You know," he said, "the Good Lord works in mysterious ways."

"Hmmm." I raised my eyebrow at Furry.

"Yeah," Furry said, still thinking. "You know, I'm about to tell you something, and I ain't really supposed to tell you what I'm about to tell you," he said very seriously. "But it's been a weird fucking day and the goddamn winds of fate are definitely swirling and I believe God brought you here on purpose today. And I believe He's talking to me, and He's telling me I should tell you about what I'm about to tell you, despite your being a pain in the ass."

I couldn't hold my tongue. "Yeah? Is that what God is telling you?" I asked. "I sure am glad I'm following you around the fucking woods since your hearing God talk to you and all. That makes me feel very confident in your sanity and your ability to keep us from getting killed by the fucking Ku Klux Klan."

"Like I said: a pain in the ass," Furry said, still studying me with a grin.

"Who isn't spoken to by God! Tell Him I said hi."

37

Dallas, Texas
1931

"WHAT'S WITH the boy?" Charlie finally asked the disheveled John Lomax to break the ice as they sat in John's office. John had smoked his whole cigarette and rolled another in silence and was already pouring himself another whiskey after downing the first.

John Lomax didn't raise his eyes as he replied. "Sad story," he said and shook his head. He didn't have the effort to think of a good way to tell what had happened to Walter so he just spit out the words like they were poison, "His parents were lynched by the Klan." His voice cracked as he said it and a look of hate came over his eyes. "And he watched it happen."

Charlie was taken aback. He had asked about the child to lighten the mood. He had not expected to hear *that* response.

John looked up just long enough to meet the eyes of Charlie Patton. He didn't have to describe what had happened. He didn't have to say what Walter had seen done to his parents. He didn't have to tell about how lynch-mobs are like an evening picnic to the perpetrators; about how whole families come to join in on the festivities; and how the young people use lynchings as a great place to pick up dates, as nothing gets the women wild like some bad whiskey and a good nigger-lynching. He didn't have to say that. He didn't have to describe what young Walter had to watch happen to his parents from his hiding place under the porch of his parent's shack. That didn't have to be told because *everybody* knew what happens.

John took a deep drag from his cigarette and blew the smoke into the whiskey glass. "I found him wandering the streets a week later, nearly starved," he continued. "He was so messed up and scared of white people that he wouldn't even talk to me when I first saw him. If he wasn't starving to death and too weak to move, he would've ran away, without a doubt."

Charlie listened in silence, not sure what to say.

"After I found him," John continued, "I took him in and haven't known what to do with him since. Been over a year."

Charlie looked at the beaten man in front of him. He looked terrible, like he hadn't slept in weeks. And he probably hadn't; not since the night of the fire that had taken his wife. The murder. Charlie watched as he ran his hands through his thin and disheveled hair and took another drink from the whiskey tumbler in front of him.

Charlie took a drink of his own whiskey and shook his head, feeling terrible for both the widowed husband and the orphaned kid. He set the empty tumbler onto the desk and sat back in his chair. "Well, John," he said, suddenly, "providing the boy wants to, I could take him back to Mississippi with me, if it's all the same to you." The words came from him to his own surprise, as if he wanted to get them out before his mind had time to think about what he was saying. "I've got a good group of folks there that'll take good care of him and bring him up right."

Lomax slowly set his glass down and raised his eyes to look at Charlie. "You'd do that? You don't even know him."

"Only if he wants," Charlie said, and then added, "and *you* want."

"Oh, I think he would very much, Mister Patton," Lomax said with the slightest bit of hope creeping into his voice. "He's a huge fan of yours." Then he shook his head sadly. "You don't have to do this."

"I know, Mister Lomax. But I'd like to."

John looked at Charlie for a long moment, then hung his head and swirled the whiskey in his glass. "I love that boy," he said. "He's a good boy. Real good." He paused. "But I ain't been fit for nothing since…" he trailed off and his head dropped.

Charlie didn't know what to say. "I'm sorry about what they

done, Mister Lomax," he said quietly.

John drained the whiskey from his glass then looked at Charlie, his eyes red from tears. "You'd give the boy a good home?"

"I'd do what I could," Charlie said. "Truth is, I've grown quite fond of teaching guitar to the pups back in Mississippi, and I'd be happy to have another. Them boys are like sons to me. And besides, there's plenty of good folks back there'll make sure he gets brought up right."

John nodded his head in appreciation. "What is it you want from me in exchange?" he asked plainly and without malice.

Charlie pulled out the blue notebook and set it on the desk. "I don't want nothing for taking the boy," he said. "I'll do that either way."

"That's mighty big of you," John said.

Charlie waved his hand, moving on. "Aside from that," he said, "I *do* have a small thing I'd like to ask of you." He pushed the blue notebook across the desk. "I want you to read this notebook and give me a chance to bend your ear about it for a few. That's all I ask."

John looked up at Charlie for a long moment. "Is that right?"

"It is."

"What is it?"

"You'll see."

John studied Charlie and the notebook for another long moment. "I think I can do that," he said finally and drained the rest of the whiskey in his glass.

Charlie smiled at the sad man and turned to the office door. "What's the boy's name? Let's ask him if he'd like to move to Mississippi."

John smiled for the first time in two weeks. "His name is Walter. 'Least that's his real name, and that's what I call him. I guess his mother -- God rest her soul -- called him Furry, and that's what he prefers, I suppose: Furry Jenkins."

Charlie nodded and yelled out the partially opened office door, "Hey, Furry!"

A moment later, they heard the pitter-patter of feet outside the door and eight-year-old Walter 'Furry' Jenkins slowly leaned his head into the office. He looked at Charlie with wide-eyed wonder and stood there and stared wordlessly with only his face out from behind the door for a long time. It was obvious that he couldn't believe he was looking at Charlie Patton, *the* Charlie Patton.

Charlie smiled at the boy and waved him in. "Come on in, Furry Jenkins."

38

Ruleville, Mississippi
2002

"I WANT to tell you this, so listen," Furry said.

"Lucky me."

Furry shook his head, but continued. "How much do you think you know about the blues?"

"I don't know, Furry. Some. Not a lot." I was grumpy and running very low on patience for blabbering.

"You know of Charlie Patton?"

I thought for a second. "They say he's the father of the Delta blues, right?"

Furry nodded. "But, you see, that's what most people think about Charlie Patton. And they're right" -- dramatic pause -- "to a degree."

"Ugh," I complained and rolled my eyes. "Is this gonna be a long one?"

"You're a little sonofabitch," Furry spouted, snapping out of his folklorist condition, genuinely offended. "If you had any idea, you'd be singing a different tune."

I rolled my eyes again. I had been listening to his delusional bum-talk all day and was getting a little sick of hearing it. Too many hours and too many miles. But at the same time, I also didn't have the energy for an argument. My legs felt like lead. "Tell your story, Furry. Tell your story."

"I'll rap you in the fucking head!"

"Ramblings of a crazy old man!" I bellowed.

"Crazy old man!? You sonofabitch!" Furry yelled. He puffed out his chest and glared. But then exhaled and dropped his head. He looked tired too.

"You know, you should be singing a different tune," he stated. "I'm an important man." He was almost pleading, wishing I would believe him.

I suddenly felt bad for the little old man. The miles had taken their toll. He looked frail in his dirty clothes, his hitched gait more pronounced. We had been through a lot in the past day together, me and Furry, whether he was a delusional bum or not. I wondered if Furry was supposed to be somewhere, maybe a shelter. He didn't look good. I just hoped he lived through this walk.

"I'm just kidding, Furry," I said, pitying the sad old man. "I didn't mean it." If Furry wanted to blabber on, I would let him.

BAM! Punch in the face!

I staggered back. "Furry, you sonofabitch!" I bent to the side and grabbed my jaw. The anger rose as I rubbed my stinging chin, but then the sight of little Furry Jenkins with his dukes up made me laugh out loud. The general pain of my body was all-encompassing anyway; a punch seemed like nothing more than a mosquito bite.

I shook my head at the feisty, little bum. "Continue your yarn, you sonofabitch. I'm dying to hear it."

"You should be," Furry said, pepping-up after the strike. "I shouldn't even be telling you this."

I rolled my eyes but kept my mouth shut. Furry, despite being just as excitable as normal, had a strange air about him as he spoke; he was really dying to tell his tale. And fighting it was proving to be more effort than it was worth. I waved him on.

"You don't know shit, you little asshole," Furry continued with a growl, "just like everybody else!" He pumped his fist at the night. "If people knew what I know, if they knew the *truth*, they would rank Charlie Patton in the realm of Einstein, and wouldn't only call him the father of the Delta blues, and the blues in general, and of *all* goddamn modern music, for that matter, but they would call him father of Civil Rights as well, the creator of a plan that in less than a hundred years has nearly stamped out a way of human life that had been around since the first nigger was stole out of Africa."

He smashed his fist into his open hand.

"Hmmm," I mumbled.

"Nearly," he said again. The life was coming back to Furry as he prepared to tell his story. It seemed he didn't have many people to listen to him and was excited to have an audience. It made me think about what Furry had said earlier in the day, about the importance of having people who care about you, who want to listen to your stories and care when you are away. I wondered if this old man had *anybody* to talk to, anybody who cared. Furry had said earlier that a story is only as good as the people who give a damn that it happened, and I could see he spoke from experience; old, wise experience. The blues. I wondered what had happened to this man's family, what family he had, what of his friends. It seemed he had been speaking in fantasy all day.

"Why would they call him the father of civil rights?" I asked, giving the old man the stage.

"Well, I'll tell you," Furry said, then prepared himself for his performance. He was excited and his voice changed as he began his tale, the pauses becoming elongated and the volume and tone varied for effect. In one sentence he was in full swing.

"So, it was nineteen-three," he started with a whisper, "I wasn't even born yet…and don't factor into this story for some time. But in nineteen-three, a twelve-year-old Charlie Patton sat in a shack in Hinds County, Mississippi, with Henry Sloan and a couple of guitars…"

39

Dockery Farms, Mississippi
1934

THE CAR pulled up to the house on Dockery Farms and young Furry Jenkins ran to greet the occupants. John Lomax and his son Alan stepped out of the car and both smiled at the sight of little Furry running toward them. The boy was smiling from ear to ear as he churned through the tall grass of the front yard, his tiny arms pumping at his side.

"Hey sport!" Alan yelled and reached out to him.

But Furry bounced straight by the nineteen-year-old and up to John in a spastic swirl of excitement. Without stopping, Furry punched John Lomax directly in the groin, then shrieked with joy and continued running past.

John went down to the ground like a sack of potatoes.

Alan doubled over in laughter and Charlie Patton chuckled as he stepped up to the man writhing on the ground.

"He just had some chocolate," Charlie offered in the form of an explanation, then added: "Also, you didn't inform me before I took him in that the child is mighty keen of punching."

A meek, "Fuck you," was all John could manage at that moment.

"Yup," Charlie chuckled, "Gotta be on your toes with little Furry Jenkins around."

Furry returned after his victory lap and both Charlie and Alan flinched as he ran between them. But he just jumped onto Alan's back and hugged him around the neck.

"Hey sport," Alan said and tousled Charlie's head.

"What kinda stories you got for me, Alan?" Furry demanded as he hung from Alan's shoulders.

"Oooo, we've been all over," Alan said. "You wouldn't believe some of the stuff we've seen, not to mention the music we've recorded."

"Tell me about the music," Furry demanded excitedly.

On the ground below them John was in pain and slowly trying to rise to his feet, having much trouble.

Furry hopped off Alan's shoulders onto the ground in front of him. "Sorry, Mister Lomax," Furry said with a grin. "I guess I got excited."

John's face was nearly blue as he wheezed, bent over at the waist. He grunted and staggered forward, swiping at Furry, who hopped out of the way and ran off in gleeful laughter. John grunted and swiped again at air and took very fast shallow breaths as he tried to make the pain go away.

Charlie and Alan watched John in amusement and the three made their way slowly toward the house as Furry disappeared into a barn.

"He's a live one," Charlie said.

Inside, and after a period of time, John recovered from his assault and he and Charlie sat at the kitchen table and caught up over a bottle of whiskey.

"So, how goes the jailhouse recording odyssey?" Charlie asked.

"It's wild," John said and raised his eyebrows, "but we're getting some really good stuff."

*

More than two years earlier, on the afternoon after their first meeting, Charlie sat across from John in John's office in the same chair he had sat in the night prior. But, on *that* day, the whole place seemed different. It was John. The life had returned to his face and his eyes danced around excitedly.

"This is fucking brilliant," Lomax said as he held up the notebook. "Where did you learn this?"

Charlie smiled. "A lot of places."

Lomax looked at the notebook in amazed disbelief and shook his head. "But I don't get what you need from me."

"Lemon Jefferson spoke very highly of you," Charlie explained. "He said you were a smart man -- and a decent one, more importantly. He also mentioned that you had compiled some world-renowned anthologies and had founded the Texas Folklore Society."

At the mention of the society John's face went cold.

Charlie continued cautiously: "He said you knew people, the right people, and could make things happen. And that's what we need. We need to get the blues on record," Charlie said. "The only way for this plan to work," he pointed at the blue notebook, "is if we have an audience. We need the music to reach beyond the juke joints of the Mississippi Delta."

"You've got records, your record is selling like mad right now."

"But this is so much more than me or Willie or any of the rest of the Triad. We are nothing but individual people, each with something to say. Our story, our blues, only goes so far on its own. We need more than just a few niggers in Mississippi to hear what we have to say. We need the masses. And that means we need to *hear* from the masses. *They*," he gestured to the wide world, "need to hear from the masses. *They* need to *feel* the blues of the masses. This sound is spreading, no doubt. That," he pointed to the blue notebook, "is spreading -- without anyone's knowledge -- and it provides a conduit for our people to speak through. For the masses to speak through. And we need to be sure that people can hear what they have to say. What the masses have to say. A handful of men cannot do this alone. Our voices can only travel so far, only live so long. The best we can hope for is to inspire others to speak as well. To spread. To record. And to show them how to get through. The world will only change when it hears our *collective* voice, and feels our *collective* blues. And only the blues can do that."

That night, he and John stayed up very late and brainstormed over a bottle of whiskey. Outside on the street, the haunting, dust covered windows of vacant storefronts were like a contagious void that spread to new buildings each day. The void of the Depression. It was a time when people needed moments like this: sitting across the table from a like-minded individual for a bottle of whiskey and some wild talk. The reaper was at the doorstep and there were very few things that could help one forget that fact. This was one; the blues was another.

Shortly after that evening, John went to New York to meet with some fat-cat publishers he knew. With some very fancy salesmanship, he landed a deal for a folk anthology. With that in hand, he then traveled to Washington, D.C., and convinced the Library of Congress, with a plea for posterity, to provide him with the field recording equipment and a spot for the recordings within its catalogue. He got everything he asked for.

On his way home, he got off the train in Mississippi to meet with Charlie and bring him the good news. And a few weeks later, with his car packed to the roof with recording gear, John and his son Alan had bumbled out of Texas to begin their expedition.

The first stop was Angola Prison in Louisiana -- to record Huddie 'Lead Belly' Ledbetter, and his *second* plea for pardon song. After delivering that song to Governor O.K. Allen, John and Alan continued down the road. And for the two years since then, they had been crisscrossing the south, making recordings of countless musicians in jailhouses, juke joints and on front porches, compiling a massive collection to be distributed for consumption and catalogued in the archives of history.

*

And now, two years later, they were back at Dockery.

Charlie grinned at John from across the table. "Well, John, they can try to kill us all they want now, but thanks to you, even if they do, they can't get rid of our message."

John Lomax raised his whiskey glass in a salute. "I am but a cog within your brilliant machine, Mister Patton," he said and downed his whiskey. "But I agree with your sentiment, they can't shut you up now."

"You gonna stay for my show tonight?" Charlie asked.

"Wouldn't miss it for all the whiskey in Mississippi," Lomax said with a smile. "Not gonna head back out till tomorrow."

"Cheers to that," Charlie said and raised his glass.

40

Ruleville, Mississippi
2002

"SO, A blue notebook, huh?" I asked. "What was in it?" I was playing along as Furry told his story. He had been talking for a very long time.

"Genius. That's what was in the notebook, pure fucking genius."

"Yeah?"

"Yeah."

"Anything more specific?"

"Wouldn't you like to know."

"Not really."

"It's Charlie Patton's keys," he said. "His manifesto, you might say."

"Manifesto?"

"It's the *invention* of the blues as you know it. And the invention of the blues as very few know it." He winked his eye. "Charlie Patton simply called it the *Blueprint*. And that's just what it was. It was a blueprint for a revolution?"

"A revolution?"

"Through the back door."

"Through the back door?"

"That's right," Furry stated happily. "Charlie Patton understood a great secret about music and its relationship with the human mind. The flute charms the viper, you know? He recognized this as a weapon to fight back, to infiltrate the very psyche of America and expose the injustices beating down his people -- without anyone ever knowing he was doing it."

I watched as Furry walked and talked with a crazy smile on his face.

"Charlie knew that black folks couldn't just fight racism head-on," Furry continued. "The deck was stacked against us on every level. But why fight the body when you can control the mind?"

"Muhammad Ali."

"What?"

"I don't know."

Furry shook his head and continued. "Charlie had the lock-picks to the mind. Musical keys, you might say. And he knew what variations of tension applied to those keys at the right moment would open a door into your very soul." He pointed at my chest. "He knew what the ancients knew, what modern science can only scratch the surface of. It was in him. And he used it to make people see and feel what he sang about, to manifest empathy through pick, rhythm, and song. What's more powerful than being able to put a man in another man's shoes?"

I shrugged.

"And the genius is, people just think they're being entertained. They let their guard down. Folks who wouldn't listen to a nigger talk for a minute will listen to him sing for hours. They'll play a record over and over without ever knowing, like Charlie did, how much of an effect certain aspects of music can have on the human mind, how much power they can have *over* the human mind -- or the doors that can be opened, the connection that can be made, the emotions that can be manipulated. That's a handy tool."

"It is."

"And Charlie Patton knew it. You think Robert Johnson made a deal with the Devil at the Crossroads?"

I shrugged.

"Robert Johnson didn't make no deal with the Devil at the Crossroads, he made a deal with Charlie Patton. That's the only reason you or anybody else ever heard of him. Charlie taught him to play the blues, him and a handful of others." Furry pointed from one finger to the next. "Willie Brown, Son House, Muddy Waters, Howlin' Wolf, Lead Belly, Blind Lemon Jefferson, Tommy

Johnson, John Lee Hooker. You might have heard of them."

I raised an eyebrow.

Furry breathed in deeply and his arms swung as he walked. "You know, Franklyn O'Connor, it feels good to talk about this."

The old bum sure could talk.

"Fuck. I feel like telling you more."

"Great."

"This is important shit."

41

Heathman-Dedham Plantation, Mississippi
1934

CHARLIE PATTON smacked the strings of his guitar and stopped. His eyes were wild as he stared at the throngs of people. The sweat dripped off his face and soaked through his shirt, his thin, boney knees pointing out in front of him from the wooden chair he was perched on. The chair rested on a slightly elevated corner of the old barn converted into a juke joint.

The crowd at the juke joint of the Heathman-Dedham plantation in Indianola, Mississippi, held for a moment, transfixed.

Charlie pulled his pick up against the strings slowly, plucking each one distinctly as he stared maniacally out at the crowd. And then he jumped up and burst suddenly into motion like a palm tree in a hurricane. He picked and strummed and swung the guitar ferociously.

The crowd went wild.

Charlie shouted out with his eyes closed:

"I see a river, rollin' like a log,"
"I wade up green river, rolling like a log;
'I wade up green river, Lord, rollin' like a log."

His hands flew about his guitar in a blur and the crowd bounced to the exotically primal rhythms being produced. He cried out:

"I think I heard Marion whistle blow;"
"I think I heard the Marion whistle blow;"
"And it blew just like my baby getting on board."

He maneuvered his guitar and his head swayed with his eyes shut tight. The crowd, the club and the earth itself disappeared from his consciousness, engulfed and erased by the white light of the blues erupting through his mind. He cried with a painful ache:

"I'm goin' where the Southern cross' the Dog;"
"I'm goin' where the Southern cross' the Dog;"
"I'm goin' where -- the Southern cross' the Dog."

The words tore holes in the listeners' souls and Charlie Patton writhed in emotion as dust from the floor burst out in tiny clouds with each pounding tap of his shoe.

"Some people say the Green River blues ain't bad;"
"Some people say the Green River blues ain't bad;"
"Then it must-a not been them Green River blues I had."

His voice had a rasp as if tangible pain were slicing from his lungs; and the crowd felt every drop. But, what the crowd felt was much different. Somewhere between his soul and the ears of his listeners, the thick, hellish pain of his sounds transmogrified into a heavenly sensation. What but the hand of God can perform this act? Who but God can turn torture into salvation? Charlie Patton could, with his guitar.

He sang mournfully:

"It was late one night, everything was still;"
"It was late one night, everything was still;
"I could see my baby up on a lonesome hill."

His head dropped as he plucked through his licks.

Then his head shot up again as he cried out at the top of his lungs:

"How long that evening train been gone?"

The sound bellowed through the room.

"How long, baby, that evening train been gone?"
"You know I'm worried now, but I won't be worried long."

He slapped and strummed his strings and his left hand slid up and down the neck with tearing vibrations. His voice dropped to a whisper:

"I'm goin' away, may get lonesome here;"
"I'm goin' away, baby, you may get lonesome here;"
"Yes, I'm goin' away, baby, it may get lonesome here."

Charlie's chest was heaving as he played the last notes and finally opened his eyes, seeming almost startled to see the crowd suddenly appear before him.

He fell back into the chair and sat silently still for a moment, looking at the crowd as they cheered. And they cheered like mad. He wiped the sweat off his forehead and tuned his E string, smiling out at the crowd. Then a man with a sad look in his eyes stepped forward and offered Charlie a swig from his bottle of whiskey as the crowd continued to clap and shout. Charlie took the bottle and turned its bottom up, pulling heavily from the green neck.

After returning the bottle, Charlie wiped his mouth with the back of his sleeve and smiled out at the crowd, drawing an eruption of cheers. Charlie tapped his guitar and stomped his foot onto the floor and stood up. He pulled the pick over the strings and began to dance about.

But then his smile faded and he stopped dancing. He watched as the man who had offered him the whiskey walked over to the garbage bin along the wall and dropped the half-full bottle into the trash. Charlie's eyes followed the man as he weaved his way through the crowd to the exit, never looking back. As the man slipped out the door, Charlie's gaze fell on the large round eyes of young Furry Jenkins sitting on a hay-bale at the back of the dimly lit room. With an excited glow to his face, the young boy waited in eager anticipation for the next song.

Charlie Patton paused only for a second before granting the

child's unspoken request. He mustered himself and grinned at the crowd and pulled the pick across the strings and whipped into motion. His mind was at ease though he knew what one never wishes to know. He had seen the end of the road. He had read the final line.

He played the blues.

42

Ruleville, Mississippi
2002

"FIRST ONE they came for was Blind Lemon Jefferson," Furry continued his story, a scowl crossing his face. "They got him in Chicago. He was found froze to death in a graveyard after playing a show that night." Furry shook his head.

I raised a tired eyebrow.

"Next was Huddie Ledbetter," Furry continued, a grin parting his lips, "But big ol' Huddie wasn't as easy to take down as a blind man." Furry laughed at the thought. "Ol' Huddie nearly gutted the two sonsabitches who came for him." He made a stabbing motion. "But that landed him in Angola State Penn in Louisiana, this time for *attempted* murder."

"Yeah?" I asked, half-listening. I was tired.

"It was at that time that Charlie Patton took his biggest risk, and made quite possibly his most gainful move," Furry said. "He took his Blueprint to John A. Lomax, a white man with connections and known black sympathies." Furry paused, then hollered: "And that's where ol' Furry Jenkins comes into the story!"

Furry hopped with excitement, and I couldn't help but smile.

"At that time I was a six year-old boy," Furry said. "And I remember it like yesterday when Charlie Patton walked through the door of Lomax's record store. My life changed forever at that very moment."

I just listened and nodded my head.

"When we got back to Mississippi was the first time I ever laid eyes on the Blueprint," Furry said. "I couldn't even read at that age, but I learned from the man himself for near three years."

A large bird rustled in the trees overhead as we passed, but Furry paid it no mind.

"Those were good times," he said. "For a while." He paused. "But in the spring of nineteen-thirty-four, Charlie was assassinated at a juke house just a few miles from where we walk right now. I saw it."

I looked over at Furry.

"A man he knew well gave him a poisoned bottle of whiskey while he was on-stage. The Klan had the man's family. They lynched the family anyway."

I didn't know what to say.

Furry didn't say anything for a while either, but just walked down the trail. Then as an afterthought, he said, "Huddie got pardoned again soon after that, again by playing the blues. I was telling you that."

"Yeah."

Another long pause and then, "Things were different after Charlie died. I was young."

I stuffed my hands into my pockets and avoided glancing at Furry.

"I'm tired," he said and stopped talking.

"Yeah."

43

Ruleville, Mississippi
2002

OFFICER RON Tweed shut the door of his cruiser and tucked his new shirt into his pants. He'd stopped back to the station and cleaned up his bloody nose and changed his shirt. His stomach was feeling better, although still uneasy, but his rage had not leveled a bit.

He had been dreading coming up to Ruleville. In his opinion, the local Ruleville cops were assholes.

"You look like shit, Tweeder," one of the officers said as Tweed walked up.

"Fuck off, Cyrus," Tweed snarled.

"Fuuuuck you, Tweeder," Cyrus snapped back. "We been standing out here all night to clean up your mess, and your fucking fugitives ain't come this way. And we're getting fucking hungry so we're shutting down. Got it?"

"Fuck you you are, Cyrus! These guys tried to fucking kill me and you're gonna stay out here till I tell you you can leave."

"Too bad they weren't better shots," Cyrus said loud enough for all his guys to hear, and then burst out laughing.

"You better watch your goddamn mouth Cyrus. Or I might just set sights on you," Ron Tweed said with snarl.

"You motherfuck--" Cyrus lunged at Ron Tweed but was held

back by the other officers. "Either way, Tweeder, they're long gone by now, give it up, you're a fucking loser. We're out of here." He signaled to the rest of his crew to pack it in.

As the Ruleville cops left in their cruisers, Tweed stormed back to his car and snatched his radio mic from its mount. "Randy, Rod, you guys get up here and help me out on forty-nine, the Ruleville cocksuckers are bailing."

"Ten-four, hoss," came the reply.

44

Ruleville, Mississippi
2002

"RIGHT UP here I'm gonna have to slip into the KwikEMart to make a phone call," Furry said as we moved down the trail. He had been mostly quiet for a long time. "I've got a guy at the rail-yard in Ruleville. He can leave a freight car open for us."

"Now it's us?" I asked. "You're coming with me?"

"Yeah, I ain't jumped a freighter in a while," Furry said.

"Anything I should do while you're inside?"

Furry shook his head. "Just keep out of sight," he instructed. "The payphone is outside so I won't even have to go in. Should just take a second."

*

Ten minutes later, Furry ran like a hell-hound down the trail and past me. "Run! You sonofabitch!" he yelled. "RUN!!"

I leapt to my feet and tore off after him.

"We've got to get over that bridge!" he yelled back.

I ran as fast as I could. "What bridge!?" I yelped. Furry's little arms were flailing as he ran at a dead-sprint.

"We're pinned between the swamp and the road," Furry yelled back. "They meet up ahead at a bridge. That bridge is our only way out of here. We need to get there before they do!"

"They?" I yelled up.

"Fucking cops!"

"What?"

"They pulled into the gas station just as I hung up."

I was petrified simply by the fear shown by Furry. "Fuckfuckfuckfuckfuckfuck," I muttered as I ran along behind him. What now?

After a few moments, Furry stopped on the trail and punched at the air. "Fuck!" he screamed.

"What!?"

"We'll never make it," Furry shouted.

"So, what do we do?" I was panicking.

Furry jutted his jaw and looked at the ground. He thought for a long moment.

"*We,*" he said finally, "don't do anything. *I'm* gonna go up to the road and try to distract them enough to buy some time for *you* to get over the bridge."

"Distract them? What the hell do you mean?"

"I'll turn myself in, keep them occupied long enough for you to get there."

"You can't do that."

"Oh shut up! Don't pretend to be a hero. We don't have time to argue about this, just do it."

"Furry, you can't just give yourself up, not now. They'll fry you."

"Bahhh, they can't do shit to ol' Furry around here," he said with a grin. "I'll get a slap on the wrist."

I raised my eyebrow.

"I will, I will," he said convincingly. Then he held up his guitar case, pausing for a moment. "Hold onto this for me," he instructed. "It's very important. Jump off the train in Memphis and find a guy named Memphis Slim, he'll be on Beale Street; you'll have no problem finding him. Wait for me there; I'll be released no later than tomorrow."

"Okay, Furry," I said, suddenly and overwhelmingly aware of the dire situation, "but I really don't think you need to do this."

"Just find Memphis Slim and tell him I sent you and tell him what happened."

I cocked my head. "The truth? You want me to tell him the truth, that you coldcocked a cop and got arrested? Or should I jazz it up a bit?"

Furry ignored the joke and I felt bad for having said it. Furry's eyes suddenly became vacant and old and his wrinkled forehead drooped over those tired eyes. Then he straightened up and stuck out his chest and tucked in the tail of his shirt to the back of his farm pants and jutted out his jaw.

"Listen, kid," he said, "I knew your father."

It hit me like a ton of bricks. "What?" was all I could say.

"I knew you were his kid the second I saw you in that parking lot. You're his spitting image. That's the whole fucking reason I even brought you to that stupid graveyard. It's where I first met your old man, when he wasn't much older than you. We don't have time to get into the rest of it now, but what you think you know about him isn't right. He loved all of you more than you'll ever know, but things don't always work out the way we hope. I owe your father my life, and so much more, plain and simple; and the world owes him, too. You come from very important lineage, Franklyn O'Connor."

I opened my mouth to speak but nothing came out. I couldn't comprehend. "Where is he," I finally stammered.

Just then we saw the flashing red lights start to flicker off the trees around the bend in the road.

"Fuck," Furry cursed, "Get the fuck on, boy! I'll tell you the rest of what I know in Memphis. Get up and get over that bridge. The Dockery plantation is just beyond. Remember this, third yellow car, four-fifty-seven a.m. And take care of that for me." He pointed to his guitar case.

I locked eyes with the little old man and all was said in that instant. Furry nodded his head, and I turned and lit off down the trail.

45

Ruleville, Mississippi
2002

I RAN down the trail, glancing back from time to time. I didn't know what to make of what Furry had just told me. I could see Furry though the trees as he stepped out onto the shoulder of the road. He stood tall and dignified, and adjusted his plantation hat and tightened his tie. I slowed slightly to watch in the last seconds as the police cars approached.

The spotlights found Furry and he didn't flinch. The cars slowed to a stop.

"All right, you got me," Furry hollered and held his hands up, using one hand to shield his eyes from the spotlight. "You got ol' Fur--"

Furry's shoulder suddenly wretched back. Then--BOOM!! The sound from a rifle shot reached me on the trail.

On the road, Furry dipped back and his hands dropped to his side and he looked down, stumbling two steps to the left, and one back, before falling forward and landing face-first with a sickening *thud* onto the cracked macadam of the dusty Mississippi highway.

I clapped both of my hands over my mouth to keep from screaming. My eyes instantly welled and I begged for it to just be a dream, a product of fatigue, a hallucination. Please don't let this be real! But I watched and it was real. Furry lay face down on the road and the flashing, blood-red lights of the two police cruisers strobed through the forest. I vomited into the underbrush.

"Hurry up and put that gun in his hands before the others get here," I heard one of the cops yell up on the road. I recognized the cop who walked forward as the one from the graveyard. He held a revolver in his hands and was wiping it with a mechanic's rag. He looked very proud of himself. He gave Furry a kick to be sure he was dead, then put the gun in his dead hand.

I started moving away, and vomited again.

"Watch out," the cop yelled back to the other two cops. "Puttin' one down range." The cop wrapped Furry's dead fingers around the handle of the gun -- the fingers that used to hold his guitar pick -- and pulled the trigger, lodging a round into one of the cruisers. He then dropped the hand and the gun, and the little old man called Furry Jenkins lay dead with a revolver in his hand on a blood-stained Mississippi highway.

46

Ruleville, Mississippi
2002

"WHAT ABOUT the other one, Hoss? The drifter?" one of the cops asked.

"Did you see him?"

"No, I only seen the nigger."

"I expect they would still be together," Ron Tweed said and looked out at the forest.

I froze. It seemed like the cop was looking right at me. He stood in thought for a moment, scanning the trees.

Suddenly he spun around. "Get up to that bridge, now!" he yelled to the other two cops. "I think this old cocksucker was just covering for the faggot."

My eyes went wide and I turned and ran.

The race was futile. I would never outrun their cars. Furry's death was futile.

I fumbled along. I cried openly. It was my fault Furry was dead.

I stopped and scanned the area around me. I wanted to curl up into a ball. I wanted to pull the Ninja Turtles comforter I had as a kid up over my head and hide from the world. This was awful. What had I just seen? I wanted to stop and cry.

Something else made me go, though. Something I had never felt. Something I couldn't even recognize because it was in a realm into which I had never previously ventured. Something made me go. All I wanted to do was stop and die, but something made me think, assess, move forward.

They could never let me live after what I just saw.

Maybe I could cross the river. Furry had been very certain and made very clear earlier that we couldn't. It was too swampy, not passable.

But the cops would be at the bridge in seconds, the road was shut down and the enemy was pressing in, flushing me out like a game fowl. The river was my only option.

What I approached a few moments later was, indeed, much more a swamp than a river. Stagnant black waters were partially canopied by tree roots and hanging white moss. I could see no sign of a flow; meaning I could not tell which way was 'across'. But I knew which way led to certain death. Backward led to certain death.

I stood on the edge of the swamp feeling somewhat like I had when I stood at the top of the tallest cliff when my buddies and I would go cliff jumping at the lake back home. My conscious mind told my legs to jump into the swamp and get the fuck out of there, and they almost would, but then the subconscious would swoop in and shut down all operations as its fail-safes kicked in and its red flags popped as my eyes reported back that they were perceiving grave danger ahead. And so it went for nearly a full minute.

Eventually my conscious mind willed itself free, and I leaped down into the chest-deep, viscous liquid and immediately started moving forward. My breath stopped the second I hit the swamp, but the adrenaline of fear coursed through my veins and I scurried through the muck with frantic desperation and mindless will, my brain reverting to the most basic of functions and commands, ignoring all else.

It was dark, darker than just the darkness that comes from night, as if the air itself were dark, as if the swamp had donned a funerary veil. I held Furry's guitar case over my head and out of the water as I stumbled along, the fear gripping me like a giant constricting snake. The water was a thick sludge and smelled of death and rotting. My pack was already wet from the rain earlier in the night and now it became mud-covered and soaked as I moved through the varying depths of the swamp. My mind avoided all thoughts of the predators that lurked in the darkness, of the venomous snakes and insects, of the hundreds of ways I could easily meet my end in the clutches of this Delta swamp. I thought only of going forward.

47

Dockery
2002

I SAW the Dockery Farms sign through the trees and looked at my watch. Four forty-seven: ten minutes until the train passed. I was covered head to toe in mud. The only thing that was clean was Furry's beat-up guitar case, which I had somehow managed to keep out of the swamp during the entire hour-long crossing. The thing was heavy. And it carried the extra weight of guilt. My eyes welled as I looked up at the weathered Dockery Farms sign.

I moved quietly through the forest along the road. On the other side of the road were the empty, gray buildings of the Dockery Plantation. The Pea-Vine railroad tracks, Furry had told me, were in the very back of the property, half a mile back, by the kudzu-covered abandoned commissary. I could hide there and make a run at the train when it came.

I moved further west and away from the bridge, walking parallel to the road. The sporadic flicker of red lights against the damp leaves of the forest told me the police were still at the bridge. My hope was that they thought I too was on the other side of the river and were searching for me over there. But to be sure, I kept moving, looking for a good place to cross the road.

The road was deserted in those dark hours of the morning, and I imagined that everyone else in the world was snuggled comfortably in bed, enjoying the clean warmth of their blankets and the safety of their homes. Dim moonlight filled the swath of the road, and the blackness of the forest around it made it almost appear to be a voluminous flow, a palpable energy filling the channel. I had forgotten that I was tired. The fear of being alone in the swamp, and now in the forest, was throttling my heart with such adrenaline that I was constantly in a state of *knowing* that something was right behind me, but turning to find nothing. Every sound presented itself as an attack. And the forest was frighteningly loud. I felt as if the eyes of the forest were watching me with macabre interest, eager to see what horrible demise awaited me down the trail. The wetness and the mud that covered me added enormous weight, and despite my best effort, I could not step quietly though the night -- and the forest seemed to grin at my attempt.

I looked at my watch: four-fifty. I had seven minutes. I didn't know how long it would take me to reach the railroad tracks at the back of the plantation, but I knew I was cutting it close. I could no longer see the flicker of the police lights and hadn't seen a single car since the road came into sight. I moved swiftly to the edge of the forest near the road. I looked up and back and saw nothing but the flow of moonlight hovering above the road.

I took off, and once I was out in the open I became fully terrified. The black forest was a walk in the park compared to the feeling I had being out from the cover of trees. I felt nakedly exposed and waited with a nauseous churn in my stomach for the rifle shot that was destined to take me out. If I had had anything to drink in the previous hours, I would have pissed myself.

After what seem like hours, but was in fact only a few seconds, I crashed into the forest on the other side. At that moment, I heard the faint call of the train whistling in the distance, though I could not tell how far away it was. Much like my reaction to the noises in the forest, my mind immediately assumed the worst: that the train was right around the bend. I began to panic. I thrashed through the forest as fast as I could. If I missed the train I was dead, literally. The sky was already starting to lighten to the east, and once daylight arrived I would be a sitting duck; I was covered head to toe in mud, carrying a swamp-covered rucksack and a guitar; I knew nothing about where I was and had nowhere to go even if I did. Once daylight came, it would only be a matter of time before they found me. My only hope would be to be caught by a decent cop. At least then I would only get tossed in jail, but would keep my life. How had it come to this: looking longingly at the prospect of incarceration over certain death? This wasn't what I had in mind when I set out from home. My loneliness seemed to weigh more than the pack and the guitar. I felt like there was no one in the world except those that were trying to kill me. I couldn't picture a single other face.

As I thrashed through the forest, I could see the outlines of the few remaining buildings of Dockery Farms to my right and I angled toward the open ground around the buildings.

I burst out into the opening a moment later and ran as fast as I could. I had to catch the train, *had* to. I was gripped with fear and ran with a nervous lumber. But I forced myself not to think of the exponential rise in danger that came with being out in the open. I just ran.

Soon, I saw the kudzu-covered abandoned commissary ahead of me and then the two strips of glimmering cold steel of the railroad tracks fifty yards beyond that. I ran as fast as my legs could carry me to the railroad tracks and stopped.

I looked at my watch: 4:57.

The train wasn't on time.

I looked around in a panic. I was exposed. The tone of the night was growing lighter by the second. Every shadow seemed to hide a pair of eyes, and all my mind could think about was the sight of Furry Jenkins lying face down on the road. I hopped on my toes and begged for the train to come. But nothing stirred down the tracks. I snapped around at a sound, but then couldn't be sure that I had heard anything at all. Then I snapped around the other way. My mind was playing tricks. I had come to the point where I no longer knew which sounds were real.

That is, until I heard the train whistle blow. I could be sure *that* sound was real, and it seemed much closer than the last time I heard it.

Then, I saw a flicker. At first I wasn't even sure if I had seen it. I turned my head back toward the buildings and the road and saw it again: a red flicker against the gray walls of the buildings.

Within seconds the flicker spread across all the buildings and seemed to fill the air. Back at the road, I could see the spiraling red lights of a police cruiser clicking between the trees of the forest, moving slowly along the road, its spotlight searching the forest. I ran to the commissary and hid behind it. Dockery Farms was the only thing on this small stretch of road and my gut told me this cop would take the time to make a loop through the grounds. My stomach was a knot and the frenetic dancing of the red lights made me gag. Oh, how I wished to be home right then. I wanted to cry.

Then I felt the ground start to rumble and heard the tin roof on the building begin to clatter. Seconds later, the headlight of the train swung around the bend down the tracks, and the massive locomotive let loose a piercing shriek into the early, pre-dawn Delta that both shattered my ears and engulfed my heart with joy. I leapt to my feet and peeked around the corner of the building. The police car was slowing to turn onto the weed-covered, crushed gravel of the shrinking Dockery drive. The train whistle shrieked again, so loud that it made the tendons tingle on the back of my knees.

I crouched into the shadow of the building as the train approached to keep from being seen by the engineer. I would have to make a fifty yard dash across open ground when I saw the third yellow car. The train was moving much faster than I had expected. Furry had said that it would be puttering through here before it picked up steam for its run north to Memphis on the main line. It was definitely not puttering.

I looked around the corner of the building again and the headlights of the police cruiser swung onto the grounds, painting a stroke of light across the farm. The rumble of the train's cargo was a sustained boom and I hid beneath the vines as the engine roared toward my position. As it approached, the train let loose another shriek that seemed to pull the oxygen from the air. The noise was so overpowering that it blotted out my vision and wiped the world away from my senses. Then, with a whooshing change of pitch, the engine rushed past, and the earthy grumble and sharp squeaks of freight cars in motion took over.

I watched the train for yellow cars while darting my eyes around the corner of the building to see where the cop was. He was slowly looping toward my position. I saw the first yellow car; it had Yazoo painted across its side in red letters. The Yellow Dog. The cop rolled along the gravel and scanned everything he passed with his spotlight.

The head-rattling rumble of the train made it hard to think; it made me want to scream. I saw the second yellow car, and my heart jumped. I peered around the corner. The cop was getting closer. I struggled to see the driver, but couldn't. I just hoped it wasn't the cop from the graveyard.

Then the spotlight suddenly flashed in my eyes. I dove back around the corner and held my head to the ground. I couldn't tell if the light had just flashed over me or if the driver had pointed it at me on purpose. I wanted to look to see, but I couldn't make myself. I couldn't force myself to gaze upon the horrors that could be approaching. Fear had completely shut me down.

And then I saw it out of the corner of my eye: the third yellow car. It was just suddenly there, galloping toward my position. I had been watching the cop and forgot to keep an eye on the train. I had fifty yards of wide-open space between myself and the swiftly moving train, and the third yellow car was almost to me.

If the car got past me at the rate it was going, I would never catch up to it. I had to meet it just right. I didn't even have a second to check on the cop. It didn't matter. This was my only chance whether the cop was watching or not.

I darted out into the open and ran like hell.

THE LAST

Mississippi
2002

I SAT on the train covered head to toe in mud, and the box car moved back and forth in a rattling sway as the wheels played a metronomic beat passing over the railroad ties below. The freight train was now on the main line, racing north toward Memphis. I stretched my legs out in front of me and leaned against the forward wall of the steel box. Three rows of small slits down both sides of the yellow car allowed me to watch the forest pass by as the sun started to lighten the scattered, billowing storm clouds that remained in the sky, the blue sky coming to life between the clouds as the morning neared.

I sighed deeply and rested my head back against the cold metal. Below one arm was my mud-covered rucksack and under the other was Furry's old guitar case. For a long while I just sat there and stared. I hadn't been off my feet but to crawl or take cover in nearly twenty-four hours. I hadn't slept in nearly forty-eight. The last I even rested was on the bench at the Crossroads---when Furry played his guitar. I hung my head. Just twenty-four hours before, Furry Jenkins had played the most beautiful of blues as the sun rose over the Crossroads. Now he was lying face down in a pool of his own blood on a muddy Mississippi highway.

To keep the tears from welling, I snapped open the latches of Furry's guitar case and pulled open the lid. The worn glimmer of the old guitar reflected the growing light coming through the slits in the sides of the car. I picked up the sturdy instrument and laid it across my lap. How I wished that I could play it, that I could play the blues like Furry Jenkins could, that I could transfer this awful ache into sound and send it off into space. I longed so badly for the blues. But I could do nothing but look at the guitar. It held so much power for those that could access it, but you must have the keys, and I didn't.

As I held the guitar in my hands, I noticed a slight line in the velvet inside the guitar case. I reached into the case and ran my fingers over the line, feeling a seam below. Curious, I pulled on the lush velvet and a small lid opened to reveal a thin compartment.

Inside, rested an old, blue notebook.

I just stared at the notebook for a long time, not sure what I was feeling. Gently, I pulled the notebook out and held it in my hands. As I picked it up, a small stack of photographs -- their edges torn and curling -- came fluttering out onto my lap from behind the front cover. There were a number of photographs in the stack, and one face remained constant in all of them, growing in age in each shot from a young boy, into a man, and then into an old man -- but always with the same worn-toothed grin. And standing beside Furry Jenkins in these photographs was a virtual who's who of blues music. Cheering and laughing, from the steps of a front porch, or the back of a juke joint, with their arms always fondly around the shoulders of Furry Jenkins, the very pioneers of blues music smiled back from the photographs, a shining testament to the man they embraced. But it was the last picture in the bunch that made me drop the rest. My tired eyes welled as I looked down at a grinning Furry Jenkins enveloped under the long thin arm of my father. They each held a beer and were raising them to the camera from in front of a dimly lit stage with a sign reading, Hopson Plantation, hanging above it. They looked happy.

I took a deep breath and lifted my head and watched out the slits on the wall as the Clarksdale Train Depot flashed by, its platform deserted but for a maintenance man pushing a broom. I swallowed the lump in my throat and turned to the left as the train sped past the intersection of Mississippi highways 61 and 49: The Crossroads. Beyond the Crossroads, and over the cotton fields, and past the old wooden church steeple, the very top sliver of the sun appeared from behind the trees and the sparrows danced forth from the forest. I rested my head back against the swaying steel wall and closed my eyes as the train whistle called out into the morning.

THE END

...OF BOOK ONE

www.RichardMBrock.com

TO THE READER

THANK YOU for making it to this point. I hope you started from the front. Despite my appreciation, I had a hard time deciding whether to tell you what is historically accurate in this story and what is stretched. Since the two tangle up into so nicely knotted a ball, I will mostly just suggest that you look these people up at your leisure and learn more. You will be entertained, I promise. But I do have a few points I'll mention while trying not to give away anything from books two and three. Charlie Patton really is considered by many to be the closest thing there is to an inventor of blues music, though the only certainty is that there is no such thing. At the very least, he is at the root of the blues family tree, which, of course, puts him at the root of all modern music's family tree. He really did learn from Henry Sloan; he really did grow up and often live on Dockery Farms; his father really did try to beat the blues out of him (before then buying him a guitar as retribution); he really was part Cherokee; he really did have a bad temper and drinking problem and at least three ex-wives (some say eight); and most importantly, he really did teach all those legends of the blues that appear in the story (though his secret connection with Blind Lemon and Lead Belly may fall a little further to the stretcher side). Lead Belly really was pardoned twice, once for murder and once for an attempt at the same, and both times pardoned after playing the blues for the respective governors. He also really did escape from a chain gang in Texas after going to jail on a gun charge when he was a young man. (Not bad for ol' Lead Belly, huh: of three incarcerations, one escape and two pardons? And as Bob Dylan correctly pointed out, Huddie Ledbetter was one of the few convicted murderers to go on to record a children's album. I highly suggest reading more on him.) Blind Lemon Jefferson really was found frozen to death in Chicago and many people suspect foul play, though nothing was ever proven. Robert Johnson really was shunned by most, including his idol, Charlie Patton, whom he followed around like a puppy, but the debate still rages as to whether it was the Devil himself who eventually taught him to play guitar at the Crossroads or if he learned from a worldlier source. Son House really was a preacher who came over to the blues and eventually learned from Charlie Patton and Willie Brown, and he really did kill a man who opened fire at a juke joint he was playing at -- and then go to prison for it. John and Alan Lomax really did make all those field recordings for the Library of Congress, and John really did found the Texas Folklore Society. The circumstances of Bess Lomax's death were dramatized for this story, though she did die at the same time. W.C. Handy's portion of the story is almost entirely true. He really did hear a man (many believe to be Henry Sloan) playing slide guitar at a train station in Tutwieler, Mississippi, and singing about going where the Southern cross' the Dog (where the Southern Railway crosses the Yazoo Delta Railroad aka "Yellow Dog" in Moorhead, MS). When Handy goes home and transcribes what he heard, that becomes the first documented blues lyric. And when he laid St. Louis Blues on those white folks a few years later, what he saw is exactly as it is described in this story, as far as I can tell. Willie Brown, Tommy Johnson, Muddy Waters, Howlin' Wolf, Bukka White, and John Lee Hooker all make very brief cameos in book one, and their portrayal is generally accurate. And for the rest, you'll just have to wait for book two and three. Thanks, again.

RMB

Oh, and don't forget to REVIEW this book wherever you can.

facebook.com/RichardMBrockAuthor
www.RichardMBrock.com

ABOUT THE AUTHOR

Richard M. Brock grew up writing stories in a small town in the Adirondack Mountains and has thereafter traveled the trails, rails, rivers, and back roads of America and beyond in search of characters and settings to use in his stories. Currently, he and his wife live in Colorado. *Cross Dog Blues* is his first novel.

www.facebook.com/RichardMBrockAuthor
www.RichardMBrock.com

CPSIA information can be obtained
at www.ICGtesting.com
Printed in the USA
LVHW020043150422
716236LV00004B/198